Rag Doll

…a theatre story

Bill Scurato

ISBN: 9781074327910

CONTENTS

ACKNOWLEDGMENTS

Thanks to my family and friends for their continuing support. Also a special nod to all my former students and fellow theatre travelers who have provided the genesis of this story.

1
You Made the Pants Too Long
January 7, 2019

Lisa Lesinski-Stratton stood before the mirror in her bedroom. Her facial features, still striking, were drawn and revealed a fraught history over the course of her barely 30 years. Her healthy lifestyle had well maintained her five foot, five inch frame. Her dark brown hair was at shoulder length, as it had been since high school. It provided an appealing compliment to her deep set brown eyes. Lisa was nervous as she applied light makeup to brighten her sad face. She would be taking a big step tonight…auditioning for a local theatre's production of *A Doll's House*. She had done theatre in high school and was a standout in her short time at Atlantic University. But that was a long time ago. In recent years her life had been totally dedicated to providing stability and security as a mostly single parent to her eight year old daughter. Charlie…or Charlene…was the love of her life. She absolutely adored everything about her.

"Your makeup looks nice, Mom," said Charlie, as she entered the room. Lisa smiled and hugged her.

Charlie was a typical eight year old…full of physical energy and bursting with curiosity about everything. She shared her mother's shimmering dark hair. But her hazel eyes twinkled with a mischievous glimmer.

“Thanks Buddy,” said Lisa, “now which shirt do you think I should wear with these jeans?” Lisa held up a crew neck purple blouse in her right hand, and a black spaghetti strap in her left.

“That one!” Charlie laughed as she pointed to the purple. “It’s more fun…it will make you look happier.”

“Okay…the purple it will be, my friend. I want to look happy”

In reality, Lisa hadn’t been happy in some time. As she put on her specially selected shirt, she watched her daughter’s eyes gleam with joy. The two of them had been through a lot lately. A sorrowful divorce had brought both mother and daughter to tears on too many occasions. But, of late, it seemed as if things had settled down. Lisa’s ex-husband, Mark, had backed off on his obsession with controlling every aspect of Charlie’s life. And last month, Lisa was promoted at the daycare facility where she worked. Mark’s child-support payments were inconsistent and sometimes non-existent. Lisa had been strapped for rent and other life essentials. Now she was a supervisor, with a welcome bump in her paycheck. Charlie was doing well in her new school and it seemed as if Lisa’s life was finally turning a corner.

“Is your homework done?” Lisa asked her daughter.

“Yup…all done. Can’t I please come to the audition with you?”

“No, I don’t think that would be a very good idea,” said Lisa. “Of course, I’d love to bring you, but these things are usually closed to anyone not auditioning”

“So I’ll audition too….please!” Charlie pleaded.

“I think we’d better take this one step at a time. They probably won’t even want *me*. I don’t have any experience…except in school.

“Are you kidding? They would be lucky to have you in their stupid play. What’s it called again?”

"*A Doll's House*"

"Sounds boring. How can there be a whole play about a dumb doll's house?"

"Well it's a little more complicated than that. I'll explain it to you later. Listen, you go to your room and get your homework…I'll be in to check it, okay?"

"Sure…whatever you say Barbra!" Charlie extended the name dramatically "Baaaaarberrrraaaa!"

"Barbra?" said Lisa.

"Sure! Barbra Streisand, silly…such a diva!" Charlie fist bumped her mom and skipped out of the room giggling.

Lisa laughed out loud as she brushed her hair, "Diva!!!"

Lisa's cell phone rang. She saw from the ID that it was her mother calling. "Hi Mom…are you on your way? I have to leave in fifteen minutes…oh…well…I'm sorry… I hope you feel better. Huh?... Oh, no it's all right. I don't have to go. It was probably a bad idea anyway… All right. Thanks. Goodnight, Mom."

Lisa called Charlie, "Hey Buddy, can you come in here for a minute…and bring your homework with you."

"Coming, Mom."

Lisa's relationship with her mother had been hot and cold…well, mostly cold. In truth, her mother hadn't been very supportive, especially through Lisa's more recent troubles. In fact, Lisa felt her mother often took Mark's side in the conflicts about Charlie.

Charlie had her notebook in hand as she entered Lisa's room. "I think I got these all right, but I'm not sure."

Lisa carefully checked her daughter's math homework and pronounced it, "Excellent!" Charlie beamed!

Lisa continued, "Listen, Buddy….I'm not going to the theatre tonight after all."

"Why not?"

"Grandma isn't feeling well, and she can't sit with you."

"Oh…Well, I'm sorry she's sick…but now I get to go with you!"

"Umm, I don't think that would be permitted," said Lisa.

"How do you know?"

"Well, I don't know really"

"So let's try it," said Charlie, "The worst that can happen, is they'll ask us to leave. And if they do…*screw* them!"

"Hey…language!" said Lisa.

"Sorry…C'mon, Mom…you've been looking forward to this …let's go!"

Lisa relented. "Okay…I guess we could try. You sure I look all right?"

"You look maaarvelous!!!"

They laughed and hugged each other.

***

During the drive to the Town Square Playhouse, Lisa and Charlie laughed and sang along to the *Barbra Streisand's Greatest Hits* cd in the car.

"But Sam, Sam, Sam! You made the pants too long!"

Mom and daughter shared the hysterical fun of the moment. Then Lisa turned off the cd and asked Charlie to listen to her monologue.

"What's a monologue?" Charlie asked from the back seat of Lisa's Civic.

Lisa glanced up at Charlie through the rear-view mirror. "It's a small section of a play spoken by one person," Lisa said. "It's recited by actors to audition in the theatre."

"Okay, let's hear your monologue"

"Here goes…" Lisa was nervous as she began-

"You...You have never loved me...... You have only thought it pleasant to be in love with me. It is perfectly true, Torvald."

Charlie interrupted her. "Who the heck is *Torvald*?"

"Her…*Nora's* husband," said Lisa.

Charlie rolled her eyes. "That's a weird name."

" It's Norwegian," said Lisa.

"Oh," Charlie said. "Go on then."

"All right," Lisa took a breath. She seemed more self-assured now.

"I have existed merely to perform tricks for you, Torvald. When I was at home with papa, he called me his doll-child, and he played with me just as I used to play with my dolls. And when I came to live with you, I was simply transferred from papa's hands into yours."

Lisa paused and took a deep breath. “Now this is the end,” and she executed with significant authority:

“You and papa have committed a great sin against me. It is your fault that I have made nothing of my life.”

Both Mom and daughter were quiet for a moment… “Wow!” said Charlie. “That was terrific, Mom. Really good!”

“Think so, Buddy?”

“Yeah…but…”

“But what, Charlie?” asked Lisa. “What’s wrong?”

“I guess this isn’t a funny play, is it?”

“No…not very funny at all. It’s about a woman who has been let down by her parents and her husband.”

“Yeah…I see that.” Charlie paused. “Kinda’ like you, Mom.”

Lisa felt overwhelmed by Charlie’s beyond her years insight. She looked up and made eye contact with Charlie in the back seat. “Kinda…you’re really something, Buddy…you know that?”

Charlie smiled. “Aw shucks! Thanks, Mom.”

There was another pause. “That was terrific, Mom. You’re gonna knock ‘em dead…”

Charlie broke into song, *“Cause…”*

Lisa joined Charlie.

“Sam, you made the pants too long”

***

Lisa and Charlie approached the entrance to the theatre. The marquee above heralded the company's current production, *Avenue Q*.

"What's *Avenue Q*?" Charlie inquired of her Mom.

"I think it's a musical show that uses puppets to tell the story," said Lisa.

"Oh, that sounds cool! Can we come here and see it? It looks like there are only two performances left."

"Oh, I don't know, Buddy, I think it's a pretty adult show."

"An adult puppet show!?" said Charlie. "That sounds *really* cool!"

"We'll see." Lisa nervously opened the front door and entered the theatre lobby with her daughter.

The lobby was colorful. A pastel paint pattern was reminiscent of an old time ice cream parlor. On the walls were four indented display boxes, each promoting an upcoming production at the Playhouse. Lisa and Charlie briefly viewed each display. *Fiddler On The Roof* depicted Tevye's three oldest daughters dancing with their mops and brooms. *Beauty and the Beast* displayed the show's namesakes…also dancing. Then came the current *Avenue Q* in which an ensemble view of the characters seemed very similar to those Charlie remembered from *Sesame Street*. Finally Lisa and Charlie approached the display box for *A Doll's House*. The main image was a birdcage, with a woman locked inside.

"This is a weird play!" said Charlie.

"It's a classic," her Mom replied.

"If you say so Mom. It just seems really, really weird."

Lisa laughed loudly as she opened the lobby door to enter the theatre auditorium. Her forceful laugh was heard and noticed by a group of actors on the stage at the front of the house. Apparently the audition had already begun.

"Oh, I'm so sorry," Lisa whispered, as she approached a counter labeled "Audition Registration." A young woman was behind the counter and quietly welcomed Lisa.

"Are you here to audition?"

Lisa was tentative. "Umm, yes…"

"How about you, Miss?" The young woman addressed Charlie. "There are three children's roles available."

Charlie eagerly looked up and smiled at her mother.

"No…just me this time," Lisa spoke quietly…nodding and smiling at Charlie. "Maybe next time."

Charlie nodded and smiled too. The woman handed Lisa two sheets of paper. "Here's an audition form. Please fill out both sides completely and sign at the bottom. And here is a rehearsal schedule. Check it for any conflicts you may have."

"Thank you," Lisa said as she gazed up at the stage. Suddenly she slightly gasped. "Is that Mr. Moretti up there?"

Lisa recognized a man whom she thought was her high school drama teacher/director, Sal Moretti.

"Yes, that's him," the young woman replied. "He's directing the play. I'm Rebecca Prescott, by the way. I'll be stage managing the show."

Lisa extended her hand. "I'm Lisa Stratton. Mr. Moretti was my teacher in high school. How long has he been directing here?"

"He started this theatre back in the '70's," said Rebecca. "It's very nice to meet you, Lisa. Is this your daughter?"

"Yes, this is Charlie...Charlene, really," said Lisa. "My sitter cancelled at the last minute. Is it okay if she sits with me?"

"Sure...no problem."

Lisa completed her form and sat with Charlie in the back of the house. They both watched what was happening onstage. The director, Mr. Moretti, was leading those auditioning through the "mirror exercise." The group was divided into pairs, each couple facing each other.

"And...action!" said Moretti.

The actors began slowly copying each other's movement, as if looking in a mirror.

"What the heck is going on?" Charlie whispered to her mom.

"The mirror exercise," said Lisa. "Each actor is trying to perfectly reflect the partner's movement."

"Why? What does that prove?" asked Charlie.

"It demonstrates an actor's attention and innovation," Lisa recited, as if engrained in her soul.

She could almost hear Moretti's voice from all those years ago.

"Remember it's not a game to win or lose. Your goal is to work together...to be flawlessly connected through observation, concentration and imagination. Focus people...*focus*!"

2
*Sh*ing a *Sh*ong of *Sh*ix*sh*penc*sh*
December 5, 2007

"Focus, people, *focus*!" Sal Moretti harped as he circulated around his theatre arts classroom at Meadow Hills High School. The designated playing space had become overcrowded, as subscription to the class had spiraled in recent years. The room was the former band facility, with two plateaus of elevated wide steps around the circumference. Here, were placed student desks. At the bottom of these steps and the center of the room, was a ten by ten foot carpeted square, which comprised the main area for performance of student scenes and presentations. Although designed for instrumental music, the space served as an appropriate lab for exploring the art of the theatre. But as the population of the class increased, that ten by ten square became overly crunched, especially in full class exercises. Moretti often had to split the class into two groups for such activities. This practice could become troublesome. Moretti had learned over the years that keeping high school students active and engaged was a key element to success. By sitting students down to "observe" for chunks of time could be inviting distraction and difficulty.

Lisa Lesinski was mirroring opposite her friend Patty Quinn. The attractive co-eds represented the most popular contingent of the school's student body. Always well dressed and well groomed; they had excelled in academics and had distinguished themselves in extra-curriculars. They were appealing representatives of the millennial generation.

Moretti complemented them as he circulated. "Nice moves ladies…smooth and focused."

Lisa smiled in acknowledgement. She had been enjoying the class very much. As a senior, she had been given the opportunity for an elective subject choice. After considering sociology and drafting, she decided on theatre arts. At first she wasn't sure it was the right selection. On the first day of school, she was surprised and somewhat concerned that she didn't know many of the other students. For Lisa, as for most kids, the social element of high school was very important. Since elementary, she was used to seeing the same faces in all of her classes. Lisa was very bright and multifaceted. She was on a definite college track and had distinguished herself in the rigorous Meadow Hills curriculum.

But this class was different. There were certainly a fair share of college bound students, but they were joined by kids from every other learning path and social group: technology, business, vocational…even some very scary looking guys who seemed to be just passing time. At first, Lisa was disarmed by this, but Moretti had developed a way of mixing everybody up in a manner that seemed to provide a comfort level for all…usually. In actuality, Lisa felt she had formed some good new friendships in theatre class, and she was quite happy about it.

Sal Moretti had been teaching for over thirty years. A "child of the '50's," he was from mixed Italian-German lineage. His blue collar parents had worked hard to send him to college. In his formative years, he may have had aspirations of becoming a professional actor, but later opted for the implied security of being an educator. In retrospect, he had totally enjoyed his teaching career and fostered no regrets for how things turned out. He believed the theatre was a powerful tool in helping young people to make life connections. He projected dark, Italian features, and was always a bit overweight. He believed much of his success had been founded in the celebration of the individual differences in people.

Moretti called, "CURTAIN!" and the mirror exercise in the ten by ten performance square stopped.

"Okay, let's have Group B down in the square," said the teacher.

With that the group which had been mirroring moved up the plateau to the desks, as the other students, who had been observing, moved down to the ten by ten. "Okay, let's form a circle," Moretti instructed, "and stretch your arms up as high above your head as you can."

The students complied with this instruction in varying degrees. The more energized kids executed a high, tight stretch while deeply inhaling. Those less motivated, lackadaisically reached their hands up to shoulder level, while looking around in fear of someone seeing them.

"All right, now drop it!" Moretti continued. The students took the cue to bend at the waist, bob, hang and sway. Moretti urged, "Get all the tension out of your body...clear your mind...get ready to work."

Moretti had found this "rag doll" exercise to be a good means of preparation, not only for acting drills, but for life tasks in general. "All right, now shake it out!" While still bent forward the kids wiggled their fingers to extract the tension. "Now, up and at 'em. Let's break into pairs for the mirror." Again there was compliance, with varying degrees of enthusiasm.

"Okay, people, I'm looking for creative, abstract movement today. Concentrate...work together...and... ACTION!" Group B was off and running.

Lisa and Patty chatted quietly as they observed. "Look at that," Lisa said, pointing to two boys working in the corner of the square. One was bending right, left and forward executing innovative arm movements and facial expressions. But his partner, one of the scary guys, was basically standing frozen, barely moving at all. "Who is that guy?" Lisa asked.

"Which one?" said Patty.

“The one with all the moves. He’s really good.”

Patty answered, “ Um, I’m not sure…Jeff something, I think. The other guy is Nick Curtiss…he’s a bad ass….and really cute!”

“You think so?” said Lisa, “Why is he not even trying to do the exercise?”

“He’s too cool,” Patty said.

The two boys in question could not have been more opposite. Jeff Townsend was an over-achiever. Although not blessed with a particularly adroit intellect, he was a hard worker. That characteristic had yielded him much high school success. He was straight-laced…regularly trimmed, chestnut brown hair…no facial whiskers …and was adorned with neat blue jeans and tan polo. On the other hand, Nick Curtiss’s jet black hair was long and curly…it dropped to the middle of his back. He sported a scraggly goatee, many tattoos, and an array of facial piercings. He wore black ripped jeans, a Metallica tee shirt, and a motorcycle jacket.

“Ugh…doesn’t seem cool to me,” said Lisa. “Why does a guy like that even take a class like this?”

“Probably nothing else he could take. He needs the credits to graduate and figured it would be easy.”

Just then Moretti stopped the exercise and complimented Jeff on his work. “But, Nick, you’ve gotta try to give something back,” Moretti said. “You look like a bump on a log.”

That garnered a few snickers from the other students, which Nick clearly, did not appreciate.

“No, don’t laugh,” Moretti admonished the class, “but Nick, you’ve gotta put forth some effort, okay?”

Nick was embarrassed by the callout. His head bowed, but when he looked up his eyes made contact with Lisa. Now Lisa, didn't know this fellow at all, but instinctively smiled and nodded.

"Now let's see just you two," Moretti said, referring to Nick and Jeff. "Okay, guys?"

Jeff sparked to attention. But Nick was still looking at Lisa.

"Ready, Nick?" said Jeff.

"Uh-huh," Nick faced his partner.

"And...ACTION!" called Moretti.

It was amazing. Nick was transformed. He was right on target with all of Jeff's energy and moves. He even created a few wild modifications of his own. When Moretti called "CURTAIN!" the entire class applauded. Nick looked up at Lisa who was still smiling at him.

As theatre arts class was winding down, Moretti called attention to a poster on his classroom bulletin board. "I just want to be sure you're all aware of auditions coming up next week for *Joseph and The Amazing Technicolor Dreamcoat*."

Melissa Matlock, the class drama queen, called out in a whiny voice, "why do we always have to do such weird stuff? What about *Hello Dolly* or *Brigadoon*?"

"Those are wonderful shows," replied Moretti, " but *Joseph* offers many opportunities for a lot of students. We want to get as many people involved as possible."

"Okay," said Melissa, "but I've been practicing *Hello Dolly* for six months.

"Well, you've got a week to get up to speed on *Joseph*, Melissa," said Moretti. "I'm sure you're up to it."

Everyone giggled, as the bell rang indicating the end of class.

"That's next Wednesday and Thursday right after school," called Moretti, as the students were rushing out into the hallway.

Waiting outside the theatre classroom door was Mark Stratton, Lisa's boyfriend. As Lisa walked out the door, Mark smiled, threw his arm around her and kissed her. Lisa happily returned his greeting. The two cantered off to their next class. Neither was aware of the gaze of Nick Curtiss.

***

At lunch, Lisa discussed the *Joseph* auditions with Patty Quinn. Lisa said she would really love to give the show a try.

"It does sound like it would be fun, but I'm sure it would interfere with cheering," said Patty.

Both Lisa and Patty had been cheerleaders since elementary school. They were co-captains of this year's squad and fully committed. Over their years of participation, cheering had transitioned from an auxiliary activity to full-fledged varsity status. Lisa had created much of their competition routine and received considerable accolades for her work.

"I don't see why we couldn't work it out so that we could do both," said Lisa. "I heard Coach Jaryn is allowing the wrestlers to do the show."

Patty said, "But, wrestling is more of an individual sport. Those guys can stagger their practice. Our team has to always be working together."

"Still," said Lisa, "I'll bet we could work it out, if we tried."

Just then Mark Stratton and Ricky Jones, Patty's boyfriend, sat themselves beside the girls.

Mark was a hometown football hero. He was a terrific athlete and had recently led his team to a sectional championship. He stood 6' 2", and weighed 185 pounds. He had thick curly blond hair, deep steel blue eyes, and was quite handsome by any standard. Mr. Esquire! Ricky Jones, on the other hand, was far less distinguished in every way. However, his association with Mark provided him many life perks.

"This looks like a serious chat ladies," said Mark. "What gives?"

Patty explained that she and Lisa would both like to do the school musical this year, but it probably wasn't possible because of cheering.

"Wait a minute," said Ricky. "You two *want* to be in the school musical?"

Both Patty and Lisa nodded.

"Why on earth would you want to do that?" said Mark. "Those people are a bunch of freaks."

"Hey," said Lisa, "there are some very nice people in that class. And Moretti is really cool."

"I heard Moretti was light in the loafers," said Ricky.

"So what if he were?" said Lisa. "Although I think it's highly doubtful in that he's married with two kids."

Mark laughed. "So, that doesn't necessarily mean--"

"Oh, shut-up," said Lisa.

"Well, it doesn't matter anyway," said Patty, "because we're cheerleaders and can't do the play."

"Hmm…I guess not," said Lisa.

***

During the remainder of the day, Lisa's thoughts kept returning to the show. At dismissal time she ran into Moretti in the hallway as she was heading to the gym for cheer practice.

"Hey, Lisa, I wanted to touch base with you about *Joseph*," said Moretti. "I was hoping you were going to audition."

"Oh, well, I'd really love to," said Lisa, "but I'm afraid I'm not going to be able to because of cheering."

"Hmm, yeah, I was afraid of that," replied Moretti.

"Is it true that some of the wrestlers are going to do the show?" asked Lisa.

Moretti smiled. "As a matter of fact that is true. We need lots of guys in *Joseph*...all the brothers you know, and Coach Jaryn is willing to share, as long as his guys get their work in."

"That's fantastic," said Lisa, "but *our* squad has to always work together. I don't think sharing would be possible."

"Yes, I guess that's true," Moretti said. "But if there's any way we could compromise, I'd be very happy to have you. Let me know."

Lisa proceeded to practice with the show still on her mind. During a break, Lisa approached the subject with the other girls. "I'd really like to give this play a try," said Lisa. "Are any others of you interested?" In addition to Lisa's friend, Patty, several other squad members indicated that they would like to audition.

Margi Manson, another senior member of the squad, was surprised. "You guys have got to be kidding. Those productions are a lot of work. They rehearse almost every day. Where would you possibly find the time?"

“Right,” said Wendy Phillips, “and *we* have practice at the same time as the play rehearses…doesn’t seem like a very practical idea.”

Wendy Phillips had been a cheerleader nearly as long as Lisa. They had cheered together since grade school. She was also a very attractive young woman…flowing auburn hair, beautiful figure…with strong dancer’s legs. Wendy was an excellent athlete. But over the years, Lisa’s achievements in cheerleading as well as in everything else, had always outshined Wendy’s. This was a point of contention.

“But maybe we could figure out a way to share the time,” said Lisa. “Obviously, we’re not going to let cheer suffer, but I’ll bet we could work out some kind of a schedule.”

“Well I don’t see how you can even consider getting involved with those people,” said Wendy. “We have a responsibility to the reputation of our whole school, and associating with the play would send a negative message.”

“I disagree,” said Lisa, “all right… let’s get back to it.”

There was a clear sense of dissension as the girls took their places to continue working on their routine.

***

At home Lisa broached the subject of the play with her mother. “I really think it’s something I’d like to try,” said Lisa. “I think it would be a good experience to work with other kids on a creative project.”

“Hmm, odd,” said Lisa’s mother.

Ainsley Weston Lesinski was a Glennville, New Jersey native. She had been a high school cheerleader herself, and had coached Lisa’s elementary school squad. To her, cheerleading was all it. She had passively allowed Lisa to pursue dance classes, but only in the mission of their value in creating cheer routines. Ainsley, who at 53, was still quite fetching, was not big into the arts. She had even questioned Lisa's enrollment in the theatre arts class.

But Lisa had found a passion in dance far beyond her mother's understanding. She had thrived in her ballet, modern and gymnastics classes. And, yes, they had brought value to her cheerleading skills, but to Lisa they were so much more.

"What's odd?" asked Lisa's father, as he entered the kitchen.

"I was thinking I'd like to audition for the school musical this year," said Lisa.

"Of course, that would be utterly impossible," said Ainsley.

"Why would it be impossible?" asked Lisa's father, Charles, "I was in my high school musical...*The Music Man*. It was wonderful."

"Thank you, Daddy," said Lisa.

"But what about cheering?" exclaimed Ainsley. "She is committed to being a cheerleader. *A cheerleader!!!* She *cannot* do both!"

Charles Lesinski, a paunch, balding banker, had learned years earlier that taking sides against his wife was not a wise thing to do.

"Hmm, I guess she's right, Sweetie," said Charles, "Sorry."

***

The next day in theatre class Moretti charged his class to create free movement to the strains of "The Benjamin Calypso," from the *Joseph* score. The song was upbeat and prompted some good energy and lots of fun for the participants. Even some of the scary boys seemed to drop their natural trepidations and got into the spirit of things. Moretti enjoyed watching the natural vitality evolve in his classroom. Lisa and Patty, both trained dancers, flourished with some particularly sophisticated steps. Afterward, Moretti complimented them on their work and suggested they might be able to help choreograph the show. The girls were flattered by the complement. As class dismissed, the theatre students exited into the hallway with exceptional exuberance.

After school at cheer practice, Lisa and Patty taught the "Benjamin" steps to several other members of the squad. The cheer girls were sparkling to the fully cranked music, when their coach, Stacy Stevens entered the gym. Stevens was puzzled by what she saw.

"It's a theatre arts routine," explained Wendy Phillips, who had followed Stevens into the gym.

Stacy Stevens sported a regal air in her walk, talk and deed. Although teaching social studies was her primary assignment at Meadow Hills, the educator regarded her classroom activities as a casual sideline. Rather, her true claim to fame was her role as varsity coach of the district's championship cheerleading squad. While short in stature, 5' 2", Stevens carried her petite frame as if a giant…taking very wide steps. Her flaming red hair was perched in tight strands on her oval head and her pug nose was permanently aimed upward. The arrogance of her personality matched her physical presentation. But in all her pomp and circumstance, Stevens was plagued with a pronounced speech impediment: a lateral lisp. Now, to be clear, this was not a frontal lisp, substituting "th" for "s"-- "*th*ing a *th*ong of *th*ix*th*penth." A lateral lisp usually replaced "s" sounds with "sh"-- "*sh*ing a *sh*ong of *sh*ix*sh*pen*sh*." Stevens was either unaware of the affliction or simply chose to ignore it. Sadly for her, not many others were oblivious. Imitating Mrs. Stevens' speech pattern was a common practice across the social spectrum of the student body… "*Sh*tudent*sh*, under*sh*tanding the United *Sh*ates Con*sh*titution i*zh* your *sh*ivic re*sh*pon*sh*ibility!" Lots of belly laughs up and down the hallways. In fact, there had even been a few reported impressionists in the faculty room.

As the energetic theatre class routine ended, Stevens smiled and nodded. "That'*ch* quite *sh*omething," said Stevens, "Did Mr. Moretti teach you tho*zh*e move*zh*?

The girls snickered as Patty explained that she and Lisa had made up the routine as part of a class exercise.

"Hmm, too bad you can't get *sh*ome of that ex*sh*itement into your competition drill," said Stevens. "Let'*sh* change the mu*zh*ic and get practi*sh*ing, okay? The smiles on the girls faded as they prepared to execute their cheer regimen.

Lisa stepped forward, "Mrs. Stevens, some of us were hoping to audition for the play this year. Do you think we might be able to share our time between cheering and the show?"

"You want to do the mu*zh*ical?" asked Stevens. "How many of you are interested in doing the mu*zh*ical?"

Lisa, Patty, Lauren Horn and two freshmen raised their hands.

Stevens counted, "1, 2, 3, 4, 5—I count five of you. *Sh*o how do you ex*sh*pect to field a competition *sh*quad if half the team is rehear*sh*ing *sh*ome *sh*illy play? No, Li*sh*a I'm *sh*orry, it'*ch* out of the que*sh*tion."

Lisa pulled a notebook out of her bag and approached Stevens, "But I think it could work. See, I worked out a schedule, where we could spend half of the time here at practice and the other half at rehearsal. Mr. Moretti said he'd be happy to cooperate."

Stevens face reddened, "Did he now? Well that's ju*sh*t wonderful. But *I'm* not happy to cooperate. Not at all. Don't you get it? Cheering is not ju*sh*t another *sh*chool activity. It represent*sh* the culture of thi*sh* community. You have to have a *sh*en*sh*e of pride. And you can't show pride when you're only committed halfway."

"That's not fair," Lisa replied, "I've been totally committed to this team for four years. I've planned and taught all the routines, organized summer practices and worked individually with girls who were struggling. I don't think it's unreasonable to adjust our practice schedule to accommodate the play. Some of the other coaches are working it out with Moretti."

Stevens was really angry now, "Well *I'm* not any other coach. I'm *your* coach. And I'm telling you that if you want to be in the '*sh*cool mu*zh*ical,' you're not going to be on thi*sh* cheer team. And that'*ch* final." Stevens stormed out of the gym and slammed the door shut behind her.

***

The next day, Stevens was paged to the high school office. When she arrived, Mrs. Loomis, the principal's secretary said that Dr. Richardson wanted to speak with her. Richardson had been principal of Meadow Hills High School for the past six years. He was known to be a compassionate educator and a very nice man. He had championed the expansion of the arts programs at the school and was particularly proud of the theatre program. While his accomplishments were embraced by much of the community, the athletic contingent was far from enthusiastic.

When Stevens entered the principal's office she was surprised to see Lisa seated and waiting.

Richardson began, "Thank you for coming Mrs. Stevens. I've just been talking to Lisa about our team's progress so far this year."

"You have?" Stevens was flat and guarded.

"Yes, she feels our team is stronger this year than last." said Richardson.

"Well it *sh*ertainly ha*zh* the potential to be," replied Stevens.

Richardson went on to explain Lisa's request to adjust the cheer practice schedule to accommodate several girls who were interested in also doing the school musical.

Richardson held up Lisa's notebook, "She seems to have done a diligent job in working out a schedule that would allow the girls to do both activities. I think it would be great if we could pull this off...really good for the school."

Stevens took a deep breath, glared at Lisa, and then softened to Richardson, "A*zh* I'm sure Li*sh*a told you, we di*sh*cu*sh*ed thi*sh* ye*sh*terday at practi*sh*e."

Lisa piped in, "Yes, but—"

Stevens brashly cut her off "And—"

Stevens then assumed a phony smile, "It would shertainly be a wonderful thing if everybody got to do whatever they wanted to do. But a championship cheer team i*zh* a proud repre*zh*entative, not only of our *sh*chool, but of our entire town. No…I'm afraid thi*sh* plan i*zh* *sh*imply not po*sh*ible. I'm *sh*orry"

In spite of Richardson's accomplishments as principal, he was not known for being particularly endowed in the cojones department.

"So I guess that's a no?" the principal asked.

Stevens smirked at Lisa and executed an exit/door slam.

"Hmm….sorry Lisa," murmured the principal. "Thanks for your suggestion. Have a good day."

3
Energized
January 7, 2019

"Lisa Stratton...Lisa? Is there a Lisa Stratton here?" came a voice from the front of the Town Square Playhouse.

"Mom, that's you!," said Charlie, as she tugged her mother's shirt sleeve.

Lisa roused out of her haze and stood up. "Yes…here…present." She handed her bag to Charlie and walked to the front of the theatre.

"Hi there," said Moretti, not yet recognizing Lisa. "So what have you prepared for us today?"

"*Nora's* act three monologue?" said Lisa, "*You have never loved me…*"

"Ah, great choice," said Moretti. "Why don't you head up on the stage and begin whenever you're ready."

"Okay." Lisa mounted the steps to the stage. She took a deep breath and began the monologue she had practiced for Charlie in the car. Although tentative at first, Lisa gained confidence as she continued. Gradually, the usual undertones in the house quieted. Lisa clearly understood the words she was saying and was effectively communicating that perception. Several auditionees exchanged approving glances. As she performed, her daughter, Charlie, was grinning from ear to ear.

When Lisa concluded the monologue, her eyes found Moretti, who was smiling at her.

"Lisa *Lesinski*!" said Moretti. "I thought you looked familiar!" Moretti apologized for not recognizing her straight on. "How have you been?" he asked.

"Well, I've had some ups and downs," said Lisa, "but things have been looking pretty good lately."

"It's wonderful to see you," said Moretti, "and your monologue was fine. If you wouldn't mind, I wonder if you could read a couple of other scenes."

"Sure," said Lisa.

She hadn't really expected to be cast as *Nora*. Well, maybe a little. But after all, Lisa hadn't been on any stage in nearly ten years. And this was her first audition at the Town Square Playhouse. Moretti had her read for *Kristine*, Nora's friend and *Anne Marie*, Nora's nanny.

The audition had gone well. Lisa was energized. At the end of the evening, Moretti walked to the rear of the house, where Lisa and Charlie were sitting. He sat in the row in front of them. "It's such a wonderful surprise to see you, Lisa," he said.

"I had no idea you would be here," said Lisa. "I live nearby and have been interested in getting involved with this theatre for some time. Oh, this is my daughter, Charlie."

Moretti shook Charlie's hand, "Well, how do you do, Charlie. Your Mom was one of my all-time favorite students…ever!"

"Hello!" Charlie responded, smiling.

Moretti told Lisa he was now retired from Meadow Hills. He explained that although he had founded the theatre many years ago, his time to engage had been limited by his high school commitments. "Anyway, it's good to see you," said Moretti as he rose from his seat, "You had a good audition. We should be able to figure the casting out in a few days. We'll be in touch." He smiled and winked at Charlie as he returned to the front of the theatre.

"He seems nice!" said Charlie.

"Oh, yeah…he's a good guy," said Lisa, as she and Charlie exited to the rear of the theatre.

*****

During the drive home, Lisa and Charlie laughed and sang along to more of *Barbra Streisand's Greatest Hits*. They both belted from the top of their lungs:

"Nobody, no, nobody. Is gonna rain on my parade…"

Then they both enjoyed a huge laugh together. "Oh, I haven't had so much fun since…I can't remember when," said Lisa.

"I had fun too, Mom," said Charlie. "When will you find out if you made the play?"

"Oh, I don't know. Mr. Moretti said they would decide in the next few days. But I'm not holding my breath. They had a lot of good people to choose from."

"Well, I think you were the best of everybody there," said Charlie. "They're nuts if they don't pick you."

Lisa smiled as she looked up at her daughter in the rearview mirror, "Thanks for your vote of confidence, Buddy, but there are many considerations to casting a show. It's complicated."

"Bullshit!" blurted Charlie.

"Hey! What did I say about language?!"

“I’m sorry,” said Charlie, “but we had such a good time tonight at the theatre. I just hope we get to go back.”

“We will,” said Lisa. “If not for this show, then for another.”

“What other?” asked Charlie.

“I don’t know right at this moment. But we will return to the Playhouse. I promise.”

As Lisa pulled into her driveway, she spotted a familiar figure sitting on the front porch. It was her ex-husband, Mark Stratton. Mark’s appearance hadn’t changed much over the years. He still conveyed abundant good looks. However, his frequent enjoyment of beer had promoted a thickening of his physical frame. His once smooth complexion had roughened somewhat, taking on a reddish leather texture. His blond hair was longer now and usually unkempt. Still to most onlookers, Mark was a very handsome man.

As he watched his daughter and ex-wife get out of the car, Mark did not look happy.

“Hi Daddy,” greeted Charlie.

“Hey there, Squirt,” replied Mark. He embraced his daughter and swung her vigorously prompting delighted laughter from Charlie.

“Where’ve you guys been?” Mark asked. “I’ve been waiting here for over an hour.”

“We went to a theatre for Mom to audition for a play,” said Charlie. “She was really good! We had a great time.”

Mark looked at Lisa in surprise. “Back to doin’ plays again, huh? Kinda late for Charlie to be out on a school night, I’d say.”

“My mother was supposed to stay with her,” said Lisa, “but she cancelled at the last minute.”

"So you took her with you! Pretty irresponsible if you ask me!"

"It's fine, Daddy," said Charlie. " I've got all my homework done and it's only a little after nine. It's fine."

"Well, I don't like it!" Mark replied. "Is this gonna happen all the time?"

"No!" said Lisa. "No. I probably won't even be cast. I just wanted to go and check it out. What did you need Mark?"

"Oh, look, uh, I'm not gonna be able to pick up the kid 'till late on Friday night," said Mark. "I've gotta run upstate to check out this cool bike this guy is practically giving away. I just can't pass up a chance like that."

Mark had become suspiciously unreliable about his weekend time with Charlie.

"How late?" asked Lisa.

"Probably pull back here around 9… 10 o'clock, the latest."

"Well, our arrangement is that you pick Charlie up after school on Fridays. I told my job I would work this Friday night."

"Can't you get out of it?" asked Mark.

"It's pretty short notice," said Lisa. "How about if I bring Charlie to my Mom's house after school. And you can pick her up there when you get in."

"That works for me," Mark said.

Mark leaned into Charlie. "I can't wait for you to see my cool new bike, Squirt." Charlie smiled at her father.

"Now… you don't have any crazy notion about riding her on this motorcycle, right?" asked Lisa.

"Crap!" said Mark. "Give me a little credit will you? I would never put our daughter in harm's way. Never!"

"Okay, good," said Lisa. "I'll check with Mom tomorrow and let you know. I'm sure it will be all right."

"Great!" said Mark, "Okay, good night, Squirt." Mark embraced Charlie and kissed her.

"Good night, Daddy. See you Friday."

Mark turned to Lisa and stepped toward her. Lisa backed away. Mark's expression turned sullen.

"Night," and he was gone.

4
Contention
December 11, 2007

Stacy Stevens was livid that Lisa had gone to the principal behind her back. The idea that a student would undermine her decision regarding the school musical was unfathomable to her. At cheer practice Stevens avoided making direct eye contact with Lisa and totally stopped speaking to her. She became highly critical of the competition routine, and specifically harped on Lisa's choreographic work at every possible opportunity. This had been going on for almost a week and Lisa had become weary of Stevens' incessant attacks. In the locker room after practice, Lisa unloaded on Patty.

"She is out of control. I don't know how much longer I can take this pettiness. Who's the adult here, huh?"

"She's been pretty rough on you, all right," said Patty. "Maybe you shouldn't have gone to Richardson."

"Maybe not, but this is ridiculous. It's getting so I hate coming to practice."

"Don't say that. You're our leader. You have to get us charged up, if we're gonna have *any* chance of being a competitive squad."

"I think I just need a break from all this *drama,*" said Lisa. "Isn't that ironic? Drama! Okay, I have a thought."

Lisa and Patty were co-captains of the cheer squad. Part of their responsibility was to set the practice schedule. Lisa suggested that the next day's practice might begin at 3:30 instead of 3:00. This type of adjustment often would occur for various reasons, such as accommodating student make-up work or tutoring needs.

"Sure," said Patty. "Why? Do you have to make up a test?"

"Not exactly," said Lisa "Here's the deal…" The girls spoke softly to each other as they exited the locker room.

The next day after theatre class, Lisa and Patty approached Moretti. Auditions for *Joseph* were scheduled for that afternoon. The girls wondered if they might be allowed to audition early in the session, so they could still arrive at cheer practice on time.

"Well, I'm not sure how early I can get to you, but I will certainly try to cooperate," said Moretti. "The wrestlers need to be processed early as well."

"Thank you," said Lisa.

"No, thank *you*," Moretti said. "I'm delighted that you two are going to do the show."

"Well, we're not sure yet," said Patty.

Moretti looked confused.

"Uhmm, after all," Lisa said, "we haven't been chosen yet, right?"

Moretti half-smiled, "Oh…right. See you at auditions…and I suggest you get here early…so we can get you out early."

That afternoon the auditorium was crowded. Moretti had managed to interest lots of kids in the show. It was truly amazing to see so many different social groups represented. Certainly there were plenty of artsy-fartsy, band and chorus kids present. But there was also a good ratio of the more disenfranchised types signing in as well. And maybe most extraordinary, was the considerable count of wrestlers and football players in the line. Incredibly, *Joseph* auditions had become a microcosm of the whole school…almost. Notably missing were the likes of Mark Stratton and Ricky Jones, the more hard core self-designated "cool" kids. Moretti explained that the audition process would be in three phases: singing, dancing and improv. Lisa and Patty rotated through the procedure fairly quickly. They both felt their strength had been in the dance phase and that their weakest showing was in singing. To be sure, try as they might, "do re mi mi-mi-mi!" both girls had difficulty matching the pitch prompts of the music director, Mrs. Lauren. But they were surprised at their enjoyment in interacting with the other students in the improv portion. When they had completed all three phases, Lisa and Patty felt exhilarated about their audition and excited about the show.

They arrived at the gym right on time for cheer practice. Stevens cast an indignant gaze at Lisa.

***

The following Friday, the cast list for *Joseph And The Amazing Technicolor Dreamcoat* was posted on Moretti's office door. Lisa and Patty had been listed as members of the featured dance ensemble. The posting advised that rehearsals would begin upon return from Christmas break.

It didn't take long for word to spread around the school that the co-captains of the cheer squad had been cast in the school musical. Stevens was outraged. Not only had she been undermined, she had been directly defied! She believed stern disciplinary action was warranted. She had Lisa and Patty paged to the principal's office. Stevens was cold as ice and suggested the girls be suspended for contradicting her authority. Dr. Richardson explained to the girls that although it was admirable that they wanted to do the show, it just wasn't feasible to do both the show and the cheer squad. He suggested that their actions in auditioning had placed vulnerability on both programs. On the other hand he rejected Stevens' contention that they be suspended. The girls were excused. They forlornly exited Richardson's office.

After school Lisa and Patty went to see Moretti. They explained what had occurred. Moretti was disappointed.

"Would it help if I spoke to Mrs. Stevens myself?" he asked.

"No..." said Patty. "That would probably make things even worse. I'm so sorry Mr. Moretti. C'mon Lisa, we'd better get to practice."

"Go ahead, Patty," Lisa said. "I'll be right there."

Lisa asked Moretti if he would consider holding off on recasting their parts for a little while. She wanted to give the matter some serious thought. He said he would be happy to in that he had managed to include roles for everyone who had auditioned for the show. So recasting Patty and Lisa would simply be a matter of shuffling things around a bit.

"Take your time and figure it out," Moretti said. "I just don't want you to bring on any more trouble for yourself, okay?"

"Right, thank you Mr. Moretti. I'll let you know as soon as possible." Lisa turned and headed for the gym.

***

Lisa decided to take one more crack at convincing Stevens to reconsider her position regarding the play. After practice she lingered until the other girls had gone home. She then made her way to the coach's office.

Steven's office was located midway between the gym and auditorium. It was notable by its 5' by 3' picture window situated beside its entrance door. Steven's almost always drew the window's venetian blinds to conceal her from students passing in the hallway.

Lisa knocked on Stevens' half-opened office door.

"Ye*sh*," said Stevens, who was sitting at her desk.

"Can I speak to you for a minute?" asked Lisa.

"Okay, but it'll have to be quick," said Stevens. "I have an engagement to get to tonight."

"Sure," said Lisa, as she closed the office door behind her. "I just wanted to say I feel really badly about how things have gone between us lately. I mean, you've been my coach for four years. I feel like we've had a good relationship. And now that graduation is around the corner, I hate to see us at such odds."

"*Sh*o… you want to apologi*zh*e!" said Stevens. "Well that'*ch* under*sh*tandable, Li*sh*a, but the egregiou*sh*nes*sh* of your act*sh*ion*zh* can*not* be fix*sh*ed by *sh*imply *sh*aying I'm *sh*orry."

"Actually, I'm not here to apologize," Lisa replied. "I was hoping to convince you to change your mind about the musical."

Stevens scowled at her.

Lisa continued, "But I can see by the look on your face, that's not going to happen, is it?"

"You are *sh*o right about that!" said Stevens.

Stacy Stevens stood up from her desk and began pacing the floor of her office like a caged animal. She could barely contain herself. She began to rant and rave. In doing so, her voice elevated in pitch and volume until she sounded like a raving banshee.

"In all my year*zh* as a coach and educator, I've never encountered a more obnoxiou*sh*, ungrateful little *sh*nit as you. How dare you approach me for con*sh*ideration after *I've* been the one brutally injured in all thi*sh*. I am the laughing *sh*tock of this faculty. Your name and Quinn'*zh* get listed on that *sh*tupid ca*sh*t li*sh*t, and I look like a blithering idiot! It make*sh* it appear that I have no control over the cheerleader*zh*… but I do have control. I *do* have control, don't I… *bitch*!"

"Mrs. Stevens!" Lisa was shocked.

People in the outer hallway heard the commotion and gathered around the closed office door.

"*Sh*tuff it!" yelled Stevens. "If it were up to me, you'd be out.-- O-U-T. I wouldn't care if we lo*sh*t every competition. Thi*sh* team would be far better off without you. But you've got an in with that gutles*sh* prin*sh*ipal and our inept athletic director, so I can't kick you out. But you'll get no con*sh*ideration from me! No con*sh*ideration of any kind! You're a bad apple, Le*sh*in*sh*ki. Now get the hell out of my… *sh*ight!"

***

Stacy Stevens wasn't always so disagreeable. When she began her teaching career eight years earlier she was enthusiastic and full of ideals. She was a newlywed with high hopes and dreams. She planned that she and her husband, Rod, would work their way up the teacher's salary guide and eventually save enough to purchase a home…and even more eventually start a family. It was an exciting time. Stevens taught Social Studies at Meadow Hills while Rod was an English teacher across the county at rival, Wainsburg.

All seemed well, until about three years ago. Rob's car, a 1980 Chevrolet Malibu, suffered ongoing mechanical problems. It had clocked over 120 thousand miles and was continually breaking down. Finally the Chevy's transmission totally failed rendering it undrivable. Stevens' 1988 Jetta was in pretty good shape, but they weren't in a good financial position to replace Rob's car. They both were paying off college loans and had run into some credit difficulty. Becoming a one car couple was less than convenient, but they really had no other option. Stevens would drop Rod off at his school every morning before proceeding to hers. They both coached after school, so by the time Stevens picked Rod up it was nearly 7 o'clock…a long day for both. But neither seemed to really mind. At some point, Rod began catching rides home with a

"Wainsburg colleague." At first, Stevens appreciated not having to pick her husband up every night.

"That's great…that mean*zh* I'll be able to cook a ni*sh*e dinner for u*sh*."

Initially, the practice was occasional…maybe once a week. But gradually it became more often and eventually, the colleague provided Rod's home commute every night. It wasn't until months later that Stevens discovered the "colleague" was female.

Again… "no big deal," she thought, "…no big deal."

Usually, Rod arrived home between 7:30 and 8:00 pm.

"Kids were late being picked up from practice," he'd say, "had to wait until their rides arrived."

This annoyed Stevens, because it was happening almost every night. Her carefully planned dinners were being ruined. But one night, Rod didn't get home until after 10:00.

"Where the heck have you been?" she asked. "I've been worried."

"Oh, I had a problem with a parent," Rob replied, "…had to meet with Principal Sharkey."

Rod explained the parent had accused him of showing favoritism on the team. The parent had called the principal and insisted the three have a sit down.

"How did it go?" Stevens asked.

Rod replied that the principal had not been very supportive. "He wanted to make sure he covered his ass with that parent…you know?"

"That'*sh* awful," Stevens exclaimed. "I'm *sh*o *sh*orry."

Oddly, Stevens hadn't considered the peculiar circumstance of a parent/principal meeting at 8:30 in the evening. Instead she was totally supportive. She gave her husband a hug and kissed him. "C'mon, let'*ch* eat," she said.

Perhaps had Stacy more closely scrutinized the strange circumstances of that evening, she could have addressed her marital problems forthright. Unfortunately, Rob's sordid affair with a married Wainsburg guidance counselor led to the end of Stacy Stevens' marriage.

Subsequently, Stevens became quite bitter, isolated and insensitive. Her only remnant of self-esteem was garnered through her coaching achievements. She wasn't about to let some "silly high school musical" take that away from her.

5
Karaoke
January 11, 2019

Lisa Stratton didn't mind working occasional evenings. Her new role as a supervisor of the Little Sprout Daycare Center, required her to rotate between the day and evening shifts. Parents whose occupation required late working hours were grateful the center was open until 10:00 each night.

Lisa had earned 3 credits in Early Childhood Education at Atlantic University, prior to dropping out. Although she had majored in dance/theatre, as per her scholarship, she had declared a minor in education. Her parents had never been sold on the idea of a career in dance for their daughter and insisted that she augment her studies with a career path on which to fall back. Now, as a single mom, Lisa was grateful that her parents' advice had helped her to secure a relatively good job. She totally enjoyed working with the pre-school children. She devised creative and meaningful activities that promoted positive engagement. Lisa was also very good at training the non-professional staff in productive child-care interactions. Since joining Little Sprout, Lisa had continued to take courses online. The owners of the facility were extremely happy with her.

Lisa also enjoyed working evenings because it gave her the opportunity to connect with Cailla McCormack. Cailla and Lisa had begun at Little Sprout at the same time, nearly seven years earlier. They shared many common goals and had become good friends. Cailla had been transferred to a permanent night shift assignment about a year ago. So when Lisa also worked at night, it was an enjoyable reunion between the two.

As the shift wound down, Cailla suggested that she and Lisa get a drink at the Cabin Tavern after work.

“Oh, that sounds great,” said Lisa, “but I’d better not.”

“C’mon, it’ll be fun,” said Cailla. “They have karaoke tonight. We could sing a duet.”

“Please…I haven’t sung in forever. No, I’d better get home.”

“Is Charlie with a sitter?” asked Cailla.

“Umm…actually Charlie is with Mark tonight.”

“She is! So what the heck… you and I are going to the Cabin!”

Lisa frowned and shook her head but, after a beat, flashed a smile. “Okay.”

By the time Lisa and Cailla arrived at the Tavern, “Karaoke Night” was in full swing…and the place was hopping. Lisa hadn’t been out socially in years and was feeling less than comfortable. She didn’t see anyone she knew, but it was clear that everyone was having a good time. She and Cailla sat at the bar and each had a beer. They enjoyed listening to the singers. Cailla thought it was funny how some participants took the songs “so very seriously,” while others were just up there to have fun.

Gradually Lisa began to feel more at ease. The crowd seemed very friendly. It was a nice environment. Unbeknownst to her, Cailla had signed them up to sing. When the KJ called their names for “The Boy Is Mine, ” Lisa yelled. “No!! No!! I’m not doing it!” Cailla pulled her off the bar stool and started walking her up to the stage. The bar patrons started applauding and cheering them on. The music began and it was clear that Cailla had a really good voice. Lisa was totally uncooperative at first, but Cailla and the crowd kept encouraging. Finally Lisa jumped in.

The two women sounded good together. As they proceeded, the performance became stronger and more energized. By the time they finished, they owned the joint. Wild applause followed their big finish. The girls received joyful high fives as they made their way back to the bar.

“Oh, that was fun,” said Lisa, as she mounted her stool. “Thank you for making me do that.”

“Sure,” said Cailla, “it was great!”

In just a short time, Lisa felt she had found a new and very comfortable spot in her life. She actually sensed a bit of guilt in her enjoyment. Lisa adored everything about her daughter. She absolutely loved being with her. But she had to admit this evening of child independence was probably good for her.

Just then the bartender placed two bottles of lager in front of Lisa and Cailla.

“Oh, no more for me,” said Lisa.

“C’mon you nursed your first all night,” said Cailla. “One more won’t hurt you.”

“I guess not, but you should have asked me before you ordered it.”

“I didn’t order it,” said Cailla.

Then the bartender piped in, “—that fellow at the corner of the bar bought them for you.”

Lisa and Cailla looked up at the young man being pointed out by the bartender. Cailla smiled and waved. The guy looked familiar to Lisa, but she couldn’t place him. Lisa threw him a half smile and toasted her bottle.

Cailla and Lisa discussed who it might be.

"*I* don't know him," said Cailla. "I'm sure of that. Looks like you've got an admirer."

"Oh, please!"

Cailla said, "Hey, come on—it's high time you got back out there, pal."

Lisa blushed as she laughed.

Cailla nudged Lisa's arm with her elbow. "Don't look now but he's headed our way."

"Shit!" said Lisa.

The young man approached Lisa and Cailla tentatively. He wasn't sure how he might be received. "Hello," he said. "I hope you don't mind me buying you a drink. I enjoyed your song very much."

"No…not at all. Thank you!" said Cailla. "I'm Cailla and this is my friend Lisa."

"Hello," Lisa said.

The young man shook hands with both women. "I'm Nick. I actually went to high school with you, Lisa."

"I thought you looked familiar."

"We were in theatre class together," Nick said. "You were a senior and I was a junior. Once, Moretti put me on the spot and you encouraged me. I always appreciated that."

Lisa's face brightened in reflection. "Yes, I remember now. But your hair was much longer then… and you had a beard, as I recall."

Nick laughed. "Yup…that was me. You remember me, huh?"

"Yes…sure, how've you been?" Lisa asked.

"Can't complain," said Nick. "I did a hitch in the service after high school. Then I went to work in my uncle's cabinet installation business."

"Well, that sounds interesting," said Cailla.

"You really think so?" Nick smiled. "I don't really find it interesting…at all. I've been going to school at night."

"Wow, good for you! Sounds like a lot to manage," said Lisa. "What are you studying?"

"I'm in pre-law. I've got a long way to go, but I'm determined… By the way, I really liked your audition the other night."

"What audition?" Cailla asked.

"Wait a minute. You were there?" Lisa asked Nick.

"What audition!" Cailla repeated impatiently.

"Oh, it was nothing," said Lisa. "On a whim, I went over to the Town Square Playhouse last week and auditioned for *A Doll's House*. I wasn't very good."

"Are you kidding?" said Nick. "You were great…at least *I* thought you were."

"Well, thank you," said Lisa. "What were you doing there?"

"I was up in the light booth. I help out there when I can. During my senior year of high school I got really involved in the tech aspects of the theatre. Moretti used to say I was his right hand man. I stayed in touch with him while I was in the Army. After I got out, he invited me to help him at the Playhouse."

"That is so wild," said Lisa, "because I recall you not being enthusiastic about theatre…at all!"

"Yeah, you're right," said Nick. "I wasn't at first. But then somebody smiled at me…and I changed."

Nick grinned as he clearly directed the sentiment to Lisa.

"Oh..," said Lisa. She was a little embarrassed, but also a little pleased.

"Well, it was nice seeing you…both," said Nick. "Maybe we'll be working together on the show, Lisa."

"Oh, I doubt I'll be cast."

"Don't sell yourself short. I could tell you were good, because all the diva girls were complaining about you," Nick laughed and he was off.

"Hmm…*veddy in-te-des-ting*," said Cailla. "I think you are the object of *somebody's* crush.

"Oh, stop!" said Lisa, as she tried to conceal a smile.

"And apparently have been for years," Cailla added. "Kinda cute, if you ask me."

"I'm not asking you," said Lisa, "although he seems to have changed a lot since high school."

As Cailla and Lisa mulled over the mysterious appearance of Nick Curtis, there came a loud disturbance at the entranceway of the bar. A rowdy group of women made their way into the club, totally oblivious to the heartfelt strains of "You Light Up My Life" being emoted with ultra-sincerity from the karaoke stage. The singer, a fifty year old short, stocky, sweaty fellow, was distracted by the intrusion and shot the girl-gang a resentful glare. As the women crowded around a nearby table, Lisa gasped.

“Oh, hell, it’s Wendy!”

Wendy Phillips had been on the cheer team with Lisa in high school. They had a dark history. Wendy was Mark’s “other woman.” Simply-put: there was no love lost between the two.

Although Phillips had generally maintained her natural attractiveness over the years, Lisa couldn’t help but notice some obvious alterations. Her brown hair was now finely streaked in purple, she sported bejeweled nose and tongue piercings, and her flimsy top was quite tight, leaving little to the imagination.

It was clear that Wendy and her posse had been imbibing prior to their arrival at the Cabin Tavern. They continued to be loud and obnoxious, spoiling a heretofore pleasant social environment. As Wendy held court with her crew, her gaze fell on Lisa. Her chatter stopped abruptly as she stood and made her way to the bar. Lisa saw her coming and offered a brave smile.

“Well, look who it is!” said Wendy. “Oh Captain, My Captain!” Wendy flashed an insincere grin as she referenced the fact that Lisa had been captain of the cheer squad in high school.

“C’mon…that was a long time ago, Wendy,” said Lisa, “How are you?”

“I’m great! I’m just great. I haven’t seen you in these parts in a long time. Where have you been keeping yourself?”

“Oh, I’m over in Lakeside…but I work at the daycare center here in town,” Lisa responded. “This is my friend, Cailla. We work together… and this is Wendy…we cheered together in high school.”

Cailla and Wendy exchanged polite greetings. Lisa was feeling uncomfortable. Then Wendy began agitating. “I was just visiting Mark. He bought a new bike tonight and invited me over to take a ride.”

“Is that so?” said Lisa.

“I don’t suppose he told you about his new bike, did he?” Wendy’s phony smile, became a gloating smirk.

“Actually he did mention something about that,” said Lisa. “How is it?”

“Oh, it’s so cool,” said Wendy. “Here look, I took a video.”

Wendy held up her phone for Lisa to see. As Lisa watched the video, her face grimaced. “Holy shit…I’ve gotta go!” She threw a twenty dollar bill on the bar and made a beeline for the exit.

Cailla was bewildered. “Let me see that video!”

“Sure…here you go.” Wendy smiled smugly.

Cailla shook her head as she viewed the images of Mark riding on his new motorcycle, with an obviously frightened Charlie holding on for dear life on the seat behind him.

6
Auld Lang Syne
December 14, 2007

To say the least, Lisa Lesinski's outreach to Stacy Stevens regarding her participation in the school musical had not gone well. In fact Lisa was shattered by her coach's vile reaction. She had never been spoken to in such an odious manner, and certainly not by a teacher. Her initial reaction was to report the incident to school authorities and seek retribution against Stevens. But as Lisa regained composure she decided to hold off on such a plan.

"It was the week before Christmas break," she reasoned, "perhaps it would be best to let the dust settle."

Lisa was looking forward to vacation. It would be her final Christmas as a high school student. She was anxiously anticipating the next phase of her life. But for now, holiday relaxation with family and friends seemed to be just what she needed. She believed the turmoil and drama at Meadow Hills High School could well wait until the new year.

Christmas morning at the Lesinski's was always enjoyable. Lisa helped her mother, Ainsley, prepare a variety of breakfast goodies for the family. These included hot cinnamon buns, buttered biscuits and freshly baked gingerbread. Lisa's Dad, Charles, turned on the television to the channel 11 yule log, which provided nice holiday music in the background.

When it came time to open gifts, Lisa's twelve year old brother Todd, received most of the attention. He was big into video gaming and was ecstatic at receiving his new Xbox system. Todd was lost to the world for the remainder of the morning. Charles was appreciative of his new recliner and Ainsley loved her exquisite diamond bracelet. Lisa's main gift was a pair of New York Knicks tickets for her and Mark, as well as a gift certificate for dinner in the city on the night of the game. In actuality, Lisa was a little disappointed. She liked the idea of spending an evening in New York City, but the gift seemed less than personal to her. Especially after she had asked for tickets to a Broadway show.

It was a little past noon when Mark arrived for Christmas dinner. He seemed to be in a happy mood. He brought a ribbon-laden six pack of lager for Charles, a lovely floral centerpiece for Ainsley and a meticulously wrapped holiday gift box for Lisa.

"How pretty," said Lisa. "Did you wrap it yourself?"

"Hell, no!" said Mark, "that is not my thing. They wrapped it at the store."

"I kinda' figured as much," Lisa said, as she carefully removed the wrapping. She opened the package to find a gorgeous cashmere sweater.

"Oh, it's beautiful." Lisa held the garment up to her cheek, "…so soft."

"My Mom helped me pick it out," said Mark.

"Well, obviously, your Mom and you both have splendid taste," said Ainsley.

Lisa was thrilled with Mark's gift. She appreciated the fact that he had taken the care and time to choose something she would like. Her gift to him was a set of fancy hubcaps for his Cavalier...about which he had been hinting for months.

"Well, I hope everyone's hungry," Ainsley said. "Time to eat."

The holiday feast was festive and high spirited. Ainsley had prepared a wonderful dinner, with Lisa's help. There was lots of laughter and good will. Lisa couldn't help but think that this pleasant scene might be predictive of things to come, with Mark as her husband in the not too distant future. She smiled reflectively at the thought. After dinner, Mark and Lisa took their leave of the Lesinski's. The rest of Christmas Day was to be spent with Mark's family...complete with a second Christmas meal.

Lisa grabbed a selection of baked goods she had prepared for Mark's family and the young couple took off. They were in a great mood as they headed toward Mark's house. Daylight was fading in the December afternoon, as the radio filled Mark's Cavalier with the sounds of the holidays. It had, so far, been a wonderful day. As they approached the high school, Mark made an abrupt turn into Meadow Hills driveway.

"What's going on?" asked Lisa.

"Oh…you'll see," Mark replied.

"There's nobody here today, dummy…it's Christmas."

"Exactly!" said Mark, as a huge mischievous grin spanned his face.

Mark drove around the back of the school to the parking lot behind the gym. Indeed, there was *no* one around…total seclusion. Mark turned off the ignition.

"What the heck…?" said Lisa.

"Oh, yeah!" Mark was beaming.

He put his arm around Lisa and pulled her close to him. He kissed her lightly. She returned the kiss. Then Mark kissed her again, but much longer this time. Lisa was somewhat taken aback, but stayed with him."

"Wow, you're kind of worked up, huh?" said Lisa.

"…you could say that," Mark replied, as he pulled Lisa even closer, kissing her passionately.

Lisa softly moaned, prompting Mark to continue. Mark's hand brushed Lisa's breast, prompting her to flinch.

"Hey…watch it, buddy!" Lisa said, only half joking.

"Sorry, I can't help myself," Mark said as he kissed her again. "I love you."

This time his hand dropped to Lisa's knee. As he started moving his hand up her leg, Lisa pushed it away.

They both were becoming physically intense.

Lisa pulled away from him. "I think we should be getting to your house," she said.

"Not yet," Mark said as he pulled Lisa toward him. He again dropped his hand to between her legs."

"Stop." Lisa whispered. But Mark continued.

"STOP!" Lisa yelled, and pulled herself as far away from him as she could. "What's the matter with you? Whatever you're thinking right now…IT'S NOT HAPPENING!"

"C'mon, it's Christmas," Mark said, "a time to be generous."

"We need to get to your house," said Lisa. "Your parents will be wondering what happened to us."

"Fine!" Mark became sullen as he roughly started the car and peeled out of the parking lot.

"Oh, c'mon…don't be mad," said Lisa.

"Why not! We've been dating for a year. Don't you think it's time you loosened up a little?"

"Well that may be what you think..." Lisa shot back, "but I'm not comfortable with that idea....at all."

"Fine! Fine!" said Mark. "I guess you're holding all the cards!"

They were both quiet as they drove to Mark's house. The pleasantness of Christmas Day was gone.

***

During the remainder of vacation, Mark and Lisa didn't see much of each other. Mark's family went off to visit relatives in New Hampshire. Lisa believed the break was probably for the best. She had been very upset by the encounter in the high school parking lot. She loved Mark, but feared their relationship was one way...Mark's way. In addition to the physical pressures he had been placing upon her, Mark was also pushing her to abandon plans of attending Atlantic University, and to instead join him wherever his football skills happened to lead. Lisa resented Mark's attitude in this regard. She had worked hard in high school, and Atlantic offered her opportunities not available anywhere else.

In addition, Lisa was still reeling from her nasty skirmish with Stevens. She was devastated. She had been a cheerleader since elementary school and had always enjoyed it. She excelled in the leadership role the sport provided her. Also, she was proud of her accomplishments in creating and executing innovative cheer routines which had proven to be highly competitive. And now, largely due to the hostile antagonism of her coach, she was seriously considering giving it all up.

She knew it wouldn't look good for her to quit cheering during her senior year, but she clearly had been provoked. Although cheering is a full year activity, it's broken down into two seasons. The official winter season would begin after Christmas. If she dropped out now, it wouldn't be like quitting per se. Also, she was drawn to the idea of doing the play. Working with new friends in her school appealed to her. She had developed a good rapport with Moretti—who had floated the idea that Lisa might help create some of the choreography for the show. She didn't think it was fair that the wrestling and track coaches were willing to share time with the play and that Stevens wasn't.

Lisa tried to talk to her parents about her dilemma, but found them less than helpful. They just didn't seem to understand. That Lisa could even consider choosing the musical over cheering sent Ainsley directly to the liquor cabinet. Charles was more sympathetic, but had no real advice for her.

When she tried to talk to Mark about the situation, she became even more frustrated. He refused to take the conversation seriously. Instead he launched into a degrading imitation of a stereotypical drama queen, which he obviously found hysterically amusing.

Lisa knew that Moretti would be at the school several days during break to begin working on the set for the show. She decided to stop by and see him. Jeff Townsend, a boy in her theatre class, was also at the school helping Moretti. Moretti led Lisa into his office. They spoke freely. He said he would love to have Lisa in the show, but totally understood the conflict she faced. He realized how difficult it was for her to choose. Moretti had held off reshuffling the dance ensemble, awaiting Lisa's and Patty's decisions. But he explained that with rehearsals beginning on the return to school, he wouldn't be able to wait any longer.

Lisa became emotional during the meeting with Moretti. She was heartfelt as she shared what she perceived as a lack of support from her parents. She also confided with the drama teacher her misgivings about Mark. She loved him, she thought, but was frustrated by his lack of consideration and support for her. Moretti again sympathized.

"Your parents have maintained a vision and direction for you for many years," he said. "It's understandable that they might struggle with your deviation from that path." Moretti also suggested that Lisa's parents had to accept the fact that their daughter was old enough to decide things for herself.

As far as Mark was concerned, Moretti could see the obvious affection he and Lisa had for each other, but he agreed that a successful relationship had to include a mutual give and take.

***

Lisa felt better after speaking to Moretti. She was still unsure as to what she would do, but it had felt good to honestly express her feelings, without the fear of being judged.

Mark's family returned from New Hampshire on New Year's Eve. Mark picked up Lisa that night as planned to go to a party at his friend Robbie Newman's house. Lisa was looking forward to spending some quality time with Mark…in hopes of putting the unpleasantness of Christmas Day behind them.

The party was a familiar scene: very loud music, lots of athletes and popular kids, no parents…and definitely no geeks. There was also plenty of alcohol.

Mark was the life of the party, drinking beer and making the rounds. Lisa sat passively in a corner nursing a soda. Her friend Patty Quinn, and a few other cheerleaders lingered nearby. It wasn't long before the subject of the play came up. Patty expressed her disappointment in not being able to participate.

"I really wanted to do it," she said. "Those dance routines at auditions were cool."

Lauren Horn, another member of the squad who had expressed an interest in auditioning asked to see the moves. Patty obliged by demonstrating the step combination. Lauren joined in as did a couple of the other girls. They all were enjoying the interaction.

Patty stopped abruptly. "I can't remember what comes next."

Lisa stood and joined. “It’s step-ball-change to the right and step-ball-change to the left, she said. “Then you repeat the whole sequence.”

“That’s right,” said Patty.

The five cheerleaders repeated the routine, laughing the whole time. From the other side of the room, Wendy Phillips rolled her eyes and laughed sarcastically at the impromptu performance.

Following the dance, the girls commiserated about not being able to do the show. Wendy Phillips, who was also a cheerleader, had made her way to the group “Oh, please….you’ve got to be kidding…,” said Wendy, “the people who are in the plays are freaks. Why would you want to have anything to do with them.”

Lisa replied, “ Not that it’s any of your business, but there are some very nice people in the drama club. I’ve made some good friends. It’s not fair that the other coaches are letting team members take part, but we can’t.”

Patty and Lauren and the other girls passively agreed.

Wendy replied, “… the cheerleaders are important to the whole school culture…the other coaches are idiots. Thank goodness Stevens has the gumption to stand up to it. The drama club is an embarrassment!”

The dispute had attracted the attention of the whole house. Mark and his pals jumped in, but they were on Wendy’s side…not Lisa’s.

“I told you not to get involved with those whack-jobs!” Mark said to Lisa, “Now look what a commotion you’ve caused!”

“*I’ve* caused,” Lisa replied. “Thanks. Thanks a lot!”

“Oh, stop!” Mark shouted, “Don’t be a damned prima donna!”

"We need to talk," Lisa said. She led Mark quietly toward the front door. "Come outside. I need some fresh air."

Mark overtly pulled away from her. "It's cold out there! Do you want me to freeze my ass off?" He let out a booming laugh, motivating others in the room to join him.

Lisa looked at him sorrowfully, as she moved to him. "Quit showing off!"

Mark's face and voice assumed a patronizing tone. "Oh, poor baby! All right! Go ahead! I'll be out as soon as I get another beer."

"Don't bother," said Lisa, as she hoisted the remains of her soda in his face.

There was a collective gasp from the partygoers.

"Hey!" Mark wasn't laughing any more.

Fighting tears, Lisa exited the front door.

"Bitch!" yelled Mark.

The room was abuzz.

Wendy brought Mark a towel from the kitchen and dabbed his face, as she led him slowly out of the room.

7
Strawberry
January 11, 2019

Lisa Stratton was trembling when she returned to her apartment with her daughter late Friday night. What had begun as a fun, carefree evening, had become disastrous. After discovering that her ex-husband had placed their daughter in what she considered to be an extremely dangerous situation, Lisa had spared no wrath in her determination to remove Charlie from harm.

She sat with her daughter on the living room sofa and warmly embraced her.

"Are you sure you're all right, Buddy?"

"I'm fine, Mom," said Charlie. "I was just a little scared, that's all."

"Your father should have known better! *He should have known better!*"

Charlie defended her dad, "Daddy didn't mean to scare me, Mom. He was just so excited about his new motorcycle, he thought it would be fun for me."

"Hmm," said Lisa.

"And, to tell the truth, I thought it would be fun too. I just didn't expect it to be so loud. The noise is what really scared me."

“At least he had the good common sense to put a helmet and jacket on you. I’ll give him that,” said Lisa.

“And after we rode around the block a couple of times, I got used to the loud noise. It didn’t scare me as much.”

“But, Buddy, your dad and I had discussed the bike. He assured me he wouldn’t put you on it. I thought you would be safe…and you were not”

“You were really mad at Daddy, weren’t you?” asked Charlie.

“Yes. Yes, I was. I *am*!”

Charlie stood and walked quietly to the living room window.

Lisa followed her and placed her hands on her daughter’s shoulders. “Listen, I know your dad loves you and he would never do anything to intentionally harm you. I know that. But tonight he took an unnecessary risk to your safety. He knew you were frightened, but he went ahead with it anyway. There’s no excuse for that.”

“What’s gonna happen?” Charlie asked.

“Well, you’re going to stay here this weekend. Maybe next weekend you can stay with Daddy, okay?”

“Okay, Mom,” Charlie hugged Lisa and headed toward her room. “Good night.”

“Night, Buddy,” said Lisa. “I’ll be right in.”

As she watched Charlie walk toward her room, Lisa brushed back a few tears. She was drained. The evening had emotionally stretched her in every direction. She had so enjoyed the karaoke at the tavern. But her good spirits crashed with the fear of her daughter being in danger. She suddenly was feeling very tired.

As she headed toward her daughter's room, Lisa checked her phone for the first time in hours. She noticed that Cailla McCormack had tried to call her three times. After tucking Charlie in, Lisa pondered whether or not she should call Cailla back. It was late…after midnight. Just then, her phone rang. It was Cailla.

Lisa's voice was drawn as she answered, "Hi, I was just wondering if was too late to call you."

"Is everything all right?" Cailla expressed the deep concern she felt, after viewing the video on Wendy Phillips' phone.

"Yes…we're fine," said Lisa. "It was just very scary. I'm sorry I had to leave so abruptly. I had really been enjoying myself."

"Well, as long as you and Charlie are all right," said Cailla, "I was worried."

"Thank you," replied Lisa. "I appreciate you're being here for me."

"Of course," said Cailla. "You sound exhausted. Get some sleep."

When the phone call ended, Lisa collapsed on the couch. She couldn't even make it to her bedroom. Cailla had been correct. Lisa was worn out.

***

The next morning Lisa treated herself and Charlie to chocolate chip pancakes topped with yummy whipped cream. "Mmmm!" For the time being, at least, they both seemed to have forgotten the strain of the previous evening.

After breakfast Charlie retired to her room and her beloved iPad. Lisa cleared the dishes and sat down at the kitchen table to pay some bills. This was a totally unpleasant task, but Lisa had avoided it as long as she could. There just never seemed to be enough money to cover her creditors. Her recent raise at the daycare center certainly helped, but Mark's child care contributions were spotty.

Each month Lisa made a game out of who would get paid and who wouldn't. Sometimes she would actually take the handful of bills and fling them down the cellar stairs. The further down the stairs an invoice traveled, the better its chances of getting paid. She knew the situation wasn't funny, but she had to laugh. Sometimes collectors would call her about bills she couldn't afford to pay.

"Well, I could send you a bad check!" Lisa would say.

The weasels on the other end of the line never…ever…appreciated Lisa's sense of humor. But she had learned that if she didn't laugh, she would probably cry. Besides, the money issues seemed minor compared to everything else she had been through.

As she gathered up her bills in preparation for her monthly stair toss, her phone rang. She looked apprehensively at the ID, fearing it would be Mark. She really wasn't ready or willing to continue last night's motorcycle battle, at least not right now. To her pleasant surprise, the ID indicated the call to be from the Town Square Playhouse. Lisa cleared her throat.

"Hello." Lisa answered in her most timbre quality.

"Hi, is this Lisa Stratton?" asked the incoming voice.

"Yes, it is."

"Hi Lisa, this is Rebecca Prescott. I'm the stage manager for *A Doll's House*. Mr. Moretti was wondering if you would be available to come in this morning for a call-back audition."

Lisa was caught off guard, "Oh…this morning?"

"Yes, around 11, if that's okay."

"Uhmm…I guess so," said Lisa.

"Great! See you soon then." The stage manager was wrapping it up.

"Except," said Lisa, "I'd have to bring my daughter along with me. I won't have time to get a sitter. Would that be all right?"

"That's fine," said Ms. Prescott. "In fact, I think Mr. Moretti wanted to audition your daughter for one of the children's roles, anyway."

"Really!" replied Lisa. " Okay, then. We'll be there."

Lisa couldn't wait to tell her daughter about the audition. Charlie was excited. Lisa told her she shouldn't get her hopes up. "There are probably lots of children up for the kids roles," Lisa said.

Charlie became very emphatic. "But none as dramatic as me!" Charlie chuckled, as she over-gestured her way across the room.

When they arrived at the Playhouse, there were only a few other people there. Rebecca Prescott greeted them in the lobby and led them down to the front of the house. There she introduced Lisa to Michael Morrison, Lindsey Ralston and Tonya Rebinski. Lisa and Charlie sat in the front row with the other three actors.

"Mr. Moretti will be right with you," Rebecca said, as she headed up the aisle to the rear of the house.

For what seemed like an eternity, the group sat quietly. Michael Morrison and Lindsey Ralston, whispered covertly to each other, while Tonya Rebinski was stone silent. This made Lisa, who was already nervous, even more uncomfortable.

Unexpectedly, Lisa spotted Moretti on the top level of a scaffolding unit far upstage.

Lisa leaned to Charlie and pointed, "Look, there's Mr. Moretti!"

Charlie noticed someone else on the scaffolding who was smiling and waving at her.

“Whose that other guy, Mom?” asked Charlie. He seems to know us.”

Lisa’s gaze returned to the scaffolding. Standing next to Moretti was her recently reconnected high school acquaintance, Nick Curtis. Lisa returned Nick’s wave.

“Yes...I do know him,” Lisa told Charlie. “His name is Nick.”

Moretti stepped downstage and spoke to the group assembled. He thanked them for coming in on short notice. He said he was certain that he wanted to cast them all, but he was not sure as to who should play what part.

“The only casting I’m absolutely convinced of is that I want this young lady right here,” Moretti said as he pointed to Charlie, “to play the role of *Emmy*.”

Everyone in the room smiled at Charlie, who was absolutely beaming.

Moretti stepped to Lisa, “That is, of course if it’s all right with Mom.”

Charlie looked up beggingly to Lisa.

“Well, thank you, Mr. Moretti,” said Lisa. “That’s wonderful. But how much of a commitment from her will there be?”

Moretti said that the *Emmy* character was only in two scenes and that Charlie wouldn’t have to come to every rehearsal. He said he would try to work out a convenient schedule. Lisa agreed to give it a try. Charlie was very excited.

Next Moretti explained his vision for *A Doll’s House*. He expressed his opinion that even though the play was written so long ago, many of its thematic principals regarding the role of women, were still pertinent today. He said it was imperative that the entire production focus on the arc of the main character, *Nora*, changing from "a child's doll" to "a free thinking and independent woman."

For the next two hours, he had the four adult actors read scene after scene and character after character. It was quite grueling. Lisa was edgy at first. She was insecure in that her only real experience had been in high school and college. Clearly the other three auditionees began the process by demonstrating a higher level of experience and confidence. But the more Lisa read, the more poised she became. She read well for all the female characters. When the session finally ended, she felt winded but invigorated.

Moretti said he would decide the cast early next week. He thanked them again for coming in. After the rigorous session, Lisa felt that she had gotten to know her fellow actors pretty well. They all seemed very nice. Charlie was tired, however, and hungry.

"Mom, it's two o'clock. I'm starving" said Charlie.

"Okay, Buddy, let's get home and get you some lunch," replied Lisa.

Just then, one of the other actors, Tonya Rebinski, approached Lisa and Charlie with a welcoming smile. Tonya was a pleasant, personable woman in her early 40's. She appeared to be a throwback to '60's flower power. Her bell bottom jeans were adorned with several brightly colored patches. She also wore lots of crafted jewelry…perhaps self-created. Her light brown hair was streaked slightly in gray and frizzled in an Afro style. Lisa thought she was pretty cool.

"Hey, Lisa, we're heading over to the Lakeside for some lunch," said Tonya. "You and your daughter are welcome to join if you'd like."

The other actors all smiled in agreement.

"Oh, thank you," said Lisa, "if you're sure we won't be intruding…"

“Absolutely not,” said Tonya. “The Lakeside is our regular haunt. You probably should get used to it.”

“Okay, then,” said Lisa, “how do we get there?”

“Just follow the caravan,” Tonya said, as the group headed up the aisle and out of the theatre.

***

The Lakeside Inn was just a mile from the Town Square Playhouse. As its name suggested the restaurant was nestled on the banks of picturesque Willow Lake. Lisa and Charlie joined the other actors in a large booth in the Inn’s lovely lounge.

“This is nice, Mom,” said Charlie.

“It really is, Buddy,” Lisa replied, “I’ve never been here before.”

“Oh, it’s great,” said Tonya, “we come here all the time…after rehearsals…after performances…it’s really our spot.”

“And the folks here are wonderful,” said Michael Morrison. “They stay open late for us after shows…so accommodating.” As he said this, Michael winked at Lisa.

Lisa thought the wink to be a bit odd, but didn’t dwell on it. After all, she had just met these folks and was anxious to fit in. At age 52, Michael was considerably older than everyone else at the table. He stood about 5’ 9” and occupied a fairly wiry frame. He sported a pencil-thin salt and pepper mustache which matched his short but well cared-for hair. He seemed to be a genial sort, but tended to take himself very seriously. He was quick to pull the discussion back to him, whenever it drifted too far away. He had considerably more acting experience than most at the Town Square Playhouse, and was quite accomplished…according to him.

"And you can't beat the food," added Lindsay Ralston. "They make a really great burger."

"How about hot dogs?" asked Charlie.

"Sure!" answered Tonya. "I highly recommend their Coney Island Hot Dogs."

"Mmm, I second that suggestion," sounded a new voice.

Everyone turned their heads to see that Nick Curtis had entered the lounge.

"They are fabulous!" Nick continued. "Do you folks mind if I join you?"

"Not at all," said Tonya, "pull up a chair."

Nick took a chair from one of the nearby tables and sat at the end of the booth.

Tonya said, "Lisa…this is Nick…he works with us at the Playhouse. Nick…this is Lisa and her daughter, Charlie."

"Yes, we've met." Lisa said.

"Hello again," said Nick to Lisa.

"Hi," replied Lisa.

"What the heck is a Coney Island Hot Dog!" asked Charlie.

"Oh, it's so yummy" said Tonya. "It's a hot dog, covered with chile, onions and mustard."

"Yuck!" said Charlie, "it sounds disgusting. Do they have plain old hot dogs?"

Everyone laughed at Charlie's assessment.

“Yes,” said Lindsay, “their plain old hot dogs are excellent as well.”

“Good…’cause that’s what I want, Mom.”

“You got it, Buddy,” replied a smiling Lisa.

The theatre folks enjoyed a jovial luncheon. Everyone seemed fairly comfortable with each other, despite Michael Morrison’s hint of vanity. Lisa was feeling particularly good about things, given the unpleasantness of the previous evening.

As the meal was winding down, the waitress asked if anyone wanted dessert.

“I’d love some dessert,” said Michael, “but I’d better not. Gotta stay trim if I’m going up on the boards.” Michael patted his stomach.”

“Besides,” added Lindsay, “you’ve got a drain to unplug this afternoon.”

Her comment confirmed Lisa’s suspicion that Michael and Lindsay were a couple. Lindsay was 36 years old and portrayed the look of efficiency. Even though it was Saturday, she dressed in a business suit and carried a briefcase. Wearing black fashionable eyewear, she appeared to be the type who was always prepared. At 5’5” and 150 pounds, she was a full-figured woman who carried herself with confidence.

At being reminded of the drain problem, Michael frowned and rolled his eyes. “Ugh…I forgot. I guess we should be going.”

“Me too,” added Tonya. “My house looks like a tornado hit it.”

“What kinds of desserts do you have?” asked Charlie.

“Well, we have all kinds,” replied the waitress.

"How about ice cream?"

"We have vanilla, chocolate and strawberry."

"Oh, strawberry! Can I Mom?" Charlie pleaded. "I haven't had strawberry ice cream since forever."

"But you had a high sugar breakfast this morning, remember?" said Lisa.

"But she hasn't had strawberry since *forever*," said Nick.

Lisa surrendered. "All right."

"Hooray!" cheered Charlie.

"But make it a small portion," Lisa told the waitress.

Charlie frowned. Nick mouthed to the waitress "not too small."

"Well we've got to get going," said Michael. He shook Lisa's hand and held on just a little longer than necessary.

"It's been very nice meeting you, Lisa," said Lindsay. "I'm looking forward to working with you…no matter how the casting turns out."

"I've gotta run too," said Tonya, "can you find your way back all right?"

"Oh, sure," said Lisa, "no sweat. Thanks everybody."

The three headed to the register to pay their bills, then were gone.

"Looks like you guys are stuck with *me*," said Nick.

The waitress returned with a generous dish of strawberry ice cream, which Charlie wasted no time jumping into.

"Oh, you don't have to wait with us," said Lisa. "She'll eat every lick of that ice cream. It may take a while."

"Hey, that's okay," replied Nick. "I've got no place to go."

As Charlie devoured her dessert, Nick and Lisa set out to catch up on old times. It didn't take long for them to realize that neither had stayed in touch with their friends from high school.

"I got a Christmas card from Patty Quinn a few years ago," said Lisa. "She was in our theatre class. Do you remember her?"

"Hmm, not really," said Nick. "to me high school is a big blank screen… but I do remember hearing about you marrying Mark Stratton—not too long after you graduated, right?"

"Yup," said Lisa, "it wasn't supposed to play out that way…but things happen."

"Tell me about it," said Nick. "I had never even heard of Afghanistan, yet there I was."

"Yikes, that must have been frightening," said Lisa.

"A little," said Nick, "but to tell you the truth, it was mostly boring. I kept thinking about what I would do when I got home."

"Well, I admire the fact that you've set your sights on such an ambitious goal," said Lisa. "I'll bet you'll be a great lawyer."

"That's a long way down the road. I hope I make it, but there are no guarantees."

"Mommy, I can't eat any more," said Charlie, " I'm sooo full."

"I'm not surprised," said Lisa, "that was a huge dish."

"It was really, really good," Charlie said.

Lisa pointed out that Charlie had ice cream all over her face. Lisa, Charlie and Nick all began laughing feverishly, when, without warning, Mark stormed loudly into the lounge.

“Here you are!” shouted Mark, “I’ve been looking all over for you!”

There were only a few other customers in the restaurant, but they all turned to the commotion.

“Well, it looks like you found us,” replied Lisa calmly.

“I’m serious…I was worried out of my mind. I went to your place, to your mother’s house…I was afraid something awful had happened to you.”

Lisa said, “I’m sorry you were worried, *I know the feeling*- but as you can see, we’re fine.”

“Uh-huh…yeah…I see that.” Mark eyed Nick suspiciously.

“I finally got the idea to stop by that theatre,” said Mark. He was clearly agitated. “They told me you had been there earlier, and they were pretty sure you had come here.”

“Mark, I think you’d better calm down,” said Lisa.

Mark grabbed Lisa’s wrist and pulled her out of the booth.
“Don’t tell me to calm down,” Mark was on a rampage. “What the hell do you think you’re doing! And who the hell is this guy! ”

Nick stood up between them, “Look, pal, nothing’s going on. We were just talking.”

“He works at the theatre,” said Lisa. “There were others who just left. We were simply having lunch.”

"All right! All right!" Mark looked at Nick, "Well I think it's time for you to go...*now*!"

Nick stood his ground and stared Mark in the eye.

Lisa turned to Nick, "You'd better go, Nick."

"Okay, then," said Nick quietly.

As he headed out, he stopped and turned back and smiled at Charlie.

"Bye Charlie!"

"Bye," Charlie replied.

And Nick was gone.

8
Retreat
January 2, 2008

Lisa hadn't seen or heard from Mark since the ill-fated New Year's Eve Party. As she prepared to return to school on January 2, she was conflicted. Lisa was emotionally torn regarding Mark. He had hurt her badly and he didn't seem to care. Yet, she had believed for some time that Mark was, "the one." She had truly thought they loved each other. But now she wasn't so sure. Lisa was also still struggling with the cheerleading/drama club quandary. After grappling with the decision for weeks, her inclination was to do the play in lieu of cheering. She knew that would be an unpopular decision with most: her parents, Mark and especially Coach Stevens. She also considered the dilemma of leaving the cheer team in the middle of her senior year. "How would it look on her college applications?" she wondered.

Lisa usually got a ride to school with Mark. But in the current circumstance, she thought it best to make other arrangements. She called her friend Patty Quinn and requested a lift, to which Patty agreed. As they rode to school, Lisa avoided talking about Mark. She felt her relationship with her boyfriend was personal. But she did take the opportunity to speak to Patty about the school musical, for which Patty had also auditioned.

"I wanted to tell you, that I've decided to do the play," said Lisa.

"What do you mean?" said Patty. "What about cheering?"

"I'm not going to cheer," Lisa said. "I'm not going to do the winter season"

“Oh, you’ve got to be kidding! You’re the frigging captain for crying out loud!”

“Co-captain,” said Lisa, “and you’re the other co-captain.”

“Yeah, but you make up all the routines, you pick the music, you teach the moves. You do everything! Stevens must be apoplectic!”

“Uhh, Stevens doesn’t know…not yet,” said Lisa. “But I was wondering if you would consider doing the play too.”

“I’d really like to…” said Patty. She paused a few seconds to consider the idea. “No! I can’t! My parents would disown me.”

“ I hear you on that one,” Lisa said. “My parents don’t know yet either.”

As Patty entered the school parking lot, Mark pulled in right behind her. When they got out of the cars, Mark stepped up to Lisa. “Hey, what’s going on? I went to pick you up and your mom said you had already left.”

“Yeah, well, I figured after what happened…” said Lisa.

Mark cut her off. “Oh please are you still whining about that!”

“Listen, I can’t talk about this right now. C’mon Patty.”

Lisa and Patty walked away from Mark and into the school.

“What’s the matter with you!” yelled Mark after them. “What the heck is the matter with you!”

***

After theatre class Lisa told Moretti her decision. She would be on-board for the featured dance ensemble for *Joseph And The Amazing Technicolor Dreamcoat*. Moretti was thrilled.

"That is fantastic news," he said. "Are you sure that's what you want to do?"

"I'm sure," Lisa replied, "but I'll probably be a couple minutes late to rehearsal today. I've got to break the news to Mrs. Stevens."

Moretti blanched. "Ugh, she doesn't know?"

"Not yet."

"Okay, I'll keep mum about it," said Moretti, "good luck."

Outside the theatre classroom, Mark was waiting for Lisa. As she breezed past him, Mark called out to her.

"Hey, will you hold on a minute!"

Lisa stopped. "Mark, I'm late."

"All right, but can we talk later?" Mark was sounding more conciliatory.

Lisa hesitated. "Um, I guess so."

The two resumed walking down the hall.

"What were you talking to your teacher about?" Mark asked.

"I…I told him I was going to do the musical."

"Oh? Stevens backed off, huh?" said Mark.

"No," said Lisa, "I'm dropping out of cheering."

Mark grabbed Lisa's arm and stopped her, "Are you out of your mind?"

"I said I don't have time to talk right now." Lisa released her arm from Mark's grip and walked briskly away.

***

When the dismissal bell rang at the end of the day, Lisa felt a pit in her stomach. She was not looking forward to facing Stevens. Their last meeting had not ended well…not at all. And she knew it was unlikely that Stevens would be gracious about what she was going to tell her. Stevens was not in her office, when Lisa arrived. But the door was open, so she was likely close-by. Lisa waited nervously in the hallway. Patty Quinn approached her.

"Have you told her yet?" asked Patty.

"Not yet, she's not in her office."

"Listen to me," said Patty, "don't do it! She's gonna cause you a lot of problems. Besides, we need you on the team. I don't know anything about choreography. What the heck are we supposed to do?"

"You'll think of something," said Lisa, "and I'll still help you if you get stuck."

Patty frowned. Just then Stevens appeared coming around the corner.

"Well, I hope it's worth it," Patty said, as she quickly headed toward the gym.

Stevens walked past Lisa and into her office. Lisa knocked on the open office door.

"Ye*sh*," said Stevens.

Lisa took a deep breath. "Mrs. Stevens, I've decided not to do the winter cheer season. I'm going to do the musical instead."

Stevens glared at Lisa and took a somewhat threatening step toward her. Then very calmly she spoke. “Well, I’m *sh*ertainly *sh*orry to hear that, Li*sh*a.” Then Stevens’ tone turned stone cold. “Get your uniform and gear to me by the end of the day.”

“I have it right here,” Lisa responded, as she placed a duffle bag in front of Stevens’ desk.

Stevens turned her back to Lisa. “Anything el*sh*e?”

“No,” Lisa said quietly.

“Plea*zh*e clo*zh*e the door on your way out.”

Lisa backed away a few steps, then turned and exited Stevens’ office, pulling the door shut behind her.

Inside her office, Stevens picked up her desk organizer and heaved it against the wall with all her might.

***

Lisa was excited about her first play rehearsal. She had attended the school productions in past years, but had no idea about how they actually came together. When she arrived in the auditorium, Moretti had already begun addressing the large cast that had assembled. He emphasized how important everyone was to the show, no matter how large or small the part.

“I know it’s a cliché,” he said, “but there really are *no* small parts. The show will only be as strong as our weakest component…so there can be *absolutely no weak components*. Everyone has to achieve his or her best potential.”

Moretti then explained that during the first weeks of rehearsal, time would be divided between singing, dancing, and other musical staging. Lisa wasn’t totally sure what all that meant, but she was anxious to begin.

"We're going to kick things off today with a vocal rehearsal," said Moretti. "As you may know, there is not one word of spoken dialogue in *Joseph*, so everyone has to sing…a lot."

"What?" thought Lisa, "No spoken dialogue…at all?"

This was a total surprise. Although Lisa had always enjoyed singing, she had no formal training. She wanted to do the show primarily because of the dancing. So when Moretti directed everyone to proceed to the chorus room, Lisa's enthusiasm wilted.

Mrs. Lauren, the music teacher, who would be in charge of the rehearsal, seemed very nice, but Lisa didn't know her well. Also, Lisa didn't read music at all. There were lots of chorus kids in the play and many tried to be helpful as Lisa struggled to learn the harmony parts of the score. The vocal rehearsal went on for nearly two hours. To Lisa it was grueling. She understood how important it was, but she really wasn't enjoying it. It crossed her mind several times during the afternoon, that maybe her decision to do the show had been a mistake.

That night Lisa broke it to her parents that she had dropped cheering for the winter season in order to do the play. Her mother, Ainsley Lesinski, became quite distraught and suggested her daughter was ruining her life. "Nothing good can come of this. I'll bet you're pulling this crazy stunt just to get back at me!"

"That is ridiculous," said Lisa.

Lisa's father, Charles, was more reasonable. But, he expressed concern about how the move might appear to potential colleges.

"I thought about that too, Dad," said Lisa. "But if I want to study dance, performing in the school musical might be considered a good thing."

"That's true," said Charles.

"Whatever…I need a drink." Lisa's mother took her leave.

Just then the doorbell rang. Lisa answered. It was Mark.

"You said, we could talk."

"Okay, c'mon in." Lisa led him into the living room.

After exchanging greetings with Mark, Lisa's father excused himself to the den.

Lisa and Mark sat on the couch and talked for a long time…maybe an hour or more. She explained the hurt she had felt on New Year's Eve. She had hoped Mark would be supportive of her in her argument with Wendy. He was her boyfriend after all. She was disappointed and sad that the support hadn't come. And it hurt even worse when he took Wendy's side.

"I'm sorry," said Mark. "I had no idea you would take it that way."

"If we're going to be together," said Lisa, "we should always stand up for each other…no matter what!"

"I can see that. But I had been drinking you know. I think that had a lot to do with it."

"Well that's upsetting in itself," said Lisa. "If you can't control yourself when you drink, that's a problem."

"Wait a minute, I don't have a *problem*!"

"I hope not." Lisa stood to indicate the talk was over. "Anyway I've got a lot of homework, so you'd better go."

Mark stood. "All right, but are *we* okay?"

"I hope so,"

"Me too," said Mark. He kissed Lisa, softly. She returned his affection.

“See you tomorrow,” said Mark

“Yup”

Then Mark dramatically gestured. “How was play practice?” he said.

Lisa rolled her eyes, “Get out of here!”

They smiled at each other as Mark went out the door.

***

Over the next couple of weeks, Lisa’s enjoyment at play rehearsal increased significantly. She loved the dancing in the show and she even became quite competent in singing the score. Moretti was delighted with Lisa’s participation. He even assigned her to choreograph the “Go-Go-Go Joseph” number…the act one finale.

Lisa took this task very seriously. She realized that most in the cast were not trained dancers, so the steps couldn’t be too complicated. She practiced at home with her brother, Todd. She figured if a 12 year old middle schooler could execute the routine, it would be a breeze for the *Joseph* cast. At first Todd hated the idea, but he eventually got into the spirit and, though he would never admit it, kind of enjoyed it. At rehearsal, Lisa’s efforts were a big hit. Her leadership skills became very obvious. The number looked great. Everyone was very pleased, and Moretti asked Lisa if she would consider choreographing some other numbers. She was flattered and quickly agreed. Lisa had regained the faith in her decision.

Meanwhile, the cheer team had not been faring so well. Patty Quinn was struggling with the competition routine. She had come up with a decent regimen (thanks to Lisa’s secret help), but had been unsuccessful in effectively teaching it to the squad members. Worse, there appeared a growing dissension among the girls. Wendy Phillips was a chronically negative influence. Clearly, the cheer team missed Lisa.

One week prior to the first competition the situation came to a head. As the girls were executing a stunt, featuring Wendy Phillips as the flyer, signals became crossed and Wendy took a harrowing fall. Fortunately she was not injured but went totally ballistic. She accused Patty of "not having a clue as to what she was doing" and suggested she resign as co-captain. A nasty argument followed, with all team members jumping in and choosing sides.

Stevens entered in the midst of the melee and assumed the persona of an uncontrolled psycho. "*Sh*top! AAAHHHH! I *sh*aid…*sh*top! *Sh*top! *Sh*top! AAAHHHH! *Sh*TOP!" She was screaming with progressively increasing intensity, as she ran from girl to girl. Her ranting was having absolutely no impact in quelling the situation. Stevens sounded like a crazy person. To an outside observer, the scene might have appeared to be a comedy sketch on *Saturday Night Live*. But in actuality, everyone involved was deadly serious.

The next day, Stevens was called to the principal's office. Dr. Richardson was looking for an explanation for the incident, about which he had received several student and parental complaints. Stevens explained what happened.

"It wa*zh* a mi*sh*communication," she said. "The*zh*e stunts require pre*sh*i*sh*e timing. *Sh*ometime*zh*e thing*zh* don't go a*zh* ex*sh*pected. The mo*sh*t important takeaway to thi*sh* i*zh* that no one wa*zh* hurt."

"Well, that may be true," said Richardson, "but it's my understanding there was a fierce and out-of-control argument that followed….and that *you* seemed unable to gain control of it!"

Stevens' face flushed, "It *sh*eem*zh* to me the account you've re*sh*eived is highly ex*zh*aggerated. I *wazh* in control, Dr. Richard*sh*on. I'M *ALWAYZH* IN CONTROL!"

"Hmm, well, the question remains," said the principal, "are we in a position to field a competition squad next week? I think not."

Stevens shot back, "You *sh*eem to forget the rea*zh*on we're in thi*sh* me*sh* to begin with i*zh* becau*zh*e of that *sh*tupid play. If you had banned Moretti from poaching Li*sh*a Le*sh*in*sh*ki, none of thi*sh* would have happened!"

Richardson sighed. "Okay…Lisa was forced to choose between the two. Had she been given the option of doing both, we wouldn't be here either."

"Of, cour*sh*e lay it all on me. With all due re*sh*pect, *sh*ir, thi*sh* whole *sh*ituation is non*sh*en*sh*e. We are pla*sh*ing a bunch of *sh*inging and dan*sh*ing weirdos on an equal *sh*tatu*sh* with the *high shchool cheer shquad!*"

Lisa stood and exited Richardson's office, "That i*zh* ab*sh*olutely ab*sh*urd!"

***

That afternoon Stevens stopped by the *Joseph* rehearsal. As she entered the rear door of the auditorium she saw Lisa onstage instructing a group of dancers. She also noticed that Moretti was working with a small group of students in an upstage area. Stevens walked down the side aisle toward the front of the house.

"Li*sh*a, may I have a word?" Stevens called.

Lisa held up her hand indicating a halt to the dancers. "Umm, I'm pretty busy right now," she said.

"I'll only be a moment," replied Stevens.

Lisa looked to Moretti upstage, who nodded to her.

"Okay, sure," Lisa said. Then to the dancers, "Let's take five."

Lisa and Stevens sat in the house, about halfway back. Stevens expressed her ongoing concern that Lisa was jeopardizing her future by dropping off the cheer team. She had given it a lot of thought, and after much consternation, was willing to allow Lisa to rejoin the squad. Lisa was surprised and quite shocked by the proposition.

“Well, that’s very considerate of you, Mrs. Stevens.”

“I’ve alway*zh* thought highly of you Li*sh*a,” said Stevens, “de*sh*pite our re*sh*ent difficultie*zh*.”

Stevens was struggling with her own sincerity. It was all she could do to force pleasantry.

“If I returned to cheering, would I be allowed to continue with the play?” asked Lisa.

Stevens dropped her head in hesitation, then looked up directly to Lisa. “I’m afraid that would be impo*sh*ible dear. The *sh*quad has fallen de*sh*perately behind. There wouldn’t be time for *thish*,” Stevens gestured disparagingly toward the stage.

Lisa stood up and moved into the aisle. “But *this*,” she said executing the same gesture, “ is what I’ve committed to be part of. Thank you, Mrs. Stevens, but I’ll stick with my original decision.”

Lisa started walking down the aisle toward the stage. Stevens was visibly aggravated as she followed her.

“Li*sh*a, *sh*top! Don’t you have any loyalty to your *sh*chool? Your team need*zh* you!”

Lisa shot back, “I feel I’m incredibly loyal to my school. I’m doing the play. I’m meeting and working with lots of new people. I’m developing leadership skills. I’m expressing my creativity. And when the show is performed for the community, I’ll be proud to be a part of it.”

Stevens approached Lisa and grabbed her by the arm…hard. “*Sh*o naïve!”

"Mrs. Stevens, you're hurting me!"

"Oh…*sh*orry." Stevens, oblivious to her action, released Lisa's arm.

Stevens started to leave…then, "I'll tell you what, you can do the play one day a week…if you in*sh*i*sh*t!"

"No," Lisa said without hesitating, "I've made a commitment to the full rehearsal schedule." Then a beat, "If I were to return to cheering, it would have to be with the understanding that it could only be on days when there was no play rehearsal."

"But…" Stevens was at a loss.

"There's no dance rehearsal tomorrow," said Lisa. I could come then."

Stevens was absolutely bristling. "FINE!" She turned away indignantly and stormed out the rear of the auditorium.

Little did Lisa or Stevens realize, that as their conversation had elevated in volume and intensity, it had drawn the attention of everyone onstage.

When the auditorium door slammed behind Stevens' exit, the entire stage burst into exuberant applause.

9
Beneath The Surface
January 13, 2019

Nick Curtis had become a highly regarded volunteer at the Town Square Playhouse. His considerable construction and technical skills made him an important asset. Although he worked a full time job and attended pre-law classes at night, Nick tried to make himself available as much as possible to help at the theatre. His contributions were very much appreciated by Moretti and the other Playhouse regulars.

Nick's status as a "theatre person," encompassed an unlikely journey. As a child he was bright, alert and energetic. His elementary teachers predicted a rosy future. But when Nick was eight years old, his mother left … no forwarding address. Obviously, this was devastating for Nick. His father, John, had a burdensome work schedule which didn't allow much time for parenting. Nick began to struggle in school, both academically and socially.

When Nick was twelve years old, his father met Sheila. She was also divorced and had two daughters. When John and Sheila married, Nick thought things would improve for him. And they did somewhat. Sheila and her daughters, Lindsey and Megan, were nice to him...or so it seemed. But as the new family evolved, it became clear that Nick was an also-ran. Family attention and considerations were always favored to Sheila's daughters…*always*. John was so relieved to have Sheila's help, he became oblivious as to what was happening. When Nick approached the subject with his father, John became angry, charging his son to be unappreciative of Sheila and all that she was doing for him.

Nick never mentioned the subject to his father again. Instead, he became totally apathetic. He struggled through middle school, barely getting by. In high school the same indifference prevailed. Most class subjects didn't interest him. He was bored. Poor academic performance was accompanied by spotty attendance and class cutting. He didn't spend much time at home, but instead associated with less than desirable cohorts. Nick never smoked or did drugs, primarily because he couldn't afford to do so. But the people with whom he hung-out were definitely into that unsavory underbelly of teenage life.

Nick's prospects of graduating with his class were poor. His high school guidance counselor placed him in a theatre class for his junior year. "It will be an easy grade," she advised. Louise Alverson had been a science teacher at Meadow Hills for ten years. After numerous student and parent complaints and countless negative evaluations, she was finally "promoted" to the guidance department. Here she was also a total disaster. In her mind, arts programs were dumping grounds in which to cast the dregs of scholastic society. As a result, such placements often fostered unmotivated negativity, prompting an obstructive toll on a risk taking environment, like theatre arts.

Nick started out in the class unwilling to try anything. His lack of high school success had made him surly and mostly unlikable. But one fateful day, a random smile of encouragement from Lisa Lesinski...a girl he didn't even know, changed his life. He became motivated and energized for the first time in years. Unknowingly, Lisa had shot him through the heart, in a totally positive way. Although the fact that she had a boyfriend discouraged him, Nick never forgot her.

He became an excellent theatre student, showing particular aptitude in the technical areas. He worked on all the high school productions, his grades improved and he easily graduated with his class.

After high school, Nick enlisted in the Army and served honorably. Following his discharge, he went to work for his uncle's cabinet making company. He also started attending community college, through the Montgomery G.I. Bill of Rights, with the goal of becoming a lawyer.

Through all this, Nick remained in contact with his high school theatre teacher, Sal Moretti. And so it came to pass that on that early January evening in 2019, Nick found himself at the Town Square Playhouse, as Moretti was conducting auditions for an upcoming production of *A Doll's House*.

Nick was working on the second floor light deck, with Tina Mason, the theatre's technical director. They were rewiring several ellipsoidal spotlights. As he pursued his task, Nick's eye caught what appeared to be a familiar face onstage. He looked up with full attention. "Yes…it was Lisa," he was certain. Nick froze and dropped his wrench. Tina Mason took note of his daze--

"What's with you?" said Tina.

"I know that girl."

Tina squinted her eyes to take a look at the girl doing the monologue. "She's pretty. Is she an old girlfriend?"

"No, I'm sure she doesn't remember me."

Tina could see the attraction in Nick's eyes. "Wow! You'd better hope she gets a part!"

Nick hadn't heard her. "Huh?"

"Never mind…now can we get back to fixing these lights please?"

***

After the Lakeside Inn confrontation with Mark, Lisa was distraught. Mark had been such an important part of her life. In some ways she knew she would always love him and be grateful to him. But she was thirty now—she wanted to move on. She wanted to expand her horizons. The positive potential of both her karaoke and theatre experiences over the weekend had been marred by Mark's baggage.

As Lisa and Charlie drove to Lisa's parents' house for Sunday dinner, they talked about the play. Charlie was excited about her part. "What kind of a costume should I wear?" she asked her mom.

Lisa answered, "Well I'm sure someone at the theatre will help us with that. But I think you'll wear a short dress. That was the custom of the period"

"Ugh! Can't I wear pants?"

"I don't think so, pal." said Lisa, "Things were very strict for women in those days. That's what the play is all about."

When they arrived at their destination, Charlie was excited to tell her grandparents about her role in *A Doll's House*. Charles, her namesake grandfather, smiled and patted her on the head. "That's my little cupcake." Lisa frowned.

Ainsley, Lisa's mother, asked Charlie how she liked her father's new motorcycle. Charlie withdrew the smile that was on her face and looked at her mom. Lisa told her parents about Friday night's incident.

Immediately, Ainsley defended Mark. "Oh, come on, I'm sure Mark was very careful. It sounds to me like you over-reacted…as usual."

"Mom!" said Lisa. "Charlie was frightened. She didn't want to ride on the bike and Mark made her do it anyway."

"She wasn't hurt, was she?"

"No, thank goodness, she wasn't hurt," said Lisa, "but Mark had promised me that he wouldn't put Charlie on that bike... Can't you take my side...for *once*?"

"It's not a matter of taking sides. There was no harm done. Sometimes I think you're afraid Charlie will enjoy her time with Mark more than when she's with you!"

"Okay, Mom, thanks," said Lisa, "thanks a lot! C'mon Charlie, we're leaving!"

Lisa grabbed Charlie by the hand and stormed out of the house. When she got into the car she started crying...softly at first and then uncontrollably. Charlie jumped up in the front seat and threw her arms around her. "It's all right, Mom," she said, "everything's all right."

Lisa snapped out of her gloom and returned Charlie's hug. "I know it is, Buddy...I know it's all right. Hey, what do you say we go to Harrison's for a root beer float?"

Charlie cheered, "Hooray!"

***

Harrison's was a drive-in restaurant...a nostalgic throwback to a seemingly simpler time. Although it lacked the youthful hustle and bustle of Mel's in *American Graffiti*, it still offered a unique alternative to the run-of-the mill drive-through window. Harrison's maintained a '50's motif and featured real life carhops providing tray service to customers in their cars. However, Harrison's carhops were not short-skirted girls on roller skates. They were more likely pimpled high school guys sporting jeans and tee shirts. But most importantly, Harrison's food was fantastic... great burgers, fries, hot dogs, steak sandwiches and, the pièce de résistance...heavenly root beer floats.

Harrison's had been a frequent destination for Lisa, Mark and Charlie during happier times. Not only did the drive-in offer great food and atmosphere…it was also cheap…a wonderful enticement for young families. Charlie loved going to Harrison's and was thrilled with Lisa's suggestion of going there, following the contentious visit with her grandparents.

No sooner had Lisa pulled her Civic into Harrison's, than a young man approached the passenger side of the car. Lisa rolled down the window.

"Hi, I'm Larry, what can I get you today?" asked the carhop.

"Should we have our regular?" Lisa asked Charlie.

"Yup!" Charlie replied.

Lisa turned to the carhop, "We'll have two hotdogs with mustard and pickle, two orders of fries, and two root beer floats."

Larry wrote down the order on a small pad and read it back to Lisa. "Anything else?"

"No, I think that'll do it," said Lisa.

"Okay, then, we'll get this out to you right away," Larry said, as he returned to the restaurant.

While waiting for their order to come out, Lisa took the opportunity to speak to Charlie about what had happened at her parent's house. "I'm sorry you saw that unpleasantness, Buddy. I just lost it."

"That's okay, Mom, I understand."

"You are incredibly wise," said Lisa. "I know how much your dad loves you…believe me I do. But we all make mistakes. I've sure made my share. And the other night, your dad made a mistake too. And I think he realizes it." Charlie nodded. "Your grandmother doesn't think your dad ever makes a mistake. She thinks everything is *my* fault. It makes me very sad." Lisa's eyes started welling up again.

"Don't cry Mom," said Charlie, "I get it. It wasn't your fault. Not at all."

There was a knock on Lisa's window. The food had arrived. Lisa paid the carhop, and she and Charlie dug in. The impending tears turned to belly laughs as Mom and daughter celebrated being together. As they were slurping up the remains of their root beer floats, a car pulled into the space right next to theirs. Lisa thought that to be odd, since the entire parking lot was empty and available. "Why would someone want to crowd our space?" she thought. Then she noticed that the driver of the car was smiling at them. Lisa popped on her glasses so as to get a better look. It was her friend, Cailla McCormack. Lisa returned the smile and waved.

"Why don't you join us?" Lisa called.

"Okay," Cailla replied as she exited her car.

Charlie hopped into the back seat as Cailla entered the passenger side of the Civic. Lisa and Cailla hugged. Then Cailla reached her hand back to greet Charlie. Lisa beeped her horn and Larry the carhop returned.

"We need to place another order," said Lisa, as she referred to her friend.

"Okay, what'll it be?" said Larry.

Cailla ordered a chicken cheese steak and root beer float. Larry wrote in his little pad and again returned to the restaurant.

"So how are things going?" asked Cailla.

Lisa's karaoke night with Cailla was only two days ago, but it seemed a lot had happened since. Lisa brought her friend up to speed on her call-back audition and her lunch at the Lakeside…including her re-meet of Nick Curtis.

Cailla's eyes bugged out. "What!...I *knew* it! I knew there was something brewing there."

"Will you stop!" said Lisa. "Several people from the theatre went. He was just one of them."

"You can deny it all you want, but that guy has his eye on you." Both Lisa and Cailla laughed.

"But you still love Daddy, right Mom?" said Charlie from the back seat.

Lisa's smile faded as she turned back to Charlie. "Of course, Buddy, I'll always love your Dad. It's just different now, that's all."

"Oh," said Charlie.

Just then, Lisa's phone rang.

"Hello" answered Lisa, "Oh, Hi…Really?...Wow!...That's wonderful….thank you so much….When?...Tomorrow at 7….Right…got it. Thanks again….Bye."

Lisa grinned silently as she hung up the phone.

"Well?" said Cailla.

"Well…what?" said Lisa.

"C'mon…you can't leave us hanging! What was that all about?"

"Well," said Lisa, "that was the Playhouse. It seems that yours truly has been cast as the lead in *A Doll's House*."

Charlie screamed with delight from the backseat. Lisa echoed her daughter's scream, as did Cailla.

As all three of the occupants were screeching with delight, Larry, the carhop, returned with Cailla's cheesesteak. "Thank you" said Cailla.

As Larry was about to leave, Lisa stopped him. "Excuse me..." Lisa glanced back at Charlie and smiled broadly. Then she looked again to the carhop, "Could you please bring us two more root beer floats?"

Larry sighed and then, "Comin' right up."

Lisa, Charlie and Cailla all laughed happily. What had been a merry-go-round weekend, ended on a distinct high note.

***

Productions at the Town Square Playhouse, usually began with a script readthrough at the first rehearsal. It was an opportunity for the cast members to meet each other and to initiate a connection to the text. It was also an opportunity for the director to communicate his vision for the play and express character insights for the actors.

Lisa was nervous as she entered the Playhouse for the first rehearsal of *A Doll's House*. As she and Charlie walked to the front of the house, she was greeted by Rebecca Prescott, the stage manager, who had phoned her with the news she had been cast.

"Hi Lisa," said Rebecca, "it's great to see you. If you would just sign these forms for you and Charlie."

"What's this?" asked Lisa

"It just allows us to take photos of you and your daughter for use in promoting the show...it's standard."

"Oh, okay" said Lisa as she signed the forms.

"Thanks, here are your scripts. You guys can just take a seat up at the table."

Lisa and Charlie climbed the steps of the stage and sat at the end of the table. There she recognized Michael Morrison and Lindsey Ralston from the callback audition.

"Congratulations," said Michael, "I guess we'll be playing opposite each other."

"Oh?" said Lisa.

"Yep…I'm *Torvold*,"

"Okay," Lisa said, "well, congratulations to you too. And how about you, Lindsey? Are you playing *Kristine*?"

"Umm, no," said Lindsey. Her facial expression was flat and sour. "I'm just your run of the mill nanny, *Anna*. But congratulations to you, Lisa. You must be *really* something to land a part like *Nora* on your first audition."

Lisa, somewhat taken back, replied quietly. "Well, I don't know about that."

As the other cast members arrived, they each introduced themselves to Lisa and Charlie. They all seemed to know each other. Clearly, Lisa was the newbie. But except for Lindsey, everyone was quite welcoming. The final cast arrival was Tonya Rebinski, another of Lisa's fellow callback auditionees. She hugged Lisa warmly and sat beside her. She would be playing *Kristine*, the second female lead in the play.

Director Moretti spoke. "Well, it appears we're all here. Welcome! I'm really glad you've all opted to do this show with us. I assure you it will be challenging. Ibsen's work requires thoughtful interpretation. Everything isn't found on the surface. We will have to dig for it. But I feel confident in this cast. I'm sure you are all very capable of achieving a gratifying and rewarding experience."

The cast nodded and smiled in anticipation.

"Now," continued Moretti, "lets ease into the readthrough. Don't try to be dynamic…just get a feel for the text. We'll have plenty of time to make choices during rehearsals. Okay? Then let's begin. Rebecca can you read the stage directions, please?"

"Sure," said the stage manager, and she began. "*A room, comfortably and tastefully, but not expensively furnished…*"

The reading proceeded smoothly for the next two hours. Every once in a while, Moretti would stop to make a comment or an actor would ask a question. Lisa was excited and stumbled over words at first, but improved as the evening continued. Charlie was frustrated at not having read a line all night. Moretti explained. "Ibsen thought it to be important for *Nora's* children to have a presence in the play, but he left it to the director to devise the words that they were to say." Charlie looked confused, along with Robbie and Stephen, the actors playing the other children. "Don't worry" said Moretti, "we're going to improvise some cool dialogue for all three of you." The three children smiled at their new director.

When the reading was complete Moretti was complimentary to everyone and expressed his confidence on a successful production. As the group began to break up, Michael Morrison approached Lisa. "Listen, if you'd like, we could get together at some point and work on our parts. We have many scenes together and it might be helpful."

As Lisa was about to answer she noticed a cold stare aimed in her direction from Lindsey Ralston. "Uhh…" said Lisa, "sure, we'll have to see how things go."

Then Michael gave Lisa an unexpected hug. "See you." He projected a toothy grin as he exited with Lindsey.

"He's weird," whispered Charlie, as she and Lisa exited up the aisle.

"Shh…" said Lisa. "I know…a little bit." Lisa and Charlie stepped outside under the theatre marquee. As they started up the street to their car, Lisa heard someone call her.

"Hey, Lisa…Charlie!" It was Nick Curtis.

"Hi," said Lisa, "were you inside?"

"Yeah," said Nick " I was upstairs working on the lights. You sounded great in the readthrough"

"Oh, thanks…I was really nervous."

"I have to improvise!" said Charlie.

"I'm sure you'll be a fantastic improvisor," said Nick.

Nick looked at Lisa, "Hey, you wanna get some coffee…or soda?

Lisa smiled but then, "Uh…it's pretty late. Charlie has school tomorrow. We'd better not."

Nick looked disappointed. "Oh…Okay. See you."

They started off in separate directions. Then Lisa stopped and called to Nick. "Hey!" Nick stopped and looked back at Lisa. "We could do it another time, if you want."

Nick answered, "Sure, let's do it another time."

As they went their separate ways both Lisa and Nick started smiling.

10
Excellent Educator
Early April, 2008

The 2007-2008 school year had not been particularly kind to Stacy Stevens. In her five years as cheer coach at Meadow Hills High School, she had ruled the roost and become accustomed to the girls' unequivocal devotion. She was highly regarded in the community and thought to be an excellent educator. Stevens had acquired an impressive competition record and the team was considered to be among the best in the state. But her ascension to near sainthood corresponded precisely with Lisa Lesinski's membership on the squad. Over the past four years, Lisa had created, produced and executed each and every competitive routine. To be sure, Stevens was quick to take credit for the team's success, but in reality, she had very little to do with it.

From the start of the current year, Stevens viewed Lisa's new found interest in the theatre to be aggravating. At first it was merely a tedious annoyance…something she'd be able to swat away like a mosquito. However, as the year progressed, the situation seemed to deteriorate. And when Lisa withdrew from the team in order to perform in the school production…that was the ultimate offense. Stevens viewed the action as a direct threat to her…personally. And then, in order to save any semblance of success, Stevens had humiliated herself by practically begging Lisa to return to the squad. The fact that she was also forced to accommodate the play's rehearsal schedule only added to Stevens' discontent.

With regard to Stevens' personal life, things had also been less than peachy. While her divorce was still stinging, she had pursued and failed at several online dating encounters. She didn't have many friends, and spent most of her out-of-school time alone. The fact that there seemed little hope for her on the romance horizon was very frustrating.

Stevens' seemingly chronic bad mood was affecting her work performance. It was certainly noticed by her students, but also by her co-workers. At one point, the principal, Dr. Richardson, summoned Stevens to his office. He gently suggested that she might want to get some help. He referred her to the district's employee assistance counselor. Stevens was highly offended by this idea and totally rejected the notion. Richardson looked her squarely in the eyes, "Today, this is only a recommendation, Mrs. Stevens."

"Well, I reject your recommendation!"

"Excuse me!" said Richardson. "I say *today* this is a recommendation. But unless your attitude improves relatively quickly, it will no longer be a recommendation…rather it will be an order!"

Stevens looked away, "Are we through?"

"Yes."

"Good!" Stevens stood and made a quick exit.

***

As the *Joseph* opening drew near, the intensity of the rehearsals escalated. Lisa was no longer questioning her decision to do the show. The satisfaction of her participation had far exceeded her expectations. She had made many new friends. It was surprising to her that although many of the students in the production had been in her class for years, she had never gotten to know them. Everyone was working incredibly hard in a most collaborative way. Lisa found herself exhilarated by the process. She had become particularly good friends with Jeff Townsend, who was playing the lead role in *Joseph*. She recognized his talent and enjoyed directing his choreography. Jeff was totally receptive and appreciative of Lisa's dance help. The two had developed a congenial working relationship which had yielded excellent results. Lisa sensed that Jeff may have been interested in her beyond friendship. But she discouraged those whims at every opportunity. She valued the new friendship, but her romantic interest remained with Mark.

And Mark had seemed to turn a corner, having become consistently attentive and supportive of Lisa in every regard. He had matured in the aftermath of the nasty New Year's Eve incident, at least it seemed so to Lisa. She was thrilled with the "new" Mark. They were happier and more affectionate than ever.

Lisa's parents also stepped up in supporting their daughter's theatrical debut. Although they still had reservations about the play, they recognized their daughter's total commitment and embraced her efforts.

When opening night finally arrived the mood in the auditorium's back hall was electric. Everyone was so excited and so nervous. There were lots of carnations being distributed as gestures of friendship and "break a leg" sentiments. Lisa, as the show's choreographer, was the recipient of many of these tokens. Jeff Townsend also presented her with a special bouquet of daisies and sunflowers. The accompanying note said, "Thanks for all your help. Love, Jeff aka *Joseph*." In front of Lisa's locker, she found another lovely arrangement of lilacs. But…no note. Lisa assumed and hoped they were from Mark.

Shortly before 8 o'clock, Moretti called the cast and crew together in his classroom. "Ok, folks, this is it," he said, "You've all worked hard and so deserve to find success tonight. Remember, no matter your role, someone in the audience is watching *you*. If everyone stays in character from beginning to end, we'll have a wonderful production. Break a leg, people! Places for Act I."

Opening night was a huge success. It was unlike anything Lisa had ever experienced. Her pre-show jitters quickly transformed to an adrenaline rush. The show seemed to fly-by, with each musical number garnering greater and greater audience reaction. As the cast took its curtain call, there was an immediate and spontaneous standing ovation, accompanied by roars and whistles of approval. When the stage lights came down and the curtain closed, the kids in the cast were visibly moved. They began to embrace each other and happy tears appeared on many faces. Lisa felt ecstatic. In the lobby she was greeted eagerly by her family. Her mom, dad, and even her brother, Todd, were surprisingly enthusiastic about Lisa's performance. Mark also showed uncharacteristic emotion.

"You were great!" he said.

"Oh, thanks, I appreciate that."

Mark held her in a tight embrace, " I mean it! The play was good…better than I expected…but *you* were fantastic!"

"We all just seemed to gel tonight," Lisa said, "everybody came through."

Lisa then kissed Mark on the cheek. "Thanks for the flowers."

"Huh?" Mark lifted his forehead. "I…I…was gonna send you flowers on Saturday night."

"Oh," said Lisa, "that's all right. I'm just glad you were here for me tonight."

As Mark drove Lisa home, she wondered who had sent the lilacs. But the excitement of the evening quickly replaced her curiosity. She felt fantastic about the show and also about Mark. It seemed like everything was finally working out for the best.

The next day at school, everyone was still buzzing about the opening. There were to be three more performances. Many students and teachers who had seen the show were giving it high praise and recommendations. However, not everyone shared this nearly universal enthusiasm.

Not in attendance on opening night of *Joseph And The Amazing Technicolor Dreamcoat*, was Meadow Hills' cheer coach Stacy Stevens. She was, instead, engaged on another clandestine encounter through the auspices of Meet.com. Over the last few years, Stevens had been on many such dates…all ending in the same way…badly. This time it was with a fellow who counted plastic bags for a living. He actually worked in a plastic bag factory. And yes, his job was to inventory the exact number of plastic bags manufactured each day. To hear him talk…and Stevens did hear him talk… a lot…it was the most fascinating occupation known to man. Another date-fail was what Stevens had come to expect.

And now, in school, all she heard was how marvelous the play had been, with particular kudos to Lisa. She became totally miffed. The more raves she heard, the more exasperated she became. She fostered deep resentment for the production because of Lisa's strong stance on participation. And even though Lisa's return to the cheer team had resulted in competitive success, Stevens still carried a bitter grudge. In each of her classes, Stevens went out of her way to minimize the value of theatrical pursuits. "I don't know about any of you," she said, "but I live in the real world. I gue*sh* it'*ch* fine to play at make believe when you're five or *sh*ix year*zh* old, but at *sh*ome point you have to grow up. I don't think we're doing the*zh*e theater ki*dzh* any favor*zh* by heaping *sh*uch prai*zhe* on *sh*uch a ridiculou*sh* and meaningle*sh* pur*sh*uit."

It didn't take long for word of Stevens' diatribe to circulate around the school. Although there may have been some who agreed with her assessment, most in the school community held the opposite view. Stevens' words were particularly hurtful to her students who were also *Joseph* cast members. Eventually Moretti found out what was happening. During lunch he confronted Stevens in her office.

"Mrs. Stevens, may I speak with you for a moment?"

"I *sh*uppoz*h*e *sh*o, although I only have twenty minute*ch* for lunch and I wa*zh* hoping to *sh*pend the time in pea*sh*e."

"Sorry," said Moretti, "but I would really appreciate it if you would refrain from talking down our show. Our kids are proud of their accomplishment. I'd think as a coach you could appreciate that."

"Oh, plea*zh*e Moretti, don't try to compare what *you* do to what *I* do. Everything about your program i*zh* phony-baloney. Not only doe*zh* our cheer team engage in var*sh*ity level competition, it i*zh* the fa*sh*e of our community. Your play*zh* are laughable. You are a wa*sh*te of tax*ch* payer money. If it were up to me, you would not exi*sh*t"

Moretti bowed his head for a beat, then looked up and advanced on Stevens' desk. "I'm so sorry you feel that way. Obviously you have no understanding of what we do. But I am urging you, for the sake of the kids in the show, please back off on bad-mouthing their efforts." He turned and exited the office. Stevens smirked as she bit into her tuna salad sandwich.

The Friday night performance went very nicely. Moretti had warned the cast about a show's tendency to experience what he called a *second night let down*. "You really have to intensify your focus," he said prior to the curtain.

Obviously, the cast and crew had done exactly that, because the performance was excellent. After the show Lisa saw that Moretti was approaching her, accompanied by someone she didn't know. "Lisa," said Moretti, "I'd like you to meet Dr. Mary Blackwell."

Lisa smiled and extended her hand. "Hello."

Blackwell returned the smile and handshake. "It's very nice to meet you Lisa. Your performance was wonderful."

"Oh, thank you," said Lisa. "Thank you very much."

Moretti chimed in, "Dr. Blackwell is the chairperson of the department of theatre and dance at Atlantic University."

Lisa's eyes widened. "Oh my goodness. I applied there. It was so nice of you to come to see the show."

"It was my pleasure, dear," said Blackwell. "Mr. Moretti suspected I would find your work impressive...and I do. It's my guess that if you choose to attend Atlantic in the fall, we will both benefit significantly." Lisa and Dr. Blackwell exchanged parting smiles. Lisa took a deep breath. She was on cloud nine.

The Saturday night performance had also gone well. Following the show, most of the cast and crew members went to Jeff Townsend's house. His parents were hosting a party for all the kids involved in the production. Mark accompanied Lisa to the gathering but felt extremely uncomfortable. He didn't know very many of these students and was certainly not friends with any of them. This was definitely not his crowd.

Mark's presence at this cast party was amazing in itself. His upbringing had not exactly fostered the idea of the big tent. He had been raised to regard the artsy kids as unacceptable weirdos...an unsurprising mindset. To be sure, Mark Stratton was the product of a highly dysfunctional home. His father, Jerry, was a high school star athlete. He had set many records at Meadow Hills High School which still remained. His photo was enshrined in the back hallway of the gym— the revered *Wall of Fame*. He was pursued and recruited by countless colleges. And indeed, Jerry Stratton enjoyed excellent success during his freshman year at Preslow University. As a full-ride freshman, he broke all previous school rushing records. But the elder Stratton fell into deep difficulty during his sophomore year...alcohol, drugs, disorderly conduct. Eventually he was asked to leave the school. After his college stint, he had difficulty adjusting to adulthood...a problem that would remain throughout his life. Eighteen years ago he married Mark's mother, Delcie, after she became pregnant. Over the years he had physically abused both her and Mark. When Mark entered Meadow Hills High School, his father and mother separated. Jerry moved across town with a woman 10 years his junior. Mark inherited much of his father's athletic prowess, but also some of his lesser qualities.

So, the fact that Mark was attending a theatre cast party was fairly stunning. He may not have totally realized it at the time, but Lisa was his salvation. Of course, he loved her…he was certain of that. But perhaps he still hadn't attained the maturity to comprehend the powerful positive influence she had on him. At the party, Mark was fairly obnoxious. He wasn't friendly or even sociable to the other company members. He tried to keep Lisa exclusively to himself, pulling her into secluded corners of the Townsend house for private chats. Lisa, on the other hand, enjoyed interacting with the other kids. Clearly she had become very popular within the group, and everyone wanted to spend time with her. Mark became sour and sulky. He wanted to leave. But Lisa was having a great time. Eventually, she gave in to his begging.

To say the least, Lisa was miffed at Mark's attitude. She had experienced a wonderful night and was anxious to share her exuberance with the other cast members. But Mark's insistence on monopolizing her attention ruined the moment. To make matters worse, Mark had no inkling as to his offensive behavior. On the drive home Lisa was silent. Mark pulled into Lisa's driveway and turned off the ignition.

"What the heck is the matter with you?" he said.

"If you don't know, I'm not going to tell you."

Mark pounded the steering wheel. "Oh, great…you're pissed at me and won't even tell me why."

"Couldn't you see how much I was enjoying myself tonight?" said Lisa.

"So…I *wasn't*"

"Oh, right…because for once the big football star wasn't the center of attention. Pretty small of you, if you ask me."

"Oh, please…" said Mark, "you think I wanted attention from that bunch of freaks?"

"Those freaks happen to be my friends. If you can't respect that and respect me, I'm not sure what we're even doing?"

"Holy crap…you're letting this play thing go to your head. You need to get a grip, Sweetie!"

"Don't call me that!"

"All right! All right! I'm sorry. If I did anything to offend you or your *friends*…I apologize, okay?"

"That sounds pretty insincere. Do you mean it?"

Mark's face broke into a dark smile. "Sure I mean it. I'll show you how much I mean it." Mark threw his arms around Lisa and attempted to kiss her.

Lisa pushed him off. "Not so fast…I'm mad at you."

"C'mon…you could never really be mad at me." Mark became more aggressive, physically forcing himself on Lisa.

"Stop…stop!" Mark showed no signs of relenting, pushing her against the passenger door of the car.

"WILL YOU STOP!!" Lisa shoved him away from her with all her might.

"All right! All right!" said Mark. "Take it easy!"

Lisa opened the passenger door. "I'm going in. Goodnight."

Mark shook his head as he watched her go into her house. "Shit!"

***

Stacy Stevens woke up early Sunday morning. She had resolved to feel better about herself. She was determined to not allow her troubles at school and her bad dates get the best of her. She went to the park near her apartment and took an invigorating run. Then she visited the local café and treated herself to a lovely breakfast. All was going well. On her return home she pampered herself with a soothing bath. But after several hours of lounging in relative bliss, Stevens suddenly became aware of a troubling realization. *Her marking period grades were due the next morning!* She had totally forgotten. Suddenly she was shaken back to reality. Grade submission was one of the most important deadlines for a teacher to meet. Failure to do so in a timely manner could result in annoying sanctions. And given her recent dispute with her principal, Stevens knew her lovely new day was about to conclude.

She reached for her briefcase and found that she had left her gradebook at school. She would have to make the short drive to Meadow Hills and retrieve it from her office. When she pulled into the school, she was surprised to see that the parking lot was full.

“Oh, shit,” she thought, “that stupid play.”

Stevens’ Sunday morning attempt to escape reality had come full circle. She had totally forgotten about the final performance of *Joseph*. This production had become the bane of her existence, and was the last thing she wanted to be thinking about. She decided to pull around to the parking lot in the rear of the school and use the back entrance. She didn’t want to witness the presumptive celebration that would follow the final curtain.

As she walked toward her office, Stevens spotted a familiar figure exiting the men’s room down the hall. It was her ex-husband. She called out, “Rod!”

Rod Stevens looked up in surprise. Squinting his eyes, he recognized his ex-wife and smiled.

"Hi."

Stevens started moving down the long hall toward him. "How did you know I'd be here?"

Rod said, "Oh, I'm not…"

Stevens cut him off, "Come on down to my offi*sh*, we can talk there."

"Oh, uhm…OK." Rod was stammering. " I'll...I'll… be down in…in a minute."

Rod gestured with his index finger, indicating he would return shortly. He then turned and headed in the opposite direction. Meanwhile Stevens practically skipped toward her office with a very broad smile on her face. She was clearly excited. She closed the venetian blinds covering the large picture window which displayed the school hallway from her workplace. She then turned on her blue filtered desk light, and switched off the harsh overhead lights. Romance was definitely on her mind.

Stevens had never gotten over Rod, and through the years had remained hopeful for a reconciliation. As she waited patiently for his return, it crossed her mind, that the forgotten gradebook was no doubt, a sign of destiny. Finally Rod appeared in the open doorway.

Stevens closed the door behind him. "There you are. I'm *sh*o glad to *sh*ee you."

She approached Rod and threw her arms around his neck. She began kissing Rod on the neck and face, and finally on the mouth.

"Whoa…whoa…whoa…" Rod pushed her away. "Stacy…I'm sorry, but you've got the wrong idea."

Stevens stopped smiling. “The wrong idea? But why did you come here to *sh*ee me?”

“I didn’t come to see you.” said Rod. “My girlfriend, Allison, has a niece who is in the play. We came to see her.”

“We?” Stevens said. “Your *girlfriend* i*zh* here with you?”

“Yes, Stacy.” Rod nodded his head. “In fact…I wanted to let you know…Allison and I are getting married next month.”

“Oh!” Stevens forced a tearful smile as she backed away from him. “Congratulation*zh*.”

“Well, I’d better get back.” Rod started for the door. “It was good seeing you Stacy.” And he was gone.

Stevens stepped out of her office into the hall, as she watched her husband walk away. She whispered, “Goodbye Rod.” She wiped her eyes as she moved back into her office, forcefully pushing the door shut behind her. Her quiet tears evolved into uncontrolled wailing. She ripped the framed diplomas, certificates and awards off the walls, tossing them as if to kingdom come. She flailed every item in her sight. Her wailing turned to a deep gasp and exhaled as a miserable screech, reminiscent of a shrieking cat. Her body was spent of all emotion and energy as she leaned on the edge of her desk, a far cry from Stevens’ early morning joy.

Suddenly she was aware of a loud commotion coming from the far end of her hallway. The final performance of *Joseph And The Amazing Technicolor Dreamcoat* had just concluded. Cast and crew members were happily meeting their families and friends in the auditorium lobby and adjoining halls. The mood was clearly jubilant. Stevens’ anguish deliberately evolved into defiant rage. Stevens spotted a large pair of pinking shears which had toppled to the floor during her outburst. She picked up the shears and eyed them maniacally.

She lightly scratched her forearm with the serrated edge of the scissor. As she watched the slight blood flow, her lips hatefully formed the word... "Li*sh*a!" Somehow, in Stevens' twisted mind, the innocent high school cheerleader had become the reason for her unhappiness and her target of blame. Shears in hand, she stepped out of her office. Upon scanning the scene, she spotted Lisa and Mark among the growing crowd. She forcefully waved and loudly called out, "Li*sh*a! Li*sh*a!"

Lisa heard her name being called and looked up. She spied Stevens waving and took a step in her direction. Stevens held her hand to the side of her mouth so as to be heard above the throng. "I need to see you. It's important!"

Lisa smiled, nodded and gave her the "Okay" gesture. Stevens stepped back into her office and laid the shears down on her desk. Lisa kissed Mark and patted him on the chest. She was clearly in a great mood. "I'll be back in a minute," Lisa said to her boyfriend. "I've gotta see what Mrs. Stevens wants...probably something about Tuesday's competition. Go keep my parents company, Okay?"

Mark cringed. "Sure...but don't be too long. Your mom tends to get all handsy with me."

Lisa laughed as she backed down the hall, "Hey, watch it buddy. You'd better not go chasing any older women."

***

Lisa approached Stevens' office door and knocked.

"Come on in, Li*sh*a"

As Lisa entered, she thought it somewhat strange to find her coach in the dimly lit, disarrayed office, seated on the edge of her desk. "What's up Mrs. Stevens. My family is waiting for me. We're going out to dinner."

"How ni*sh*e," said Stevens, "I won't keep you long, dear."

Stevens got up off the desk and walked to her office door, closing and locking it. She then backed Lisa deeper into the office. "I ju*sh*t wanted to congratulate you on what ha*zh* apparently been a huge *sh*uc*sh*e*sh*."

Lisa continued backing up, "Oh, thank you. Yes, the show has been well received. It was a remarkable experience."

Stevens backed her to the rear wall of the office. "Oh, it's been a remarkable experien*sh* for me too." They were now nose to nose. "You, see—this fucking play ha*zh* ruined my life, Li*sh*a!"

Lisa's eyes widened. "Huh?" Lisa tried to escape her close encounter, but Stevens threw both hands against the wall on either side of her, trapping Lisa in place.

Stevens gritted her teeth. "Oh, ye*sh*—I was a re*sh*pected educator. I wa*zh* known as a fine coach and an ex*sh*ellent teacher."

Lisa tried to escape her entrapment, but Stevens' grip was tight. "You're still that."

Stevens grabbed Lisa's arms. "Oh…no, it'*ch* all changed Li*sh*a. I'm a laughing *sh*tock now. And do you know why I'm a laughing *sh*tock?"

"You're not a laughing stock." Lisa was trembling.

"Oh, ye*sh*, I am. And it's all becau*zh*e of *you*! You and your *sh*tupid play! You're a bitch Li*sh*a. You're an A-1 bitch. And now, you're going to pay!"

Lisa pulled her arms free and shoved Stevens forcefully away. She ran as hard as she could, but Stevens was right behind her. As Lisa attempted to unlock the door, Stevens grabbed her by the hair and yanked her to the floor. Lisa was sprawled out on her stomach with Stevens sitting on her back. Lisa was screaming, but by now the outer hall was jam-packed with people from the play, loudly laughing and talking. The screams could not be heard.

Stevens grasped Lisa's long, beautiful, dark-brown hair with both hands and banged her head into the floor. She did this repeatedly, shouting "Bitch!...Bitch!...Bitch!" with each strike. Lisa kicked and screamed to no avail. She kicked so hard, the pink character shoes she had worn in the play flew off her feet. Stevens continued beating her head against the concrete floor. Lisa felt dizzy, and was drifting in and out. She recognized the distinct laughter of her director, Sal Moretti, in the hallway just as she lost consciousness. Lisa was out cold.

***

In the auditorium lobby, Mark was making nice with Lisa's parents, Ainsley and Charles Lesinsky. Several audience members had approached them, complementing Lisa's performance. Charles' happy face reflected his pride. Even Ainsley, who had not exactly been supportive of Lisa's participation in the show, was enjoying all the attention. As the well-wishers began to thin out, Ainsley took a deep breath. "Whew! Well, I must confess, I never thought this play would be such a big deal."

Mark smiled. "Yeah, who knew?"

Charles put his arm around his wife. "And it sounds like our daughter will be up for a big scholarship to Atlantic. I like the sound of that!"

The auditorium lobby had practically emptied. "I wonder what's keeping her?" said Ainsley.

Mark turned his head in the direction of Stevens' office. "The cheer coach said she wanted to see her."

"Well, it's important that Lisa remain on good terms with her," Ainsley said. "Our reservation isn't until 8. We've got some time."

***

When Lisa regained consciousness, she found herself bound to Stevens' desk chair. There was duct tape binding her wrists to the arms of the chair. Her ankles were strewn together as well. Also a large strip of tape covered her mouth. Lisa squirmed in the chair and tried to yell, but her voice was muffled.

Stevens brandished the pinking shears in front of Lisa's face. "I *sh*ugge*sh*t you *sh*it *sh*till and *shut up*!" Lisa obeyed. Stevens depressed the point of the scissor in Lisa's cheek causing it to bleed. "I really hope you enjoyed your little game of make believe, Li*sh*a! I hope it was worth it!" Stevens grabbed a large clump of Lisa's hair and cut it off with the shears. Tears began falling from Lisa's eyes. She believed she was going to die.

***

In the lobby, only Mark and Lisa's parents now remained. Charles was pacing. "Where *is* she? We need to get to the restaurant."

Ainsley linked her arm around Mark's. "Do me a favor handsome, and see what's keeping her." Ainsley placed her palm affectionately on Mark's face.

Mark forced a smile. "Sure Mrs. Lesinski, I'll check on her." Mark started down the long hallway toward Stevens' office. As he walked, Mark called out. "Lisa!....Lisa!"

Both Stevens and Lisa heard Mark's call. Stevens had, by now, cut off much of Lisa's hair. She had also perforated a large section of skin on Lisa's forehead. Significant blood was dripping on Lisa's face and clothing. When Lisa heard Mark's call her eyes widened and she again attempted to yell.

"Shh!" Stevens held her index finger to her mouth with her left hand. With her right hand she pressed the point of the scissor to Lisa's throat.

Mark arrived at Stevens office. The window blinds prevented him from seeing inside. He knocked on the office door. “Lisa....Lisa are you in there? Your dad wants to get going.” There was no answer from within. Mark knocked again. “Lisa? ... Mrs. Stevens?” No answer.

Mark shook his head in confusion and started back to the lobby. But after a few steps he returned to the office quietly. He got down on his knees in front of the window. There was a thin space between the bottom of the venetian blind and the window sill. He crooked his head to try to see in the space. It was such a tight opening, he could see very little. But as he continued to maneuver across the width of the space, he caught a glimpse of something. He could barely make it out in the dark room, but after focusing his eyes, he was quite sure it was one of the pink shoes Lisa had worn in the show. Mark sprang to his feet and started banging loudly on the office door.

“Lisa! Are you all right? Lisa answer me!” Nothing. Mark turned in a circle. He was slightly panicking but subsequently his head cleared. He ran halfway down the hall to where he knew there was a fire extinguisher. He yanked it from its wall-well and ran back to Stevens’ office. Again, Mark banged on the office door, calling for Lisa. There was no response. He stepped to the office window, back-swung the extinguisher and forcefully crashed it through the glass...shattering it in every direction. As he attempted to climb through the jagged opening, Stevens lunged at him, striking his head with the pinking shears. She then grabbed his head and pulled it to the floor. Both Mark and Stevens were lacerated by the shards of glass. Blood was everywhere. As Mark and Stevens wrestled for control, he caught a glimpse of Lisa, with her clumped butchered head and bloody face.

“Let go, Stratton!” screamed Stevens, “let go of me!”

Mark had managed to get one arm around Stevens’ neck in a choke hold, causing her to gasp for breath. With the other arm, he wrestled away the shears and tossed them out of reach. Lisa’s loud cries were still muffled by the duct tape. Mark yelled for help.

Moretti was still in his office, behind the auditorium stage, when he heard Mark's shouts. He immediately began running up the long corridor toward Mark's voice…which he quickly determined was coming from Stevens' office. Running from the opposite end of the hall were Lisa's parents. When the shocked Moretti realized what was happening, he climbed through the disintegrated window and helped Mark restrain Stevens.

"What are you doing?" said Stevens as Moretti grabbed her arm, "let me go! The*zh* kid*zh* attacked me!"

"I don't think so, Stacy."

Moretti opened the office door allowing Lisa's parents to enter. They were shocked to find their daughter bloody and brutalized.

"Oh, my baby!" cried Ainsley as she began releasing Lisa from her bondage.

Charles found Stevens' phone on the office floor and called 911.

Stevens was wailing out of control. "Let me go! I wa*zh* the one who wazh attacked! I wa*zh* defending my*sh*elf! I'm an ex*sh*ellent educator! *I'm an exshellent educator*!"

Mark and Moretti held the screaming Stevens fast until the police and emergency squad arrived. The EMS personnel attended to Lisa and conveyed her on a stretcher to the waiting ambulance for transport to the local hospital. Mark and Lisa's parents also left in the ambulance. Because the police found it difficult to take the thrashing Stevens into custody, it was necessary for them to place her in a restraining jacket. As she was rolled out on a stretcher, Steven's continued to sob, "*I'm an exshellent educator*!"

Moretti watched in disbelief as Stevens was wheeled away from her office, screeching her innocence. He re-entered the cheer coach's office, which was now a crime scene. He picked up one of the framed certificates that Stevens had flung to the floor. It was her Coach of the Year Award. As Moretti laid the frame on Stevens' desk, he recalled his heated encounter with her just two days ago. Now it was fairly certain that Stevens' career as an teacher was over…to say the least. Moretti was strangely sad.

***

Eventually, Lisa recovered from her injuries and ultimately her hair grew back. But she was socially wrecked for weeks. She became fearful to the touch…anyone's touch. However, at the same time, her gratitude to Mark became unbounded. She would never forget his bravery in saving her life.

As Lisa grew older, that gratitude may have confused her emotions and affected her life in an unpredictable and irreversible manner.

11
Integrity
Mid-January, 2019

Michael Morrison, at age 52, was still waiting for his ship to come in. Acting was his life and always had been. He spent many years trying to make it in New York, with little luck. Feedback from his unsuccessful auditions had been fairly consistent. Inauthentic.

In 1992 he married Leslie Newman. They lived in a small apartment in the city. Leslie was also an unsuccessful actor. She auditioned for whatever was available: plays, movies, television, commercials, corporate events…anything and everything. Michael, on the other hand, was quite selective. He only went for roles that were "right for him." Because theatre work for both had been rare, Leslie decided to apply for and secure a job at a radio station, WJKL, a country music outlet in the heart of the city. She worked in the traffic department generating program logs and scheduling commercials. She was good at this and became a valued employee. She eventually branched out and began writing and producing commercial copy. She even voiced some of the spots. She was making fairly good money. Life was improving for her and her husband. Michael still auditioned sometimes, but this became less frequent. Leslie thought she could get him an interview for a sales position at the radio station. Michael was not enthusiastic about the idea, but acquiesced to Leslie's pleading. Because everyone at WJLK loved Leslie, Michael was given the job. Salespeople often work flexible schedules. They make calls at the convenience of their customers. Michael took advantage of this and spent a lot of work time at home on his couch. Eventually, he was called on the carpet for his poor performance and it seemed certain he would be fired. But again, due to the company's affection for Leslie,

Michael survived the axe. In the fall of 1994, Leslie gave birth to a son, Edward Prescott Morrison. It was decided that Michael would give up his sales job to become the primary caregiver. At first Michael was delighted. He didn't enjoy radio sales at all. He was convinced that fatherhood would bring him a much easier and happier life. But after six months of daddy-daycare, he had had enough. He complained that his acting career was ruined by his marriage and subsequent parenthood. One day, he packed his bag and took off. Neither Leslie, nor their son, Edward, ever heard from him again.

Michael ran and ran… to Los Angeles, Chicago, Atlanta, Miami—and so on. Auditioning for parts and being sent home empty handed…for years—fifteen years. He lived hand to mouth—often sleeping in homeless shelters. Finally he landed in Lakeside, New Jersey, where he was given the role of the judge in the Town Square Playhouse production of *Witness For The Prosecution*. It was a small part but finally he had been cast…in something. Of course there was no pay in the community theatre show, so he continued to live on odd jobs. He finally found part time employment at the local Super Gas service station on Main Street. With this working wage he was able to rent a room. Michael found that he learned a lot and his acting improved at Town Square…to the point where he was cast in some significant roles.

Unfortunately, this degree of success overly fed his already bloated ego. His fellow actors often had difficulty in dealing with him. One night, he noticed a quiet, somewhat insecure, actor playing the role of Rachel Brown, the minister's daughter, in the Playhouse production of *Inherit The Wind*. He approached the girl, Lindsey Ralston, and offered himself to her…as a mentor. Lindsey, who was 16 years younger than Michael, became totally drawn to him. She quickly fell in love with him, she thought. Three months after meeting, Michael gave up his rented room, and moved in with Lindsey. Michael continued to guide and teach Lindsey in all matters of life. As this *Svengali* relationship evolved, she became exceedingly dependent on him. Soon after moving in, Michael quit his job at Super Gas, in order to pursue a writing career in conjunction with his acting. Lindsey worked each day as a paralegal at a local law firm in Glennville.

As the *Doll's House* rehearsals began, Michael and Lindsey had been cohabitating for about a year. Lindsey had become concerned about Michael. Whenever she asked him to share "his writing" with her, he refused, saying it was a work in progress and couldn't be seen until complete. Also, she became suspicious of other behaviors. He received strange phone calls in the middle of the night—calls that he couldn't or wouldn't explain to any satisfaction… "an audition"… "a writing issue"… "an investment opportunity." One day her office closed early due to a power failure. When she arrived home, Michael was nowhere to be found. When he finally came in, around midnight— he would only say he was meeting with a colleague.

So, when Michael made the overture to Lisa, of working together on the *Doll's House* script, Lindsey's antennae went up, and not in a good way. Lisa sensed Lindsey's annoyance and put Michael off. But at one point in rehearsal, director Moretti also suggested that the two might benefit from extra rehearsals together. Lisa was reticent, but agreed to the suggestion.

"Okay," Lisa said, "but I don't have a lot of free time."

Michael pulled out his planner. "Are you ever free during the day?"

"Well, sometimes I work evening shifts. I could possibly be free during those days."

"Perfect," said Michael, "how about this Thursday? Say about 2, at my place?"

Lisa swallowed hard. She really didn't want to do this, but she relented. "All right, I'm on nightshift Thursday. I guess that would be okay."

Lisa arrived to rehearse with Michael at exactly 2 o'clock. Michael greeted her warmly, hugged her and offered her a glass of wine.

Lisa passed on the wine. "I think we should get right to it."

"Sure," said Michael.

They decided to begin with the first scene in Act I of *A Doll's House*. In it, *Torvald* patronizes his wife, *Nora*, as his "little skylark" and his "little squirrel." At the same time he admonishes her for spending too much of *his* money. *Nora* is oblivious to her husband's patronage and flirts with him in order to secure additional household funds.

Lisa was still somewhat uncomfortable in this strange setting but began reading *Nora's* lines. Michael stepped close to her to read *Torvald.*

Nora: If you really want to give me something, you might--you might--

Torvold: Well, out with it!

Nora: You might give me money, Torvald. Only just as much as you can afford; and then one of these days I will buy something with it.

Torvald: You're my expensive "little bird," Nora. But I dare say, you are well worth it. [Embraces and kisses her]

Lisa had been aware of the kiss in the stage directions and had been nervous about it. She was relieved when they had skipped over the action in the rehearsals at the theatre. But at Michael's home rehearsal, he laid a wet one on her.

She was shocked and pulled away. "Whoa. I wasn't expecting that."

"What do you mean?" said Michael, "it's right in the script."

Michael argued that they needed to get used to doing it so it would seem authentic. Lisa wasn't convinced, but reluctantly agreed. They tried it again.

Nora: You might give me money, Torvald. Only just as much as you can afford; and then one of these days I will buy something with it.

Torvald: You're my expensive "little bird," Nora. But I dare say, you are well worth it. [Embraces and kisses her]

The kiss was longer this time. Lisa was definitely uncomfortable, but got through it. Then Michael suggested they do the scene once more. Lisa asked if they could move on to another scene. But Michael felt they should repeat the same scene in order to get it perfectly right. Again, Lisa acquiesced. The third time through the scene clearly went better. The lines flowed more smoothly, and the characters definitely seemed fuller. As the kiss section approached, Lisa flinched a bit but prepared herself. Michael's embrace was tighter and the kiss was harder. Then Michael's hands slid downward from Lisa's back and landed squarely on her butt. He then pulled Lisa's lower body very tightly against his. It was obvious that Michael Morrison was no longer 'acting" with his "intellect."

Lisa pushed him away. "Hey, what the heck are you doing?"

Michael shrugged. "Oh, don't be such a baby! I was *in the moment.* I believed that's what *Torvald* would have done. It's a method thing."

Lisa grabbed her bag and headed for the door. "Fuck off, Michael!" And she was gone.

***

Lisa was trembling as she left Michael. She had been physically molested by her leading man. She didn't know what to do. She wondered if she should quit the play. "Perhaps that would be best," she thought. But then she considered how that decision might impact Charlie. Her daughter had been so excited about acting in a play with her mom. And what about Moretti? He had passed over many of his regulars to cast her in a major role. What would he think if she dropped out so early in the rehearsal period?

Lisa was torn. She wanted to stay with the show, but the prospect of facing Michael again made her physically ill. At work that night she was quiet and despondent, not her usual self at all. Her friend Cailla McCormack could tell something was wrong. As they closed up the daycare, Lisa confided in her. She told her friend what had happened and that she was probably going to quit the show.

Cailla stepped to Lisa and grabbed her by both arms. "That is crazy talk. Why should *you* drop out! You should report that creep and get *him* kicked out…if not arrested."

Lisa stepped away from Cailla. "I don't want to do that. I'm the new kid on the block at this theatre. I'm afraid I would be perceived as a trouble maker."

"That's bullshit," said Cailla. "*He's* the troublemaker. My guess is, he's pulled this crap before. Somebody has to call him to task. Otherwise he'll keep right on. You'd be doing that theatre a favor."

Lisa half smiled. "I know you're right, but I'm not sure I can. I've gotta think about it."

"Okay, you think about it…hard and long." Cailla hugged Lisa. "And I'll think about it too. There must be some way to get back at this prick."

Lisa began to tear up. "Thank you Cailla. You're a good friend. I feel better now that I've told someone."

When Lisa got home, Charlie had already gone to bed. Lisa's mother, Ainsley, who had been sitting with Charlie, sensed that Lisa was troubled.

Ainsley put on her coat to leave. "What's with you?"

"Nothing," said Lisa. "Did you check Charlie's homework?"

Her mother nodded. "Yes, it looks fine to me. But I don't really understand that math. She has all the right answers, but I don't have a clue about all those little blocks she draws next to the problems.

"That's all right Mom, I'll check it. Thanks for sitting tonight. See you on Tuesday?"

"Tuesday, right. Goodnight." Ainsley was out the door.

Lisa did not have the kind of relationship with her mother that would allow her to share the hurt she felt inside. But hurt she felt, nevertheless. When she looked in on Charlie, she was tempted to wake her. At age 8, her daughter seemed a wise old soul. But Lisa resisted the notion and simply kissed Charlie on the forehead.

Lisa didn't sleep well that night. She tossed and turned, scrutinizing her dilemma and its possible consequences.

The next morning she still wasn't sure what she would do. She and Charlie had a pleasant breakfast, as they prepared for school and work. When the school bus approached, Lisa kissed Charlie and bid her have a great day. Charlie mounted the steps of the bus.

"You too, Mom!"

As the bus departed with her daughter, Lisa again began to cry.

***

It took all the courage Lisa could muster for her to attend rehearsal that night. As she and Charlie walked toward the theatre's marquee, she spotted a familiar face in an out-of-place setting. It was Cailla McCormack.

"Hey, you!" Lisa hugged her friend. "What the heck are you doing here?"

"I haven't been able to get you off my mind," said Cailla. "Hi Charlie!"

Charlie smiled. "Hello Mrs. McCormack."

"Lisa, I need a quick moment with you before you go inside." Cailla clutched at Lisa's elbow.

Lisa told Charlie to head in to rehearsal and that she would be in directly. Charlie waved goodbye to Cailla and entered the theatre.

Cailla's eyes widened. "Listen, Lisa, you can't drop out of this play. This is your chance to turn a corner in your life. You've earned it!"

"I know, but the thought of working with Michael ---"

Cailla interrupted her. "So make him quit."

"Huh?" said Lisa.

"If you don't want to report him," said Cailla, "find a way to make *him* quit. Threaten him…or better yet, embarrass him."

"You don't know this guy. He has a huge ego. I doubt if he'd be easily embarrassed."

"You've gotta try," said Cailla. "You can't let him win. You're too good a person."

Lisa embraced her. "Thank you Cailla. You're the best."

Lisa entered the theatre, bolstered by Cailla's encouragement. On the other hand, she still had no idea what she would do."

Lisa was walking down the house right aisle when she encountered Moretti.

"Evening," said the director.

"Hi." Lisa stopped walking.

"What's up?" Moretti asked.

Lisa looked around. There was no one else in earshot. If she was going to report Michael, this would be the time.

Lisa bit her lip. "Oh…no. Everything's okay. I'm just a little nervous."

Moretti patted her on the back. "You'll be fine. Just like riding a bike." Moretti smiled and started up the aisle. "Go ahead. I'll be right down."

Lisa saw that Charlie was sitting with the other kids in the show. They seemed to be getting along well, so she sat several rows back. Most of the cast had arrived and were seated up front. Then Michael came striding down the aisle. He paused briefly next to where Lisa was seated. He glowered at her without speaking. Lisa turned her face front. Then Michael continued down the aisle and took his seat. Suddenly another voice was heard.

"Can you scooch over? I need to speak with you."

Lisa turned to see that it was Lindsey Ralston, Michael's girlfriend.

"Sure." Lisa moved in one seat, and Lindsey sat beside her. Lisa could feel the blood rushing to her head. It felt like something bad was about to happen.

"So," said Lindsey, "how did your rehearsal with Michael go yesterday?"

Lisa shifted in her seat. "Oh, it went."

"Yeah, that's what Michael said."

Lisa looked at her. "What do you mean?"

"Look, Lisa," said Lindsey, "you don't need to try to hide it. Michael told me."

"*What* did he tell you?"

Lindsey folded her hands in her lap. "Well, according to Michael, your rehearsal had hardly begun when you made a pass at him."

"*What?!*"

"Oh, yes….he told me everything. He said that you threw yourself at him sexually and that he had to practically throw you out of our…*my* house."

Lisa was dumbfounded. She turned her focus to Michael, who was jovially holding court in the front row. She could barely believe the disdain she felt. Lisa then turned back to Lindsey. As she was about to respond, Lindsey continued. "Before you say anything, Lisa, understand this. If you are about to tell me that Michael is lying, I will absolutely believe you."

"What?"

"Oh yes, I've been down this path before…and I've had enough. It was Michael who moved on you, wasn't it?"

"Yes!" said Lisa.

"That's what I thought. Thank you."

Just then Moretti called places for Act I, scene 1…the infamous kissing scene. Michael sprang to his feet and quickly took his place onstage. Lisa was slow to rise. She had been fearing this moment. When she reached the stage, she avoided making eye contact with Michael.

So let's begin with Torvald's line, *" Is that my little lark twittering out there?"* said Moretti as he sat in the front row.

Michael stepped to dead center stage. "Righteo."

"Actually, I'd like you to come in from up-right, Michael," said Moretti.

Michael furrowed his brow. "Really, I thought center stage would provide a more dynamic opening statement."

Suddenly, Lindsey's voice was heard from the house. "The director said up-right, *Shithead.* Last time I looked you were not now nor were never likely to be the director!"

A quiet buzz worked its way through the other cast members. Lisa could barely keep a straight face. Moretti was also taken back.

Michael stepped downstage. "*Excuse me!*"

"You heard me," Lindsey answered.

Moretti stood as he regained his sensibility. "All right. Umm. All right. No, Michael, I want you to enter from up-right. It'll allow for a good build up in the scene."

Michael reluctantly did the staging as directed. Moretti then continued to block the scene. Lisa conscientiously wrote all her stage movement in her script. She was feeling confident about what she was doing, but, as *Nora*, she still hadn't made eye contact with her *Torvald.* As they approached the end of the scene, Lisa got nervous. The kiss was coming up. As Michael began to lean in, Moretti stopped.

"Cut!" said the director. "We'll skip the kiss for right now."

Lisa breathed a sigh of relief. Michael stepped to her, looked her squarely in the eyes and lecherously smiled.

"All right, let's take it from the top," said Moretti. "And action!"

As the two actors walked through their movement, it was obvious that something was wrong. The stage picture was out of balance. The movement was ragged, clumsy and rough. Michael stopped and stepped to the edge of the stage.

"I'm sorry Sal, but I can't work like this. Lisa is constantly getting in my way."

Before Moretti could answer, Lindsey piped in from the house. "It's not her, *moron*, it's you that's in the wrong place.

"How dare you call me a moron you ingrate. After all I've done for you."

Lindsey responded, "Oh, yes…all you've done…like *lived* in my house, *eaten* my food, and *spent* my money."

"Oh, please!" Michael turned upstage.

"Not to mention the fact that you've cheated on me time and time again."

Lisa tried to change the subject, "I don't think it's me, Mr. Moretti. I'm pretty sure I'm in the right spot."

Moretti checked his prompt book. "Yes, you are correct, Lisa."

"What is going on here?" Michael stomped his foot. "I am a professional! I've been on stages all over the world. I will not be humiliated by a bunch of wet-behind-the-ears *amateurs*!"

"Calm down, Michael," said Moretti.

"Sal, I'm calm, I'm perfectly calm." Michael took a deep breath. "But if you want me in this role, you'll have to bounce these two." He pointed to Lindsey and Lisa.

"What an *asshole*!" shouted Lindsey.

Moretti stepped onstage, "Michael, I don't appreciate threats and I'm certainly not going to put up with one from you. The director turned to Lindsey, then Lisa and then back to Michael. "Now I don't know what happened between the three of you, but I can take a pretty good guess. Michael, *everyone* is replaceable, and right now the one most replaceable is *you.* I'm sorry. You can leave your script with Rebecca on your way out."

Michael slammed his script to the floor. "Unbelievable! What a two-bit operation. You're making a huge mistake, Sal. As for me, I'll be far better off…elsewhere. And with me I take my talent and I take my experience."

Everyone could see that Michael was gearing up for a dramatic departure. He took wide strides toward the edge of the stage, but he misjudged his depth perception and as he delivered his exit line, "But most of all I take my integrity." He stepped off the front of the platform and fell squarely on his face.

***

Fortunately (or unfortunately) depending on your point of view, Michael was not injured as a result of his front header off the stage. Red in the face, he gathered himself to his feet and muttered his way up the aisle and out the lobby door. After about three silent beats, most of the cast burst into hysterical laughter. The only exceptions were Lindsey, who sat solemnly in the house and Lisa, who quietly moved to Charlie and put her arm around her.

Moretti pulled out his cell phone and within 20 minutes, Michael's replacement arrived at the theatre. David James was an experienced actor and scenic designer. He had initially considered auditioning for *A Doll's House*, but had backed off due to a busy schedule. When Moretti called and asked him to assume the role of *Torvald*, he gladly accommodated. The other cast members knew David well and were delighted that he was stepping in.

Moretti introduced David to Lisa. The two seemed to quickly strike a congenial working relationship. Incredibly, the evening's rehearsal proceeded as if nothing unusual had happened. After a sputter start, *A Doll's House* was off and running.

***

Along the way, Lisa's casual friendship with Nick Curtis began to evolve. Nick sensed that Lisa was cautious about her personal space, and proceeded slowly. On evenings when he was working at the theatre, Nick would sometimes approach Lisa and chat a bit. They engaged in lightweight, friendly talk about weather and such…nothing too serious. These interactions were pleasant and enjoyable to both. Nick also became friendly with Charlie. They would speak and joke about all kinds of things…video games, TV shows, school…everything. After a few weeks, all three felt comfortable with the amicable connection that had seemed to develop.

One night, as rehearsal was winding down, Nick resolved to up the ante a bit. Charlie had not been required to attend the evening's rehearsal, so Nick decided to ask Lisa to join him for coffee.

Lisa smiled at Nick. "Oh, that would be nice, but…"

"C'mon," said Nick, "you're daughter's not here. You don't have to worry about school in the morning. Let's get some coffee."

"I'd really like to…I would…but my Mom is home sitting with Charlie. I don't want to take advantage of her."

Nick lightly took Lisa's hand. "Hey, it's still pretty early. And I promise we won't be long. It'll be fun. You deserve to have a little fun, right?"

Lisa looked at her watch then at Nick. "Okay, I guess so. But just for a little while, right?"

Nick raised his right hand as if in court. "I swear, your honor."

Nick drove Lisa in his Chevy Cruze to the Tasty Diner. The establishment had been operated by the same Greek family since the 1970's. They sat in a retro-style booth, sporting bright red shiny upholstery. A mini-juke box was at the end of the table. Nick dropped a quarter in the machine and punched up K-3.

"What are you playing?" asked Lisa.

"*Don't Stop Believin*' by Journey," Nick replied.

Lisa wiggled her nose. "That's a weird choice."

Nick smiled. "Hey, no self-respecting Jersey guy can sit at one of these diner jukes without punching up that song"

Lisa tilted her head in confusion.

Nick continued, "*The Sopranos*? The series finale?"

"Oh, I've never seen *The Sopranos*," said Lisa.

Nick whistled. "Whoa...you've got to be kidding! You've never seen *The Sopranos*? Well, we'll have to correct that situation.

They both laughed and agreed they would get together for a *Sopranos* marathon sometime in the future. Lisa and Nick spoke of many things that night in the confines of the nearly empty Tasty Diner. Nick revealed the rough going of his early life, his senior year rally, and what he regarded as the positive benefits of his military service. Lisa opened up about the challenges of her marriage, separation and divorce.

"I never talk about this stuff," Lisa said, "especially to anyone outside my family."

Nick took a sip of coffee. "Well, I'm pleased that you feel comfortable enough with me to share."

"And I'm talking so much," said Lisa. "I can't believe I'm being such a chatterbox."

"Well, my jaw's been flapping too."

Lisa looked up at the clock over the diner counter. "Oh, my goodness it's after 11. I need to get home. My mother is going to freak out."

"I didn't realize it was so late," Nick said as he laid a ten dollar bill on the table. "This has been fun."

Lisa got out of the booth and put on her coat. "Yes…it has been…fun"

As Nick drove Lisa back to her car, he suggested they might do coffee again sometime. Lisa nodded and agreed that would be a definite possibility. Nick pulled up behind Lisa's parked car.

Lisa turned to Nick. "Well thanks for the coffee."

"Anytime."

As they looked at each other, a kiss crossed both their minds. But then…awkwardly…

"Well goodnight, Nick."

"Goodnight, Lisa."

Lisa got out of Nick's car, into her Civic and off she drove. As she pulled away, a distinct and deliberate smile emerged on her face. Nick was smiling too.

***

When Lisa arrived at her apartment, she found her mother in a highly agitated state. "Where the heck have you been," said Ashley, "I've been worried sick."

"I'm so sorry," said Lisa, "I had coffee with a friend. I didn't realize it was so late.

"Well, you *should* be sorry. That was highly inconsiderate of you."

"You're right, Mom. I should have called."

"You certainly should have." Ainsley eyed her daughter with suspicion. "So who is this friend?"

"Oh, just someone from the theatre. He works on the technical crew."

"*He*?" said Ainsley, "so this was a date."

"No…not really…well maybe." Lisa half smiled.

"Does Mark know you're dating?"

Lisa rolled her eyes. "I wouldn't say I was dating. I had coffee with a guy. No big deal."

Ainsley shook her head. "That is not going to get you back with Mark!"

"Who says I want to get back with Mark?"

"He's the father of your daughter…I'd think that would mean something to you."

Lisa tossed her script on the living room coffee table. "Of course it does. Mark will always be part of my life. But, Mom—I'm working hard to move on."

"Well, if you ask me, you're being foolish."

"I'm not asking you. And I'd really appreciate it if you didn't tell Mark about this."

Ainsley stepped to her. "Oh! So you're hiding it!"

"No, I'm not exactly hiding it," said Lisa. "It's just that it's something brand new and I'm not even sure what it is yet. It may be nothing…or it may be something. But until I figure it out, I'd just as soon keep it on the QT."

Ainsley put on her coat. "Well, you're a big girl. I can't tell you what to do. But I know what *I'd* do."

"I'm sure you do. Thanks Mom. Again, I'm sorry I was so late. See you Thursday?"

"Sure," said Ainsley as she walked out the door, "good night."

"Night."

Lisa went to Charlie's room. She watched her sleeping child with wonder. "How am I so lucky?" she thought. She bent over and kissed her daughter on the forehead. "Sweet dreams, Buddy."

She checked her watch as she left Charlie and entered her living room. It was a little past 11:30. Lisa wondered if Cailla might still be up. She decided to risk it and picked up her phone and called.

Cailla answered. "Everything all right?"

"Yeah, I'd say so!" Lisa smiled from ear to ear. "I'd definitely say so!"

12
Mein Herr
June 2008

Graduation night for the Meadow Hills High School class of 2008 was special to Lisa Lesinski. Certainly, most people hold fond memories of graduation. But Lisa's senior year had been transformational, to say the least. She had always been a good student, so her high class rank was no surprise. She had been a varsity athlete for all four years, so her sports honors were also expected. But Lisa surprised everyone by her senior year achievements in theatre arts. She received high praise for her performance in the school musical, but even more recognition as a student choreographer. This latter accomplishment went far in earning her a generous scholarship to the Theatre and Dance Department at Atlantic University.

But beyond her official attainments, Lisa was grateful and happy to be alive for graduation day. The brutal attack by the school's cheer coach had resulted in long term consequences. Although she had recovered relatively quickly from her physical injuries, Lisa had struggled to regain a healthy mental capacity. She had engaged in intense counseling and in recent weeks had shown positive signs of improvement. Also, her hair had grown back… somewhat.

Through all this, she felt as one with her boyfriend, Mark Stratton. Although Lisa believed she had been in love with Mark prior to her attack, his courageous rescue convinced her that he was indeed the *one*. Mark certainly returned Lisa's affection and shared her joy on graduation night.

But Mark's future plans were not as resolved as were those of his girlfriend. There had been interest from several colleges for Mark to play football, but his poor academic record was a concern. In the final analysis he had only one firm offer. He had accepted provisional enrollment at Wington University, near Wheeling, West Virginia. But the college attached a provision to his scholarship that required his participation in a mandatory tutoring program. The school made it clear that Mark would have to maintain satisfactory grades in order to play ball. Mark was uncomfortable with this arrangement. He had never been a good student, and wasn't sure he would be up to the task. Lisa did everything she could to build Mark up. She told him of her confidence in his ability and was certain of his success. He remained reticent but was determined to give it his best shot.

Lisa and Mark had a great summer together. They both obtained summer jobs at the high school. Lisa worked in the office and Mark was on the painting crew. They had lunch together every day. Most evenings they would go out...movies...mini golf...or just hanging out with friends. On many Saturdays, they headed to the Jersey Shore. They were both enjoying life and feeling very happy.

In spite of all this joy, Lisa and Mark had still not been intimate. Lisa was well aware that her point of view may have been considered very old fashioned, but something inside her fostered an insistence that sex be saved for marriage. It wasn't a matter of religion. Lisa considered herself spiritual but not religious. It was, in fact, an intense personal reflection. In spite of her pronounced appreciation and commitment to Mark, her avowed abstinence remained intact.

Mark had come to accept the state of affairs, but wasn't very happy about it. He sometimes found himself so frustrated that he questioned the relationship. He hadn't forgotten the night of the infamous New Year's Eve party, when Lisa left in a huff. That evening, following Lisa's premature exit, her fellow cheerleader Wendy Phillips delivered an explicit sexual offering to Mark. And he had accepted. Although Mark had enjoyed the interaction, he was not interested in Wendy for anything other than the physicality. When school resumed in the new year, Mark quickly made-up with Lisa, much to Wendy's disappointment. Lisa had never learned of the incident, and Mark wanted to keep it that way. In spite of the sex issue, Mark loved Lisa and believed her partnership would bring him success in life.

As the summer began to wind down, both Mark and Lisa looked to the future. Lisa had received several calls and emails from Dr. Mary Blackwell, the department chair at Atlantic. In addition to advising Lisa's course of study, Blackwell recruited her for the dance ensemble for the school's production of the musical, *Cabaret*. She sent links to several online dance videos for Lisa to view. She also suggested that Lisa arrive on campus a week early, so as to get a head start on rehearsals.

At first Lisa was resistant to this idea. Her summer had been so enjoyable, she didn't want it to end early. But then she realized that Mark would also be leaving early for football camp in West Virginia. She wrote back to Dr. Blackwell that she would indeed be reporting as requested.

On their final night together before going off in separate directions, Mark and Lisa went to *Ernie's*, a very fancy restaurant, for a grown-up dinner date. The evening was a goodbye gift from Lisa's parents. The couple had a wonderful time. They laughed wildly as they fed each other the elegant shrimp appetizers. Lisa feigned disgust at Mark's very rare steak. And they both "oohed and aahed" at the decadent chocolate fudge cake.

Lisa placed her hand on her stomach. "Ugh, I am absolutely stuffed."

Mark stuck his fork in her unfinished dessert. "Oh…too bad…more for me."

They both laughed happily. Then both became serious. "I can't believe this is it," said Lisa

"I know." Mark swallowed the last of the cake. "The summer has flown."

"I'm gonna miss you." Lisa looked away, not wishing to show her emotion.

Mark reached across the table and took her hands. "Hey, we'll visit each other, right? My first game is in three weeks. And when is your play?"

"End of October," said Lisa.

"Sure…and before you know it, we'll be home for Christmas."

Lisa smiled. "I hope it all goes that quickly."

As Mark drove Lisa home from the restaurant, the car was quiet. The cd player which usually blared the strains of Kanye West and Bow Wow was turned off. The young couple didn't converse. Every so often one would turn and look to the other with deep tenderness. When Mark pulled up to Lisa's house, the emotion within each was overwhelming.

"Let's just call this whole thing off!" said Mark.

Lisa smiled. "Call what off?"

"Your college, my college, football, dancing…all of it. Let's just stay here and keep on doing what we've been doing all summer."

"Mark?!"

"Hey, I love you," Mark said, "and I've never been happier than right now. I know you feel the same way. So why should we risk losing that? Let's just stay here."

Lisa kissed Mark on the cheek. "I love you too, totally. But I'll still love you when we finish college. I have goals and you do too. I really think we'll be happier in the long run, if we accomplish what we set out to do." She kissed him again. "You know that's true."

"Hmm, I guess so." Mark kissed Lisa passionately and she responded in kind.

"Okay, we've both got big days tomorrow." Lisa moved as if to open the car door.

"Wait…" Mark pulled Lisa close to him. "I'll always love you."

"Me too."

Mark lovingly kissed Lisa once more.

Lisa exited the car. As she walked to her front door she wiped the tears from her eyes. Mark felt numb as he drove away.

***

Mark's arrival at Wington University for football camp was not particularly remarkable. Most of the other players were more local…from West Virginia, Pennsylvania and Ohio. But Mark's roommate was another Jersey boy, Randy Marchello, from South Brunswick. The two "Garden State" transplants hit it off right away. They both were excited about playing ball in college, but uncertain about their new very non-Jersey environment.

To be sure everyone on the team was friendly and congenial. The fact of the matter was that Mark and Randy seemed just as strange to them as they were to Mark and Randy. The pattern of speech was different. The locals didn't really have southern accents, but just a different style: "yinz" meant *you*, "ahr" meant *hour*, and "ndat" meant and *whatever follows*. There were lots of other regional affectations. Of course, the Jersey guys were cited for "whutter" instead of *water*, and "cawfee" for *coffee*. Pretty quickly though, everyone got used to each other and a sense of camaraderie seemed to take hold.

The head football coach for the Wington Hilltoppers was Roscoe Bodean. He was a local boy who had made good in the NFL and returned in glory to his alma mater. Bodean had played four seasons as a middle linebacker for the Buffalo Bills until his career was cut short by an achilles tendon injury. This was his third year as head coach and he was looking forward to a successful season. He regarded his two freshman wide receivers from New Jersey as important factors in that success. He was a tough coach with high expectations.

Mark was used to being the star of the team. The fact that the other guys were just as good as he was a bit confusing. On one hand, it was fun to play with other high caliber athletes, but on the other…he kind of missed being the center of attention.

***

Lisa's arrival on the Atlantic University campus was greeted with high anticipation. Dr. Blackwell had informed the upper class dancers of what she called "an exceptional new prospect" for the program. The girls greeted Lisa with open arms. Her roommate, Lauren Benke, seemed especially nice. She was a senior and had been a featured performer in the school's productions every year. She took it upon herself to show Lisa around the campus and introduce her to the other girls in the troupe.

Lisa was surprised to find out that she was the only incoming freshman chosen for the mainstage performance company. "Blackwell usually doesn't use freshman in the productions," said Lauren Benke, "you must be really hot stuff."

Lisa did a double-take. "You've got to be kidding. I had no idea I was the only freshman…believe me, I'm no hot stuff."

"Most of us have been together for at least two years," Lauren said. "We lost Katie Johnson to graduation last year. She was fantastic. It looks to me like Blackwell sees you as her replacement."

Up until now Lisa had felt nothing but excitement for her new endeavor. But all of a sudden she was feeling some pressure. Yes, she had taken dance lessons, but not that seriously. Up until recently, her only performance experience had been as a cheerleader. It sounded to her like most of these girls had studied with big time teachers for a long time. For the first time, she wondered if she had made the right choice.

The *Cabaret* production would feature eight dancers, comprising the Kit Kat Club ensemble. This unit would perform with the *Emcee*, on many of the musical numbers in the show. The production was set in 1931 Berlin, as the Nazi's were gaining power. So in spite of the upbeat illusion of the dances, many numbers suggested darker overtones.

The first rehearsal was held on the day Lisa arrived on campus. Leaving her little time to settle in. For the first few weeks, the girls would be working in a rehearsal hall in the basement floor of the Hall of Fine Arts. In high school Lisa's rehearsals were always on the mainstage, so she was surprised at the confines of the facility. The room was fairly small…maybe 20 by 20 feet. It was also dimly lit and the walls were painted black. There was a ballet bar along one side of the room, and mirrors all the way around. Dr. Blackwell, who would be directing the production, introduced the group to the show's choreographer, Lynette Ritchie.

Ritchie, who graduated from Atlantic a decade ago, had achieved some impressive success. She had worked in the dance ensembles of several national tours, and had recently been a featured dancer in the Broadway revival of *Miss Saigon*. Her return to Atlantic as choreographer represented an expansion of her marketable repertoire.

She stood about 5' 3" and probably weighed around 115 pounds… kind of petite…but solid. She was obviously in great shape. Her short, black curly hair framed a very pretty face. She was personable, but focused. During her first meeting with the ensemble dancers, she discussed a little of her philosophy.

"Theatre is a collaboration," she said. "Over the summer, Dr. Blackwell and I have had many chats regarding her vision for the show and how important the dances would be in conveying that vision."

Ritchie made it clear that the work would be challenging but fulfilling. Lisa's excitement grew as the choreographer outlined her plan of attack for *Cabaret*. "We'll start out with full day rehearsal sessions. When classes begin, we'll obviously have to pull that back, but you can expect to be here at least six nights a week."

"Whoa," thought Lisa, "that's a little more than I was expecting." But Lisa was charged up. She liked Ritchie and she liked the other girls too. As rehearsals progressed, she felt she was working as hard as she had ever worked in her life…and she found it totally satisfying.

***

At Wington, West Virginia, Mark had settled-in well as a Hilltopper wide receiver. The team had won its first three games, and Mark had figured positively into much of the effort. He was working hard and was well regarded by his teammates and coaches. He was disappointed that Lisa hadn't made it to his first game, or any of his games for that matter. Her rehearsal schedule simply would not allow it. Similarly, he would be unable to see her in her production. Although the couple's summer plans had been diverted, Mark and Lisa eagerly anticipated seeing each other over Christmas vacation.

While Mark had been excelling on the football field, the same could not be said for his academic performance. He was really struggling in all of his classes. English Composition, Biology and especially Economics were not going well at all. The mandatory tutoring sessions had been less than productive. Although Mark usually attended them, he wasn't really motivated to receive the help. He was tired and distracted. Some of the upperclassmen on the team told him not to worry. They assured him that as a star of the team, the coaches would see to it that he passed his courses. And they were right. At the end of the semester, Mark had miraculously attained a solid 3.0 average. Mark thought, "Wow! College is all right!"

***

Cabaret had been progressing well. The dances were innovative and engaging. The principal actors had also been working diligently. With three weeks of rehearsals remaining, the prospects for a top-notch production were promising.

Lisa was enjoying the work immensely. She had struck a great rhythm with the other dancers and totally admired Ritchie as a choreographer. She felt she had learned so much in a relatively short time. But academics were a challenge for her too. She loved her classes and professors, but the rigid rehearsal schedule, made it difficult for her to keep up. Typically she would attend classes from 8 to 4, rehearse from 6 to 11, and study from midnight until 2 or 3 in the morning. Although she was enjoying it all, Lisa was feeling pretty run-down.

It was the practice of the university's theatre department to sometimes contract professional actors to perform with the students in the productions. The idea was that the underclassmen would learn from people employed in the industry. The practice, although solid in theory, had yielded varying results over the years. Most often the collaboration worked well, but occasionally it became problematic. It always depended on the true sense of professionalism in the guest artist. For *Cabaret,* things became dicey, to say the least…and Lisa found herself smack dab in the middle of it.

Olivia Clarke, from New York City, was the professional actress engaged to portray *Sally Bowles* in the Atlantic production of *Cabaret.* In her late 20's, she was indeed a beautiful woman. Tall and slender, Clarke displayed elegant features. Her long, flowing, auburn hair could be noticed from across any room. Her sculpted face was accentuated with lovely high cheek bones and the cutest button nose. And could she sing! Her lovely soprano voice had been featured in over a dozen regional and touring productions.

The entire cast eagerly anticipated the arrival of Olivia Clarke for the final two weeks of rehearsals. She was living the life that many of the students were striving for…to earn a living doing the thing they loved. The theatre department hosted a meet-and-greet the day the actress arrived on campus. To Lisa, Clarke seemed pleasant enough…all smiles and wide eager eyes. But as the evening progressed, there was something about Clarke's demeanor that troubled Lisa. She couldn't put her finger on it, but something just didn't hit her right. "Why would she come to the event in full stage make-up?" Lisa wondered. And it became clear that she had the same, somewhat patronizing greeting, for everyone.

"Hi there….oh you are so cute," Clarke repeated over and over again.

As they walked back to their dorm following the meet-and-greet, Lisa mentioned her impression to her roommate, Lauren Benke. "Is it me or was there something not right about her?"

Lauren stopped walking. "What do you mean? I thought she was terrific."

"Okay, so I guess it *is* me."

As they resumed walking Lauren continued. "You've got to remember, these guest artists aren't like us. They're professionals, so their confidence is consistent with their achievements. You'll get used to it, and you'll learn a lot."

Oh, okay, thanks." She remained unconvinced but yielded to Lauren's experience.

***

The next day full cast rehearsals began with the guest artist. Everyone was blown away by Olivia Clarke's excellent vocal renditions of "Don't Tell Mama," "Maybe This Time" and of course "Cabaret." It appeared that she would be a perfect enhancement to a show already showing excellent potential. However…

It was primarily based on recordings of Clarke's singing as well as her considerable experience, that had prompted Dr. Blackwell to hire her for the Atlantic show. There had been no formal audition. But as rehearsals progressed, it became clear that Clarke's acting left a void. She was playing *Sally* sexy, which was expected, but ignoring the underlying vulnerability of the character. Even after Dr. Blackwell's private coaching sessions, Clarke seemed clueless. But worse, she didn't seem to be making any effort to accept Blackwell's direction. "I'm sorry, but I just don't see it that way," was often her response.

Clarke was also unreceptive to Lynette Ritchie's choreographic direction. As a matter of course, she rejected every dance idea presented her. It was frustrating to the choreographer, because most of the musical numbers had been designed around the *Sally Bowles* character. A weak *Sally* defeated the whole concept. Finally, Ritchie decided to dumb everything down. Olivia Clarke, as *Sally Bowles*, remained the center of attention, but the steps and combinations were simplified…*really* simplified.

The women in the ensemble were disappointed. They had worked diligently to create a high caliber presentation. Now they felt totally diminished. Despite Lisa's early reticence about Clarke, it was she who stepped up to rally the troops. "Okay, so we're not doing what we had originally planned…so what! We're all capable and flexible dancers, aren't we? What matters is the best interest of the show. And as of this moment, that means adjusting our performance to accommodate our director's vision."

The other girls took Lisa's words to heart. Although they were still miffed about the changes, they rose to the occasion. Lisa had very quickly and unintentionally become a leader in her university dance troupe. This was not unnoticed by Dr. Blackwell, Lynette Ritchie and even Olivia Clarke.

With only a few days before opening, *Cabaret* was, for the most part, coming together. The remaining obstacle was the chair dance in the *Mein Herr* number. This song had become iconic, primarily due to Liza Minelli's performance of Bob Fosse's choreography in the film version of the musical. The *Sally Bowles* character, as well as the Kit-Kat Club dancers, rhythmically pulsated... on, with, around and on top of chairs... in a very sensual capacity. But underlying the sexuality, the song possesses a subtlety intended to empower *Sally*.

The multi-tasking of the number was challenging. Lynette Ritchie had devoted more time and effort with the dancers on *Mein Herr* than any other song in the show. The work had paid off. The ensemble's performance was spectacular. But, as had come to be expected, the guest artist was struggling.

It wasn't that Olivia Clarke wasn't appealing...she was. She exuded a fantastic presence which snapped every audience eye to her like a magnet. In most situations, such an immediacy is an asset. But in this case, it drew attention to the fact that Clarke was insecure in her performance. She knew all her lines and her singing was exceptional...but when it came to *Sally Bowles*, she just didn't own it.

Clearly, the deficits might have been corrected, but Clarke was totally resistant to any direction. Eventually Dr. Blackwell gave up and opted to focus on her singing, which was fine. Blackwell also had to concentrate on delivering the production as a whole. She had run out of time and patience with Clarke and privately regretted the hire.

Meanwhile, Ritchie was still hopeful that *Mein Herr* might reach its potential. Olivia Clarke knew the steps to the dance. She could execute them perfectly...but there was no life. Although she would never admit it, Clarke seemed to know she was deficient. Her lack of confidence was clear. As they worked on the number the night before final dress, the choreographer stopped the rehearsal.

"Okay, hold up everybody. Olivia your steps are looking good…looking great."

Olivia Clarke half-smiled. "But…"

Ritchie walked closer to her and lowered her voice. "But, I'm just not feeling it. You need to view this chair as a *man*…a *man* you are manipulating with your sensuality."

"I'm sorry, but I just don't see it that way."

"Olivia, you can do this. I know you can. You've just got to put yourself out there."

Clarke knocked over a chair. "How dare you patronize me. Who do you think you are?"

Ritchie picked up the chair. "I'm not patronizing you. I just want your performance to be as good as it can possibly be."

Ritchie moved out into the house and asked Clarke to join her.
"Just come out here and watch. I'll show you what I mean."

Clarke reluctantly followed the choreographer off the stage and into the house.

"Lisa, will you stand-in for *Sally*?" asked Ritchie. She explained to Clarke that Lisa had occasionally filled in as *Sally Bowles* during the earlier weeks of rehearsal.

As they went through *Mein Herr* this time, there was an obvious heightened energy, seduction and meaning displayed. When the run through of the number had completed, the room became very quiet. Olivia Clarke mounted the stage and slowly approached Lisa. "Well, that was really good," she said.

Lisa smiled. "Oh, thank you. Thank you very much."

Then Clarke got into Lisa's face. "Does it make you feel good to show me up?"

Lisa stepped back. "What? No! I was just trying to…"

Ritchie, who was still out in the house, jumped in. "She was *not* trying to show you up, Olivia. She was merely trying to help…and she was doing so at my request."

"Is that so!" Clarke stepped to the edge of the stage "So I guess you're out to get me, too!"

Ritchie quickly stepped up on the stage. "Listen to me. You're wrong about that. We have done everything possible to accommodate you. Frankly, we've restaged every number in order to accentuate your strengths."

"Except *this* one," said Clarke.

"Well, yes, except this one," replied Ritchie. "The style of this song has become an embodiment of the show. The audience is going to expect the chair dance."

Clarke stepped to stage right as she considered what Ritchie had said. "Well, I think you had better rethink it. I want a new concept…and I want it tonight." Clarke started off stage but as she was about to depart, she stopped. After a long beat, she turned to the group and pointed to Lisa. "And I want *her* the fuck off of my stage." She took a step toward Lisa. "You're a nobody, Sweetie…and take it from me…you'll always be a nobody." Then Olivia Clarke exited with angry intensity.

***

Dr. Blackwell was stunned at hearing what had happened at the dance rehearsal. The pressures on a director during tech week of a show are incredibly intense, and Blackwell had been feeling it.
"That little bitch has got some nerve!" said Blackwell to Lynette Ritchie. "We're paying her good money to spread a sense of

professionalism to our undergraduates. What we're getting instead is total immaturity and the exact opposite of professional behavior."

"Well, I can change the choreography," said Ritchie, "though I think it's a mistake. But we need to draw the line on Lisa. That kid has done nothing wrong. It is imperative that she stay in the show."

"I totally agree," said Blackwell. "Clarke is working for *us*. I'm not about to let her dictate the terms."

The next morning in Dr. Blackwell's office, the director met with Olivia Clarke. She explained that, although she thought it to be ill advised, the choreographer was willing to re-stage the *Mein Herr* number.

"Good," said Clarke. She smirked in victory as she rose to leave.

"But…Lisa Lesinski will be remaining as a featured dancer in the show," said Blackwell.

"Excuse me!"

"I'm sorry, Olivia, but Lisa is one of our most promising students. I see no reason whatsoever to exclude her."

Clarke gasped dramatically. "You need a reason? Okay, I'll give you a reason. If *she's* in the show…*I'm* not!"

"Olivia!"

"Goodbye, Mary. Sorry it didn't work out. I'll be in my room if you change your mind." And she was gone.

***

Mary Blackwell was in crisis. It was the day before the scheduled opening of a major production and her female lead had issued an ultimatum. Olivia Clarke's behavior went against everything the director stood for. Blackwell believed strongly that the theatre was a collaborative team-effort and that every member of the team was important. On the other hand, a production of *Cabaret* without a strong *Sally Bowles* was inconceivable.

In Blackwell's mind, there were three options. One…she could succumb to the diva's demand and eliminate Lisa from the cast. Two…she could terminate Olivia Clarke and attempt to cast another *Sally Bowles*. Three…she could cancel or postpone the production. None of these solutions were very appealing, but it was essential that a decision be made right away. Cancelling the show was the least appealing choice. Thousands of dollars had already been spent on licensing, set creation, musicians, etc.—not to mention the contractual obligations guaranteed in hiring Clarke. For an institution struggling to hold on to its arts financing, cancellation would be disastrous. Dismissing Lisa from the cast might have been the simplest and least damaging solution. The "star" would be mollified and the show would go on as scheduled. Easy-peasy. But…Mary Blackwell absolutely hated the prospect of giving-in to Olivia Clarke's demands. She wondered if, indeed, she might be able to find a replacement to play *Sally Bowles* on 24 hours' notice.

Blackwell summoned Lynette Ritchie to her office. She explained the three options she was considering and asked the choreographer's advice. "Wow," said Ritchie, "there's no easy answer, is there?"

"Not really," replied Blackwell, "but my gut reaction would be to show Clarke the door and find another *Sally*."

"Yeah, well, sure…but who are we gonna get…on such short notice."

Blackwell said, "I suppose we could hire another burned-out *professional*, but that's what got us here to begin with…let's face it." Then the director stepped to the cast list that was stapled to her bulletin board. "Do you think there's anyone in our cast that could step in?"

Ritchie also moved to the board. "Hmm, I don't know..." She perused the cast list. "Honestly, the only one who I think might have a shot would be...Lisa."

"Shit, really?" said Blackwell. "Well, that's ironic. Do you think she can sing it?"

"She could sing it. She sure doesn't have Olivia's voice...not by a long shot. But I think she could get by."

Blackwell sat at her desk. "I don't know. That's a lot of pressure to put on a first semester freshman."

Just then there was a knock on the office door. "Come in," said Blackwell.

Lisa Lesinski entered.

"Hello, Lisa," said Blackwell, "we were just talking about you."

"I can just imagine. I just wanted to tell you how sorry I was about all the trouble with Olivia."

Dr. Blackwell stepped to Lisa and hugged her. "Lisa, you have no reason to apologize. You have done everything we have asked of you...and your work has been excellent."

Lisa smiled. "Well, I've been trying my best. I don't know why, but I always seem to make people angry. I don't mean to, but I do."

"That's ridiculous," said Ritchie. "You're too hard on yourself."

Blackwell led Lisa to a chair in front of her desk. "Sit down, we have something we want to talk to you about."

Lisa sat. "I know. You want me to drop out of the show. Actually, that's why I'm here. I thought I would just quit, and save you the trouble of firing me."

"No, that's not what we had in mind," said Ritchie.

"Not at all," said Blackwell. "As a matter of fact, we would like you to consider opening as *Sally Bowles* tomorrow night."

Lisa did a doubletake to Blackwell. "Wait, what?"

Ritchie explained, "We believe you are our best possible replacement for Olivia."

"And it's very short notice," said Blackwell, " so we'll understand if you decline. But we're hoping you'll at least give it a try."

Lisa stood up and walked to the office window. Ritchie moved to her and put her arm around her. "It's all right Lisa. You don't have to do it. But we're not going to let Olivia get away with her nonsense."

"That's right," said Blackwell. "If you don't feel you want to do it, we'll try to come up with another solution."

Lisa was wide eyed as she turned to her director. "It's just that it's *tomorrow night*! I'm not a great singer... and my acting experience is zilch. I don't want to let you down."

Blackwell and Ritchie assured Lisa that she would not in any way be letting them down. If she was willing to try, Blackwell would have her excused from her classes and they would rehearse all day.

Lisa returned slowly to the chair and again sat. "All right. I'll try. But if you think I'm terrible, you have to promise that you'll pull the plug."

"I promise," said Blackwell.

Dr. Blackwell instructed Lisa to meet her in forty-five minutes at the basement rehearsal hall in the Fine Arts building. She also cautioned Lisa to keep everything quiet. She would announce the cast change at the evening rehearsal, but she didn't want the news to get out before then. Lynette Ritchie would also clear her day's schedule in order to work with Lisa. Next Blackwell called Drew Orbach, the show's rather flamboyant piano accompanist, and informed him of the situation. Orbach told Blackwell that he was teaching until noon, but would join the team soon thereafter. He added, "Oh, this is exciting! I absolutely hated that Olivia bitch. I'm at 9's and 10's…"

As the day's rehearsal wore on, Blackwell and Ritchie were hardly at 9's and 10's. Lisa was giving it everything she had but things were not going very well. It was a frustrating struggle and everyone was feeling the pressure. Between musical numbers, Lisa tried to learn the considerable dialogue required of the part. She was retaining a lot of it, but her obvious uncertainty took its toll on her character delivery. At one point in the mid-afternoon, Lisa reminded Blackwell of her promise to "pull the plug" if she was "terrible."

"In no way are you terrible," said Blackwell.

"But I'm not exactly killing it either, am I?"

Ritchie chimed in, "Hey, this is hard. You're doing fine."

Lisa stepped away. "It's a good thing you two don't play poker."

Then Drew Orbach got up from his piano and walked to Lisa. "Listen to me, Honey. You'll be fine. You might not hit every note as precisely as 'Cruella De Vil,' but you are a hell of a lot more likable. Believe me, you will be fine."

Lisa smiled. "Thank you Drew. That means a lot."

Orbach fanned himself with both hands, "Oh stop it Sweetie, you're gonna make me cry."

Everybody in the room had a good laugh, which at the time, was critically needed. As they were about to resume rehearsing the door opened and in walked Olivia Clarke.

As the actress looked around the room, it became obvious to her what was happening. "Excuse me, Mary," said Olivia, "but can I speak with you for a moment?"

"I'm quite busy, Olivia."

Clarke stepped to the director. "Yes, I can see that. I'm sorry, but I promise I'll be brief."

Blackwell headed toward the doorway, "All right, we can talk in the hallway." Clarke followed her but stopped and eyed Lisa before exiting out the door.

As Blackwell and Clarke met, Drew coached Lisa through some of the songs. As they were about to begin work on "Don't Tell Mama," Blackwell re-entered the room. The expression on her face was grave.

Everyone looked to Dr. Blackwell in dire anticipation.

"Well?" said Ritchie.

Blackwell said that Clarke had apologized for her behavior and wanted to be given another chance.

"When hell freezes over!" said Ritchie.

Drew Orbach moved to the choreographer. "That's right. We're better off without her."

"What do you think, Lisa?" asked Blackwell.

Lisa looked to the floor. "Does she still want me out of the show?"

"No, I told her that was not an option. I said the only way we would even consider letting her back in, was if you were also in."

Lisa looked up. "And…?"

"She said that would be fine."

"That's big of the bitch," said Orbach.

"Not only that," Blackwell took Lisa's hand. "I told her she could only return if you agreed."

"Me?"

"Yes, you. *You* are the one who has been violated here. I'm perfectly willing to abide by whatever you decide."

Lisa walked to the piano and sat backwards on the bench. Then she looked up. "I appreciate the confidence you've shown in me…I truly do. But I think it would be best for Olivia to do the part.

"Are you sure?" said Blackwell.

"Yes." Lisa stood and moved to Blackwell. "That's how you planned it, so that's how it should be done."

"All right then," said Blackwell. "She's waiting in the hall to talk to you. One way or the other, she wants to apologize to you."

"Oh."

"You're a class act, kid" said Blackwell and she began applauding. Lisa smiled as Ritchie and Orbach joined in the ovation.

***

Cabaret was both a critical and box office success for Atlantic University. Olivia Clarke's vocal performance was considered the highlight of the production. But the Kit-Kat dancers also scored considerable raves for their creative energy and innovation. Lisa earned the respect and gratitude of her fellow cast members as well as her directors. When her parents came to see the show, they were quite impressed. Afterward they beamed at their daughter with pride. To top it all off, Lisa earned a perfect 4.0 grade point average for the semester. In spite of all the strife, Lisa, like Mark, thought college was “all right.”

13
Revelations
February, 2019

As rehearsals progressed for *A Doll's House* at the Town Square Playhouse, Lisa Stratton's excitement and nervousness accelerated. The casting of David James as *Torvald* had been incredibly beneficial to the production. He was a big man physically…tall. In his mid 40's, James was handsome, sporting distinguished blond, slightly whiting hair and a well-trimmed moustache which he had raised for the role. Despite his looming presence, David was quiet and totally unpretentious. He brought a sense of stability to the production, following its somewhat tumultuous beginning. Lisa thought him to be incredibly kind and generous with her. He put her at ease…such a contrast from the previous *Torvald.* Lisa's confidence in the role of *Nora* grew with each rehearsal.

Personally, things were looking up for Lisa too. Charlie was totally enjoying her first theatre experience as *Emmy*, *Nora's* daughter in *A Doll's House.* She had struck good friendships with Robbie Fenske and Stephen Manickus, the two other kids in the show. But most of all Charlie enjoyed spending such special time with her mom. "I wish the show would never end," Charlie told her mother.

"Why?" asked Lisa.

"Because I feel like we're making something really cool…you and me. We're together…and it's fun."

Lisa put her arm around Charlie. "We'll always be together."

“I know, but it’s the whole thing,” said Charlie. “I wish I could just go to the theatre instead of school.”

“Oh, c’mon, you like school.”

“If you say so, Mom.”

Though Charlie’s school comment troubled Lisa, she was delighted that her daughter was so enjoying her theatre experience.

Lisa’s friendship with Nick Curtis had also been blossoming. Their coffee rendezvous had been repeated several times, each with pleasant outcomes. Lisa enjoyed his company very much. There was no pressure…which was exactly what Lisa needed. One night, Lisa, Nick and Charlie got together for dinner at the Tasty Diner before rehearsal. They all enjoyed themselves. Charlie liked Nick and considered him a fellow theatre-person. But, unknown to Lisa, Charlie began to suspect that Nick and her mother might be becoming more than just friends.

***

Meanwhile in a quiet room at New York-Presbyterian Hospital in Brooklyn, Leslie Newman Morrison, lay near death. Michael Morrison’s ex-wife was the victim of severe complications to pneumonia. At her side was her twenty-four year old son, Edward. Leslie had been drifting in and out of consciousness. Her breathing was painful. The doctors had cautioned that the end was near. Leslie opened her eyes and reached for her son. “Eddie, I need to tell you something.”

“Rest, Mom. Save your strength.”

She squeezed his hand. “You have been the joy of my life. You know that, right?”

“Sure Mom, I know.”

Leslie closed her eyes for a moment, then reopened them with difficulty. "Your father is alive."

Edward knelt beside his mother's hospital bed. "No, Mom, no...He was killed in a car accident…a long time ago."

"Eddie…he left us. He left us when you were just a baby. I'm sorry I didn't tell you."

"Mom!"

"I was so hurt, I didn't want you to know about him," said Leslie. "I always thought I would tell you…someday. But I didn't think it would be like this."

"Where is he?" asked Edward.

Leslie weakly shook her head. "I love you Eddie." Leslie closed her eyes.

"I love you Mom."

As his mother took her final breaths, Edward wept in grief. But, at the same time, an angry hollowness began to permeate him.

***

Lisa felt a sense of trepidation as she vacuumed her living room rug. She had broken with her usual drowsy Sunday morning routine by rising at the crack of dawn and insanely cleaning every nook and cranny of her place. Charlie was spending the weekend with her father and Lisa was having Nick Curtis to her apartment for the first time.

In her mind, Nick was still no more than a friend, but in her heart something more seemed to be happening. He was sweet and kind to her and Lisa appreciated having a shoulder to lean on. After weeks of Nick's *Soprano* talk, they were finally beginning what he hoped would be a binge of the New Jersey based mob TV series.

Lisa had never seen the show and in reality, had no desire. She had been totally bored by *The Godfather* and *Good Fellas*. The genre simply didn't appeal to her.

But because it was Nick's favorite, she determined to give it a try. Her doorbell rang at 2 o'clock, right on time. When she opened the door, she was surprised at what she saw. Nick was dressed in casual slacks and a button down shirt. This was quite a noticeable contrast from his usual jeans and tee. It was also obvious that Nick was the recent recipient of a haircut. His long, tangled strands had been replaced by a styled Ivy League coiffure…short on the sides but longer on the top. And Nick's stubble was clean shaven. Lisa thought he looked great…but really different.

"Excuse me, do I know you sir?" joked Lisa.

Nick, who had a bouquet of purple lilacs in his right hand, smiled broadly. "Well, what do you think?"

"I like…I like very much," said Lisa, as she ushered him in.

Nick presented his bouquet. "These are for you."

"Why, thank you kind sir. They're beautiful. Let me get them in water."

As Lisa fetched a vase, Nick told her that he had given her this same type of bouquet once before.

Lisa frowned. "Really? I think you're thinking of someone else."

"No it was definitely you," said Nick, "don't you remember?"

Lisa shook her head in total puzzlement. "I really think you are mistaken."

Nick explained that many years ago, he had placed a bouquet of lilacs in front of Lisa's high school locker on opening night of *Joseph And The Amazing Technicolor Dreamcoat*.

"Wait! That was *you*?" said Lisa. I remember those flowers very well. I could never figure out who they were from. Why didn't you leave a card?"

"Hey, I wasn't even sure you knew who I was," said Nick. "I had quite a case on you then, but you were already with Mark…so I kept my distance."

Lisa gave Nick a hug. "Well, thank you…belatedly and currently. I love lilacs."

The two sat down to a *Soprano* style luncheon of lasagna, garnished with a little red wine. Lisa was happy with her culinary result. Although she had never previously attempted the dish, she had been confident in the recipe and coaching supplied by her friend, Cailla McCormack.

After lunch the two settled into Lisa's living room loveseat, along with the remains from the bottle of wine. Nick navigated Lisa's TV streaming box to *The Sopranos*, season 1, episode 1- *Pilot*. As the program progressed, Nick chatted about the various characters in the show as they were introduced.

"Gee, this is just like watching a DVD commentary reel" feigned Lisa.

"Okay, I'll pipe down," said Nick, "I just wanted to get you up to speed. These characters can be confusing."

Lisa laughed. "I'm just pulling your leg." She was surprised in that she really enjoyed the show. She found the complication of the characters appealing. When the episode concluded Lisa and Nick sipped the last of the wine and discussed Tony Soprano's panic attacks.

"I'll give you a little spoiler alert," said Nick, "they may have something to do with his overbearing mother."

"I can sure relate to that," said Lisa. "I love my mom, but sometimes…" She rolled her eyes. "I wish I could talk to her about things…but I can't. We just don't have that kind of relationship."

"That's too bad," said Nick.

Lisa smiled. "That's why I like hanging out with you. You don't judge me. I feel comfortable talking to you."

"Ditto," Nick replied.

Nick's mind sputtered. "If there was ever a lead-in," he thought, "this was it."

He leaned in to kiss Lisa for the first time. And to his relief and joy, she didn't resist.

"… that was nice," he said.

Lisa smiled. "Yes, it was."

He leaned in again. But just as they were about to repeat, the apartment door flew open. In stormed Mark, followed closely by Charlie.

"Whoa," Mark surveyed the impending kiss. "Well isn't this special."

Lisa stood up. "You know, you really need to knock before you come barging into my house."

Charlie moved to hug Lisa. "Hi Mommy."

"Hello, Buddy." Lisa looked at Mark. "Is there something wrong?"

"You're damned right something's wrong," said Mark, "but I'm not gonna talk about it in front of this guy." He stepped to Nick. "I think it's time for you to go home, pal!"

"I'll go if that's what Lisa wants," said Nick.

Lisa touched Nick's arm. "Maybe you'd better. I'll talk to you later."

"Okay." Nick moved to the door. "Bye Charlie."

"See ya', Nick," said Charlie. And Nick was out.

Mark sat on the loveseat and picked up the empty wine bottle and gave it a whiff.

"Umm, looks like it was a good party."

Lisa moved to the opposite side of the living room. "All right …so what's so important?"

Mark produced a piece of paper from his shirt pocket.

"I found this in the kid's back-pack. It's a note from her teacher. Apparently things aren't going so well in school."

"What?" Lisa stepped to Mark and took the note.

"Read it and weep," said Mark. "The kid's become inattentive and distracted. The teacher wants us both to come in for a conference as soon as possible. And look at the date on the note."

"…beginning of last week?" Lisa stepped to Charlie. "Buddy, why didn't you give this to me?"

"I'll tell you why!" Mark jumped in. "She was afraid if she showed it to you, you'd pull her out of that damned play."

"Is that true?" Lisa asked her daughter. Charlie nodded her head. "Sweetie, you have to let me know what's happening. I can't help you, if I don't know."

Lisa turned to Mark. "I'll call the school tomorrow and set up the appointment.

"Well, if you ask me, this play is the problem," said Mark. "She's getting home late every night…not getting enough sleep…probably not doing her homework."

"She does her homework every night. I check it."

"Well, I think you should pull her out of that play anyway," said Mark.

"No!" said Charlie.

Lisa stepped to Mark. "The play is almost over, just a couple more weeks. It really means a lot to her."

Mark shook his head. "Let's see what the teacher says. Let me know when the appointment is." He stepped to Charlie and kissed her. "Goodnight Squirt." Mark moved to the door and looked back at Lisa. "Let me know."

When Mark was gone, Lisa pulled Charlie on the loveseat with her. She told her daughter she would try her best to see that she could stay in the play, but from now on, she had to promise to tell her of any problems she was having in school. Charlie agreed.

Lisa went to her freezer and scooped a dish of chocolate mint chip ice cream for each of them. The evening concluded sweetly…but the afternoon's romantic moment was a distant memory.

***

Edward Morrison sat wistfully in the Brooklyn apartment that he had shared with his mother. The funeral earlier that day had left him limp. Only a handful of people had attended. His mother had no family to speak of. Her few friends were scattered among the many jobs she had held over the years.

Leslie Newman Morrison had flourished at WJLK radio for a decade. She advanced from commercial production assistant to sales manager. Her income was healthy and she was able to provide a private school education for her son. But in the late aughts, the technology boom took its toll on the music industry and ultimately terrestrial radio stations as well. Eventually, WJLK was sold to an overseas entity. With the transition came a totally automated format and a massive reduction in staff.

Leslie's termination wasn't unexpected, but still devastating. She had difficulty finding work and lived on unemployment benefits for over a year. She was forced to give up her Manhattan apartment and move to a smaller place in Brooklyn. Also, she had to pull Edward out of private school and enroll him in a public middle school.

Edward was a quiet, shy student who fell between the cracks in the overcrowded classrooms of P.S. 176. Although he got by academically, his achievement fell short of his potential. Socially, he was invisible. Though he had inherited his father's good looks, he lacked Michael's survival instincts. As he advanced through his high school years, Edward became more passive and unassertive...a loner.

Leslie's experience in voicing radio commercials secured some occasional work…but those opportunities were few and far between. For the rest of her life, she took whatever employment she could find…secretary, waitress, janitor… in order to provide for her and her son. She often went without, so that Edward could continue his education. In doing so, Leslie neglected her personal health and well-being. Though her proudest moment was the day of Edward's graduation from City College, it was shortly thereafter that her personal neglect precipitated the illness from which she would not recover.

As Edward sadly pondered his mother's premature demise, he could not stop thinking about her deathbed reveal. "Your father is alive." As sad as he was at losing his mother, he couldn't rid himself of an intense resentment.

"How could she have kept this from me," he thought.

As he went through Leslie's things, he came upon a photo book containing pre-marriage pictures of his mother and father acting in a 1990 community theatre production of *Barefoot In The Park*, in Huntington, Pennsylvania. As he perused the photos, he was struck by his physical resemblance to his father. The more he studied the old photos, the more frustrated he became.

To Edward, his parents looked so happy in those pictures. He wondered what had happened. "Why had his father left? And why had he never heard from him?" And another thought crossed his mind, "Why had his mother been left to scrimp and save on her own…to the point of literally killing herself!"

This last notion would plague Edward's peace of mind for the foreseeable future.

***

Lisa waited for Mark in front of the Oxford Street Elementary School. As she paced the sidewalk waiting for her ex-husband, her cell phone went off. She could see by the ID that it was her friend Cailla McCormack. Lisa took the call. "Hey…what's up?"

"I was just wondering if you met with the teacher yet?" said Cailla.

"I'm about to go in now. I'm waiting for Mark…he's running late."

"Well, I just wanted to let you know I was thinking about you," Cailla said. "I'm sure everything will be fine."

Lisa looked at her watch. "I hope so. I wish Mark would get here. It's almost time for the conference. I just can't understand why Charlie clammed up on me. It's not like her."

"Well, she's been through a lot lately, you know?" said Cailla.

"I know, but everything seemed to be going so well…all right…it's time. I'm going in without him. I'll let you know how it goes."

"Okay, good luck." Cailla hung up.

As Lisa started up the front walkway of the school, Mark arrived on his motorcycle. Lisa turned toward the street and waited for him to join her.

"Cutting it a little close, aren't you?" said Lisa.

"Hey, I'm here. Let's get this over with."

Lisa and Mark waited in a conference room for Charlie's teacher. When Mrs. Adamcyk entered the room, Lisa stood up to shake her hand.

"Please sit," said the teacher, "I'm glad you could both make it."

Stella Adamcyk had been an elementary school teacher for nearly twenty years. In her mid-forties, she was stylish in her appearance. Her short blond hair was well maintained and her dress was coordinated and professional. She moved and spoke with an animated energy honed over years of engaging and guiding young children. When she spoke, her care and sincerity became obvious.

"I'm sorry that it took us so long to get back to you," said Lisa. "As I told you on the phone, Charlie hid your note from us for almost a week."

"Yes," said Mrs. Adamcyk, "why do you think she did that?"

"She was afraid we would pull her out of this play she's in," said Mark.

"Oh, I've heard all about the play," said Mrs. Adamcyk. "Charlie really seems to be enjoying it."

"Yeah, but if it's causing her problems in school, she *should* give it up," said Mark.

"But, what *is* her problem?" asked Lisa. "Have her grades dropped?"

Mrs. Adamcyk opened her grade book. "No...not at all. As a matter of fact, her academic performance has actually improved since she started *A Doll's House*."

Mark gritted his teeth. "What!"

"Well, that's good to hear," said Lisa, "but again I ask, what is the problem?"

The teacher closed the gradebook and set it aside. She explained that she was concerned about their daughter's state of mind. She recalled that in the beginning of the year, Charlie was shy and reserved. "I chalked that up to her being in a new school," said Mrs. Adamcyk, "but it didn't take long for her to become acclimated and outgoing."

The teacher went on to explain that in recent weeks, Charlie had reverted to her previous introverted demeanor. "I wanted to make you aware of the change," said Mrs. Adamcyk. "And I wondered if you would want her to speak to the school counselor."

"That's a *no*!" said Mark. "I think she's just tired from being out late every night with this stupid play."

"It's not just that she's tired, Mr. Stratton. She's withdrawn. That wonderful smile of Charlie's has disappeared."

Lisa addressed her ex-husband. "Well, maybe she *should* talk to the counselor. If there's a problem we want to know about it, right?"

Mark stood and started for the door. “There is nothing wrong with my kid that getting her out of that play won’t fix. We’re out of here!”

Lisa stood. “Thank you Mrs. Adamcyk. Thank you very much. We’ll discuss it and I’ll call you.”

Lisa and Mark exited the conference room in silence. When they got outside the school, Lisa didn’t hide her annoyance. “You were very rude in there.”

The couple walked to the street. “Hey, that was a total waste of my time. The kid’s just not getting enough sleep. I already knew that.”

“But, there may be more to it,” said Lisa. “Charlie’s been through a lot of changes lately.”

“Yeah, well who’s fault’s that?” Mark mounted his motorcycle.

“I think we should talk about this. Let’s go to the diner,” said Lisa.

“I don’t have time,” said Mark, “but I’ll tell you what I think. First, pull her out of that play…*now*... and second, stop confusing the poor kid with your new *boyfriend*.”

“What?! How dare you!”

Mark started the motorcycle and shouted above the engine, “The poor kid is scared. She doesn’t understand why she’s lost her family. Wise up…dump him!”

Mark peeled out onto the street and was off.

***

Edward Morrison became consumed with the knowledge that his father was probably still alive. He was obsessed with finding and confronting him. He continued to scan his late mother’s papers in hopes of discovering clues, but this proved an exercise in futility.

Clearly, Leslie Newman Morrison had expunged most references to her ex-husband from her documented life.

Edward found it exasperating to execute internet searches as well. “Michael Morrison” was an all too common name, generating thousands of search results. However, he continued to dedicate a portion of each day to the Google start page. Every so often he would find a link to someone he thought could be his father. These most often had to do with theatre or acting. Usually, they would turn out to be referring to old productions. Edward’s attempts to follow-up to these links had proven negligible.

Then one day, Edward found an online press release indicating that a “Michael Morrison” was to play the lead in an upcoming production of Henrik Ibsen’s *A Doll’s House*, at the Town Square Playhouse in Lakeside, New Jersey. “Hmm could this be the guy?” he thought. “I’ve never been to New Jersey.”

***

When Charlie Stratton got home from school, her mother sat her down at the dining room table. Lisa shared with her daughter the crux of the conference held that day with Mrs. Adamcyk. “Your teacher thinks something is bothering you.”

“I’m fine,” replied Charlie.

“Really? I hope you know you can tell me anything.” Lisa reached across the table and took Charlie’s hand. “I’m here for you…and I’m on your side, no matter what.”

“Do I have to quit the play?” asked Lisa.

“I think your dad thinks the play is the reason you’re having trouble in school.”

“I’m *not* having any trouble in school. I get good marks on all my papers.”

"But your teacher says you're so quiet," said Lisa, "…not outgoing anymore."

"It's just that school is kinda boring," said Charlie, "… I mean, I like my teacher, but we have a big class and she doesn't have much time for me."

"Okay, well that's good to know. I'll talk to Mrs. Adamcyk about that." Lisa smiled, but Charlie wouldn't make eye contact with her. "Anything else bothering you?"

Charlie's eyes began to water. She got up from the table and ran into her room. She jumped on her bed and buried her face in her pillow. Lisa followed closely behind.

"Charlie…what is it?" said Lisa as she sat on the bed. "Buddy, you can tell me."

Charlie sat up next to her mom and spoke through her tears. "I'm so worried about Dad." She embraced her mother as her eyes gushed.

"Don't worry Buddy, Daddy is fine."

"Now, sure…but what about when you marry Nick? What then? He'll never be able to come back to us. I won't see him anymore. He won't have anybody to take care of him. He'll be all alone!" Charlie became overwrought with emotion.

Lisa squeezed her daughter. "Buddy…Buddy…what are you talking about? Daddy will always be here for you...always! And where did you get the idea that I was going to marry Nick?"

"You act like you like him," said Charlie.

"I do like him…but only as a friend. You like him too, right?"

"Yes…but does Nick know you only like him as a friend?"

"I'm sure he does," said Lisa. Now *she* had to fight back the tears. "The main thing for you to know is that Daddy and I love you very much... and we will forever."

Charlie smiled at her mom.

"Hey," said Lisa, "it's such a nice day. Why don't we take a walk in the park."

"Okay," Charlie grabbed Lisa's hand and they were out the door.

***

That evening Lisa worked the night shift at the Little Sprout Daycare Center. After work, she and Cailla McCormick stopped at the Cabin Tavern for a quick drink. Lisa told her friend about the day's developments. Cailla expressed her concern for both Lisa and Charlie.

"What a mess," said Cailla. "What are you gonna do?"

"I don't know. I'm really at a loss."

"Well, do you like this guy?" asked Cailla.

"Yes."

Cailla took a swig of her beer. "Then you have to explain to Charlie, that you need to move on in your life. And right now, Nick is gonna be a part of it."

"I can't do that to her," said Lisa. "She's confused and very upset. And, she's too young to understand."

"So?" said Cailla.

Lisa reflected as she placed her coaster on top of her glass. "I'm going to break it off with Nick. I have to. Charlie's well- being has to come first. And it will."

14
Rise and Fall
Late '08 and early '09

Both Lisa and Mark looked forward to being home for Christmas. In spite of their initial plans to see each other during their first college semester, busy schedules had prevented any visits from occurring. Mark had become a valued wide-receiver for the Wington University Hilltoppers, which required a tough regimen of games and practice. Lisa also found the rigors of college life, particularly during *Cabaret*, prohibitive to any potential meetups with her boyfriend. So it was with great joy that the couple reunited for the holidays. They spent every day together and their mutual affection had never been greater. The fact that they had enjoyed success in their initial college experiences only added to their happiness.

On New Year's Eve, they spent a quiet evening at Lisa's house. Her parents had gone to a party and her younger brother, Todd, was spending the night with a friend. So Lisa and Mark were alone. They were happy and peaceful…a sharp contrast to the previous New Year's Eve that had precipitated such an ugly scene between the two. Neither spoke of that fateful night, which seemed so long ago, but each possessed a painful memory.

As the witching hour approached, the couple opened a bottle of champagne to usher in 2009. At the stroke of midnight, they stood and toasted each other. They set down their glasses and Mark got down on one knee. Lisa's eyes widened as she covered her mouth with both hands.

Mark produced a small box from his pocket. He opened it to reveal a lovely diamond ring. "Lisa Lesinski…I love you. I love you now…I'll love you tomorrow...I'll always love you. Will you marry me?"

Lisa wept as she took Mark's hand and pulled him to his feet. "I love you too. Yes, Mark Stratton, I'll proudly marry you."

Mark placed the ring on Lisa's finger. They smiled and laughed in jubilation. Then they sealed their engagement with a kiss.

The Lesinski family was thrilled with the news. Lisa's mother, Ainsley, started planning the wedding immediately. "Hold on, Mom," said Lisa, "it's quite a ways away. We have four years of college to finish first."

"Well, it's never too early to begin making arrangements," replied Ainsley. "The best venues have long waiting lists."

Lisa laughed. "Okay, Mom, knock yourself out."

"Does that mean I get your room?" asked Lisa's brother.

Lisa gave Todd a noogie on his head, "I guess so, but…again…it's at least four years from now, Bro."

The remainder of Christmas vacation flew by. Lisa and Mark visited many family members and friends to share their good news. At each stop they were greeted with hearty congratulations and best wishes.

All too quickly, the day arrived for Lisa and Mark to travel back to their respective schools. They met for a bittersweet farewell breakfast at Hiller's Diner in Glennville. Afterward they slowly walked to Lisa's car in the parking lot. "I don't want to go back," said Mark.

"I know, it's been such a wonderful Christmas." Lisa put her arms around his neck.

“At least in the fall, I had football. I’ve got nothing to distract me from missing you now.”

“Well, you have your classes, don’t you? You can devote your full concentration there.”

Mark frowned. “Please…I’m gonna be bored to death.”

“But you did so well last semester.”

“Yeah…” Mark didn’t want to go there.

Lisa looked at her watch. “Well, we’d better get going. We both have some driving to do…I love you, Mister.”

“I love you too!” Mark kissed Lisa. “Drive safe.”

“You too.” Lisa got in her car, Mark in his.

Both felt sadness as they drove off.

***

It was 7 o’clock in the morning when Elsa Gest unlocked the door of her office on the Wington University campus. Other than the custodian, she was alone in the school’s administration building. She walked to her desk and pulled a shiny, new executive name plate out of her bag. She gave it a quick polish with a handkerchief and placed it prominently, front and center… “Dr. Elsa Gest, Dean of Students”

She was excited about forging forward in her new position. After years of serving as a public high school principal, Gest was anxious to expand her administrative skills in higher education. At age 49, she had achieved significant success, through her diligence and attention to detail. Somewhat short in stature, about 5’2”, Gest was a powerhouse of discipline. Staff and students alike, feared her wrath. She dressed expensively and professionally. Her straight black coif, revealed random streaks of gray and was helmet-like…reminiscent of fighter pilot headgear. Gest wore thick glasses, which were essential to her ability to function. But these too were quite stylish…forest green…complimenting the "wild blue yonder" image. During her job interview, Dr. Gest suggested several areas of observed deficiency at Wington. In view of her successful candidacy, she assumed she was expected to address the cited problems as soon as possible. The Wington University community, returning for the second semester, had no inkling of the changes about to occur.

***

Mark Stratton arrived at his dorm slightly after 3 o'clock in the afternoon. The drive from Glennville, had taken a little more than five hours…a fairly typical running time. He considered himself fortunate that he hadn't hit much traffic, and there had been very little construction delay on the Pennsylvania Turnpike. When he got to his room, he discovered that his roommate, Randy Marchello, had already arrived. The two Jersey boys sat and shot the breeze about their respective holidays. Randy had worked most of the semester-break at his father's warehouse. He had been grateful for the opportunity to earn some spending money. Mark told Randy of his engagement.

Randy slapped Mark on the back. "Well, you sly S.O.B. congratulations!"

"Thank you," said Mark. "She's a great girl. I'm really lucky."

Randy suggested they go out for a beer to celebrate. Mark agreed and they were off to the Bucket Bar.

***

Lisa arrived on the Atlantic University campus in the early afternoon. Her drive back to school was considerably shorter than Mark's. Her dorm was quiet as she carried her belongings up to her second floor room. Her roommate, Lauren Benke, had not yet arrived, nor had any of her other friends. The peaceful surroundings gave Lisa some time to reflect on the substantial happenings of her life over the past few weeks.

For the first time in a long time, Lisa felt content. She was happy. Her engagement to Mark enhanced the prophesy of a storybook future. Her ensuing college career was also rosy. She had gained universal admiration among her peers and professors by her intrepid actions during *Cabaret*. In addition, she had emerged as a leader in her department. Her previous difficulties with Stacy Stevens and Olivia Clarke, seemed like distant memories. Still a freshman, Lisa had settled-in as a highly respected member of the Atlantic University community.

***

At Wington, the athletic department was abuzz. Word was out that the new dean of students was about to lower the boom on team eligibility requirements. This made all the coaches nervous. Although the school had always held the athletes to minimum academic standards, it was assumed that rules would be bent in order to keep good players playing.

"I've seen 'em come, and I've seen 'em…go," said Wington Athletic Director Charlie Sturgis. Sturgis was a big man…6'4", and 380 pounds. He always wore the same garb: black sweat pants, brown Wington sweatshirt, 20 year old black sneakers, and a vintage baseball cap. In addition, he was rarely seen without a black cigar sticking out of his mouth. But Sturgis claim to fame was his punctuated speech pattern. Whenever he spoke, the AD would sporadically shift his weight to his right leg… tip his left toes…and export a stream of free-flowing flatulence. As he exercised the well-oiled routine, Sturgis would momentarily pause his words so as to seemingly totally enjoy the moment. "I'm tellin' ya'," said Sturgis, "this lady is trying to make a quick… name for herself. It ain't gonna work. I'm tellin' ya', once the Alumni Association gets…wind of what's going on, things will go right back to…normal. Nothin' to worry…about." The athletic director smiled with gastric satisfaction.

Although Sturgis comments were a source of somewhat comic relief, head football coach, Roscoe Bodean, was still concerned. He called a team meeting to address the issue. He informed his players of the new dean and her eligibility policy. He impressed upon the squad members to take their studies seriously. “Spring practice is right around the corner,” said Bodean, “and I don’t want any of you knuckleheads sitting on the bench…or worse. Hit the books now, while you’ve got some extra time.”

For Mark, the situation was particularly daunting. Not only was his academic performance linked to team eligibility, it was crucially connected to his scholarship. He was well aware that his excellent first semester grades were bogus. He had been assured that the coaches would protect him academically. And so far this seemed to be the case. But now there was a new sheriff in town…with a different point of view. Even his coach seemed troubled.

It wasn’t that Mark didn’t want to succeed in his classes…he did. He was simply never held to any kind of academic standard. Even in high school, the teachers would often give him a pass, in light of his “football hero” status. He really never had any reason to apply himself. In light of Mark’s scholarship requirement, Lisa had tried to encourage him to succeed. “You are a very bright guy,” she would say. “There’s not a reason in the world why you can’t do well, if you try.” So when Mark brought home his 3.0 grade point from the first semester, Lisa was so proud of him. Of course, he didn’t reveal his true performance of .075.

Mark took his coach’s warning to heart, and set out to do better. He began to take his tutoring sessions seriously and was trying his best to keep up with his reading assignments. To his surprise, he was totally absorbed in his art appreciation class. The teacher, Dr. Pace, was quite personable, and had an uncanny ability of bringing the works of Rembrandt, Matisse, and Gauguin to present day relevance. Mark was even asking questions and contributing to the class. Though early in the semester, it seemed that he might be turning things around.

On the first of February, 2009, Coach Roscoe Bodean submitted his roster for spring football practice to the Wington University administration offices. That afternoon, there was a knock on the coach's office door.

"Come on in," said Bodean.

Through the door ambled Athletic Director, Charlie Sturgis. "Got a minute, Coach?"

"Sure thing, Charlie," said Bodean, "what's up?"

The AD started delivering his shift and tip routine. "Well, I just got off the phone with Dean…Gest."

"Uh-oh, trouble?" asked the coach.

"I'll be damned if I…know," said Sturgis. "She says there's some kind of a problem with your roster list. She wants to see you in her office right…away. Ahh!"

"She didn't say what the problem was?" asked Bodean.

"Hell, no…not a clue. Probably that time of the…month." Sturgis howled with laughter. But Roscoe Bodean didn't join in. He was anxious.

***

Mark was finishing up his presentation on the work of George Seurat for his art appreciation class. He had worked hard on the project and had somewhat surprised himself by how much he had learned. If anyone had previously asked him about the concept of Pointillism, he would have no doubt looked at him as if from Mars. Now he considered himself a mini-expert on the technique made famous by Seurat.

As Mark returned to his seat, Dr. Pace, complimented him on his presentation. "That was real good, Mr. Stratton. You gave the class a fine overview of Seurat and provided great examples of his paintings in your slides. Excellent!"

Mark felt absolutely fantastic. He had never received such a complement off the football field. He thought that perhaps Lisa had been right. All he really needed to do was apply himself. He couldn't wait to get back to the dorm and call his fiancé. They had a happy conversation in which Lisa expressed her exuberance about his accomplishment.

***

Later that afternoon Coach Roscoe Bodean was ushered into the office of the new dean of students, Dr. Elsa Gest.

"Would you care for anything?" asked Gest, "coffee, tea, water?"

"No thanks, I'm fine," replied Bodean.

Dr. Gest then explained her concern about his submitted spring football roster. She noted that the coach had apparently utilized what she called his "athletic prerogative" to change the first semester grades of several players on the list. "So…what have you to say for yourself?" asked the dean.

"What's to say?" said Bodean. "It's a practice we've been using here for many years. This university makes a lot of money off its athletic teams. That money is contingent on those teams winning. If our best players become ineligible the teams don't win and the school loses thousands of dollars. It's that simple. So… if a kid is in academic trouble, we help him out a little. It's no big deal."

Gest glared at the coach. "So you admit to changing the grades of Leonard Pearce, Harold Fenimore and Mark Stratton."

"Yes, I did," said Bodean, "*as has been a tradition of this school forever*. These guys need to play in order for us to win."

"Well, I'm here to tell you that *forever* just ended."

Gest explained her view that any tampering with grades was unacceptable and would no longer be tolerated. She believed such practice diminished the academic integrity of the university. "Not only that, I am hereby directing you to rescind the changes you facilitated in the first semester grades of the three students in question."

Bodean stood up. "Wait…wait one minute. That's not fair! If I do that, our team is likely to lose every game. And what about the students? It would be changing the rules in the middle of the game. Those kids could lose their scholarships!"

"If that's the case," said Dr. Gest, " then so be it. We have to start somewhere. It's a new day, Mr. Bodean."

The coach retook his seat. "What if I refuse?"

"Well I would hope it wouldn't come to that," said Gest. "But if it does, I will have no choice but to relieve you of your position at Wington."

"*What?*"

"I've spoken to the Board of Directors and Alumni Association and they've cleared me to take that course of action if required. I urge you to consider carefully your decision. Good afternoon, Mr. Bodean."

***

The next day, Mark found himself seated in the athletic director's office along with Leonard Pearce and Harold Fenimore. Also present was Coach Bodean. The AD, Charlie Steiner, explained that due to a change in the academic policies of the college, the three students present had become ineligible for football activities.

"The harsh reality is, your first semester grades are being changed back to what you actually earned," said Steiner, "and those grades were piss-poor...as you...know."

Coach Bodean spoke. "I'm sorry fellas. I know this stinks, but apparently there's not a thing we can do about it. The university has officially withdrawn your scholarships. "

The three students gravely looked at their coach and then to each other. Steiner handed each player his amended first semester transcript. "All right. That's it guys ... if you can make-up some credits in community college or someplace else, we may be able to take you back next year...but there are no guarantees..." Steiner stood-up and released a loud, sustained surge of intestinal gas.

The coach and AD shook hands with each of the mortified players. Stunned, they quietly exited the office.

***

Lisa was celebrating her 19th birthday by having dinner with several of her friends at the Graph House, a seafood restaurant located five miles west of the Atlantic University campus. It had been an enjoyable evening of chowder, flounder and several bottles of white. Earlier in the day, Lisa had received birthday greetings from her parents and several of her hometown friends. She was a little surprised that she hadn't heard from Mark, but given his new found academic enthusiasm, she wasn't particularly concerned. "He must be busy with his classes," Lisa thought.

Suddenly her cell phone rang. She was excited to see by the ID that it was Mark calling. Lisa excused herself from the table at the restaurant and stepped into an adjacent hallway to take the call.

"Hey! I was wondering if you were gonna call," Lisa answered the phone joyfully. There was no response. "Hello...Hello!" She could hear distorted music and lots of remote voices, but not Mark.

Finally Mark yelled, "LISA...LISA IS THAT YOU?"

"Yes…it's me. Where are you?" said Lisa.

"I'm sorry, Lisa…I'm so s..s..s-sorry"

It was clear to Lisa that Mark had been drinking. "How much beer have you had?" she asked. The joy in her voice was gone.

"I LOVE YOU…LISA"

"I love you too, …but I'm worried about you. You can't drive like that."

"LISA…I'm coming home."

"What?"

"They took away my scholarship. I … flunked out. I'm sorry!"

"Oh, no," said Lisa. "That makes no sense."

"I'm so, so, so sorry!"

Lisa put Mark on hold and called his roommate, Randy Marchello. Randy told Lisa what had happened with the scholarship. "Oh, shit!" said Lisa. "Do you know where he is now?"

"No…I haven't seen him since about 4 o'clock," said Randy.

"Well, I have him on hold and he's very drunk. You have to find him before he tries to drive."

"He's probably at the Bucket. I'll go out there and get him right away, Lisa."

"Thanks, Randy."

Lisa hit the hold button. "Mark are you still there?"

"I'M SO SORRY!" said Mark.

"It's okay, we'll figure it out. It's gonna be all right. Listen, Randy is on his way to get you. Promise me you won't try to drive."

"Okay, I promise," said Mark. "I LOVE YOU, LISA!"

"I … love you too. I'll call you later."

Lisa hung up the phone. She had totally forgotten it was her birthday.

***

The next weekend, Lisa made an unscheduled visit home. She knew Mark had become despondent and wanted to be with him. Saturday morning they met at Hillers Diner, as they had just two weeks earlier in happier times. They talked for a long while. Mark told his fiancé how he had really begun to enjoy being a college student and was realizing some success. Now he felt totally discouraged and bewildered as to what he should do.

"Look, it's not the end of the world," said Lisa, "they said they'd take you back if you made-up the classes, right?"

"Yeah…well, they said they *might* take me back. No guarantees."

"Hey, that's *something*. So we need to get you registered at the community college," Lisa said.

"No good," said Mark, "they're too deep into the semester for new students. I'd have to wait until summer session."

"All right…so get registered for the summer. That would still give you time to make-up classes before fall."

Mark frowned. "I don't know. It seems like a long shot. Besides, I want to spend the summer with you."

“Umm…about that,” said Lisa. “There’s something I want to talk to you about.”

“Oh, God…are you breaking our engagement?”

“Of course not!”

“Good,” said Mark, “because I don’t think I could take that right now. So what’s up?”

Lisa explained that the University was sending a select dance ensemble on a ten city performance tour of Europe during July and August. Lisa had been chosen to participate through a highly competitive selection process. She would receive a generous travel allowance as well as ten academic credits.

Mark’s face turned sullen. “So, are you gonna do it?”

“I’d like to do it. I’d really like to. It’s an incredible opportunity…don’t you think?

Mark shoved his coffee cup to the side. “So not only am I flat on my face…I’m being trampled by my ‘so-called’ fiancé.”

“Hey, come on,” said Lisa, “that’s not fair. I’m here for you, aren’t I?”

“Shit…I’m gonna need you here for me for more than a weekend.”

“I know that, and I *will* be. But I don’t know how I can pass this up. I have to think about my own future too, right?”

Mark threw some cash down on the table and got up from the booth. “Whatever…let’s go.” He fleeted out of the diner, leaving Lisa behind.

“Hey…wait.” she hurried to catch up.

Neither Lisa nor Mark spoke during the ride home. Mark stopped his car in front of Lisa's house and waited for her to get out.

"So that's it?" said Lisa. "We're not gonna talk about this?"

"Nothing to talk about. You've made up your mind."

"Be reasonable," said Lisa, "you need to make up your credits this summer. If I'm on the tour, you won't have any distractions."

"Right…you're right," said Mark. He leaned across the front seat and kissed her on the cheek. "See ya."

Lisa opened the passenger door. "Am I going to see you tonight?"

"I don't know, I doubt it. I might be busy."

"What!"

"No, I might have a line on a job." Mark smiled. "Hey, I've got to pay my rent you know? I'll see you tomorrow before you head back to school."

"Okay…bye." Lisa stepped out of the car but then leaned back in. "I love you."

"Me too," said Mark.

Lisa closed the door and Mark sped away.

***

After dropping Lisa off, Mark drove aimlessly through the rural outskirts of town. He was dejected. He couldn't believe how fate had turned so against him. After an hour or so, his emotions calmed. He thought perhaps he should go back to Lisa's and apologize for his impulsive behavior. He knew that she was still the best thing that had ever happened to him. As he navigated to within a few blocks of Lisa's house, he spotted a neon sign for the

Cabin Tavern. Mark looked at his watch and decided he would have time for a quick one…a slight bolster before encountering his miffed fiancé. He nosed the Cavalier into the Cabin's gravel parking lot.

The Tavern was fairly quiet as Mark straddled one of the unoccupied bar stools. He ordered a lager and began to sip. The beer was comforting and immediately began to buzz his head. Such indulgence should have triggered caution in Mark…but it didn't. He was unaware at the time, but this tinge of a high would evolve to a ruinous element in his life. He was on his second beer, when Mark became aware of someone's hands covering his eyes from behind.

"Guess who?" came a female voice.

"I give up," said Mark.

"It's me!" Wendy Phillips removed her hands and revealed herself by hugging Mark enthusiastically. "Hi Handsome! How are you?"

"Hi Wendy," said Mark.

"Happy New Year!" Wendy winked knowingly. The sensual twinkle in her eye recalled the secret sexual liaison between her and Mark from New Year's Eve '08.

Mark half-smiled. He understood her reference, if reluctantly.

"Happy New Year to you, too," said Mark. "How have you been?"

Not too bad," said Wendy, "I'm working at the Big Depot now…for about six months. I'm a cashier. It's all right." She flirtatiously smiled. "I get bored though. So what's up with you?"

"Lisa and I got engaged," said Mark.

Wendy's smile faded. "Oh, that's nice."

“On New Year’s Eve,” Mark added.

“Well, congratulations.” Wendy sat on the barstool next to Mark.

***

Over the next weeks and months, Mark and Lisa didn’t see much of each other. Lisa was busy at school managing a challenging academic load as well as preparing for the summer dance tour. Mark struggled to make good in the work-a-day world. He had secured a minimum wage bus-boy job at the Hiller Diner. He worked the evening shift, 4 p.m. to midnight. To say the least, he wasn’t exactly enjoying the experience. It was a big step down from being the town hero. But his mother insisted that he pay rent at her house, and his father declared that living with him “was out of the question.” And of course, he couldn’t afford to get a place of his own.

Every night after work Mark found himself on what had become his regular stool at the Cabin. He had graduated from his regular lager to several boilermakers (whiskey shot and beer chaser) each night. He became regularly intoxicated…quiet and mostly to himself. His mother’s house was close by, so he walked home every night. The next day he would pick up his car at the Tavern and drive to work. As this pattern prevailed, Mark began having a drink or two before work as well as a much larger quantity after his shift. Sometimes he would remain at the bar straight through his working hours. As a result, Mark was let go.

He was almost relieved at his firing. He hated the job and thought he could surely find something better. Unfortunately, his reputation had begun to precede him. It didn’t take long for word to get around the small town of Mark’s lack of dependability and control. His mother figured out what had happened when he failed to provide her rent money. She essentially told him to find another job quickly, or move out.

Mark didn’t tell Lisa of his difficulties. Even though she tried to phone him each night, he often would let the call go to voice mail.

He was embarrassed. Mark's relationship with Lisa was deteriorating and he knew it. It seemed his only consolation could be found at the bar. Because he was still somewhat considered a local celebrity, he didn't have to worry about paying his tab. Lots of old men and young women, lined up to buy him drinks. He became a happier drunk… at least on the outside.

Wendy Phillips was also a regular at the Cabin Tavern. She often flirted with Mark, knowing full well he was engaged to Lisa. Mark had consistently resisted her advances. But, one night, after much alcohol, Mark revealed to Wendy that he had yet to have sex with Lisa. "*What!*....you're not serious!" said Wendy.

Mark quietly laughed as he downed his drink. "Another one, please, Walt." The bartender provided a glass of lager and a shot of whiskey.

"You poor baby," said Wendy, "no wonder you're here drinking every night."

Almost immediately Mark regretted the fact that he had shared such a personal detail with Wendy. He wasn't particularly enthralled with his sexual status…or lack thereof. But after much soul searching, he had arrived at the conclusion that his respect for Lisa and her wishes outweighed his physical aspirations. Meanwhile, Wendy's coquettish overtures revved into high gear. Every night her bar stool inched closer to his. She could barely keep her hands off him. Mark enjoyed having someone to talk to and he feared his resistance to Wendy's advances was weakening.

Eventually Mark looked forward to the nightly companionship of Wendy Phillips. She seemed to understand what he had gone through and was a good listener. But each night, when Wendy offered him a ride home, he declined and walked the several blocks to his mother's house.

Wendy had also arranged for him to have a job interview at the Big Depot. Mark was very appreciative, since his mother was becoming impatient with his rent-free arrangement. Although the supervisor was impressed with Mark and was ready to hire him, the company's pre-employment drug and alcohol screening came back positive. He was out.

That night, sitting at the bar, Mark was as low as he had ever been. Wendy, sensing his vulnerability, accelerated her accessibility. "I'm here for you…you know that, right?" said Wendy.

Mark chugged his shot. "I know. Thanks."

"I mean…in every way," Wendy placed her hand on his leg. "I'm here for you in every way."

Mark looked at her and smiled. "You are, are you?"

"I am… and you know I could make you feel a lot better."

Mark held up his shot glass to the bartender indicating a refill. "I'll bet you could."

"It could be our secret," said Wendy, "nobody has to know."

Mark downed his refill. "I...I think I'd better get home." He reached for his wallet, but Wendy put money on the bar to pay his tab.

"All right…whatever you say. But I'm here when you're ready." Wendy got up from her stool. Mark got up too and as they walked out of the bar together, they discovered it had been raining.

"Are you sure I can't give you a lift?" said Wendy.

Mark pulled down the brim of his hat. "No…I'm fine."

As Mark was about to start his trek home, Wendy grabbed his arm.

"Oh, shit…I think my keys are locked in my car."

Mark sighed. "Ugh, all right. We'll need to get a coat hanger."

After borrowing a hanger from the Cabin, Mark jerried open Lisa's car door. "Thank you so much, said Wendy, "now I insist on giving you a ride home."

Mark looked up at the dark sky. The intensity of the rain had increased. "Okay, I guess so. Thanks." Mark got into the passenger side of Wendy's car. Wendy started her engine.

Just then the intensity of the rain escalated. It pummeled the roof of Wendy's car and obliterated the visibility out the front window. Wendy turned off the ignition. "I think we have to wait until this let's up a little." Then she turned deliberately to Mark, leaned across the seat and kissed him.

Mark weakly surrendered his resistance.

.

15
Destined Reality
Early March, 2019

Edward Morrison benefited from handsome birth features. He stood 5’10” tall and weighed 175 pounds. But his potential good looks were tarnished by a lack of interest and care. His sandy blond hair was clean but stringy. He combed it straight back every morning (just wet…no product) and within a few hours it tangled in all directions. He didn’t devote much time to shaving and on any given day, his face revealed a bevy of nicks and cuts. He wore ’60’s style, thick, black glasses which did no favors for his appearance. Also, his posture was poor. He was, in fact, quite the nerdy geek. His physical image, coupled with his introverted personality, resulted in an unsurprising lack of social interaction in his young adulthood.

Edward was a research librarian for the Hunter, Dawson & Scott law firm in lower Manhattan. He had worked there since graduating from City College three years earlier. His job consisted of locating articles and case law references requested by the various departments of the firm. It was a perfect job for Edward, because he was required to have very little personal contact with anyone. Each morning he would retrieve the requested information from his email account. He then spent the day finding, summarizing and analyzing the appropriate data and resources. After completing each assignment, he delivered the requested materials to the appropriate attorney…again through email. The job could be challenging at times, but Edward was good at it. His work was highly regarded throughout the organization. But in spite of that, to most at Hunter, Dawson & Scott, Edward was a name without a face. There were a few friendly colleagues, but no real friends. The firm had sent flowers for his mother's funeral, but no one had attended the service. Upon his return to work, there were no verbal condolences, as one might have expected.

As cold as that might seem, Edward didn't mind. In fact, he preferred the detachment…at least that's what he told himself. The only real friend he had ever had was his mother. And now she was gone. Edward's already shaded personality grew even darker. His work was a distraction to his depression and it kept him going during the day. But at night and on the weekends, things became tougher. Edward tried to pursue various activities to occupy his off-time…reading…video games…even sports. He began following the New York Mets. But the televised games were slow and chocked full of commercials which drove him crazy. Nothing seemed to hold his interest.

Edward's only satisfying focus settled on his newly discovered father, Michael Morrison. His thoughts became consumed by theories of his parental history. He became obsessed with understanding why his father had abandoned his mother. It haunted and debilitated him. Eventually this obsession evolved to detestation. He convinced himself that his mother's demise was directly related to his father's desertion. Edward Morrison resolved to avenge his mother's death. He set his sights on the rural New Jersey community of Lakeside…the home of the Town Square Playhouse, where he believed he would finally confront Michael Morrison.

***

Lisa Stratton's budding relationship with Nick Curtis had been troubling to her daughter, Charlie. Lisa was totally surprised and shocked to learn of this. When ex-husband Michael had suggested as much, Lisa dismissed the idea as ludicrous. But when Charlie finally opened up to her, she was devastated. Her daughter was the most important aspect of Lisa's life. "How could I not have recognized her pain ?" she thought.

The Town Square Playhouse production of *A Doll's House* was scheduled to open in just a couple of weeks. Lisa was already feeling considerable pressure as the lead actor in the show. This would be, after all, her first performance since her college days at Atlantic. She really didn't need any additional stress. But as rehearsal wound down one night, she determined she would have to deal with the "Nick" issue.

After giving rehearsal notes to the cast, director Sal Moretti reminded the company of the upcoming tech week and the necessity of clearing schedules for the home stretch. Because Charlie had not been called for rehearsal that night, Lisa knew that Nick would ask her to join him for coffee at the diner. And she was right. As she started up the aisle toward the exit of the theatre she saw Nick moving in her direction.

"Hey, great job tonight," said Nick. "You're really hitting your stride."

Lisa smiled. "Oh, I don't know... I'm pretty terrified, if you want to know the truth."

Nick hugged Lisa. "Oh, c'mon, you're gonna be great. Let's head over to the diner and unwind, huh?" Nick took Lisa's hand and started leading her up the aisle.

Lisa suddenly stopped and pulled back her hand. "I need to talk to you about something."

Nick looked puzzled. "Okay…what's up?"

"Let's sit a minute," said Lisa. They sat in the last row of the Playhouse. Lisa put her hand on Nick's shoulder. "Look, I want you to know, you've done nothing wrong."

"Oh, shit!" said Nick.

"Charlie is going through a tough time. She's worried about losing her family… and what's going to happen to her dad."

Nick looked away. "Well, I can certainly understand that but…"

Lisa cut him off. "And she's convinced that you and I are going to get married and leave Mark all alone."

Nick turned to face her. "But…I…."

"I know," said Lisa, "but she's so young, and doesn't understand any of this."

"Right," said Nick.

"I think, for her sake, you and I are going to have to shut things down…at least for now."

"Hmm…yep…so that's that!" Nick got up and rushed out without looking back. "See ya' around." He was gone.

Lisa sat stunned. She was disappointed. She truly believed Nick would be more understanding. She sadly shook her head, got up, and left the theatre.

***

Lisa invited Mark to her place for dinner the next night. She thought it would be good for Charlie if the three could share a pleasant evening together. Lisa had worked hard all day in preparation. She rolled out all the special occasion table dressings and dinnerware. She also conferred with her personal food connoisseur, Cailla McCormack, on the menu for the evening. They had come up with what they thought to be a dandy selection: shrimp cocktail, New York Strip Steak, and chocolate mousse. Both Charlie and Lisa were excited with anticipation.

When the doorbell rang, Lisa checked herself in the mirror. Although she knew her marriage to Mark was over, she still loved him on many levels. She wanted to look good for him. Moreover, she wanted the evening to be a success, for Charlie's sake. When

Charlie opened the door, Lisa's excitement depleted like a popped balloon.

"Hi Daddy!" said Charlie.

"Hey, Squirt!" Mark picked Charlie up under her arm pits and spun her around. Charlie and Mark laughed joyously. Mark put Charlie down and looked to Lisa. "I brought Wendy along. I hope you don't mind."

Lisa forced a grin. "Of course not. Hello Wendy, welcome."

Lisa was furious. The entire purpose of the evening was to assure Charlie of her family stability. Wendy's presence was, to say the least, counterproductive. Beyond that, three steaks had been prepared…not four. Still, Lisa presented an undaunted front. "Why don't we all have a seat in the living room. Dinner will be ready in a few minutes."

Charlie helped Lisa serve the hors d'oeuvres…little meatballs and hot dogs on toothpicks.

"Can I get you a drink?" Lisa asked. "Iced tea? Cola?"

"I'll have a beer," replied Mark.

"Me too," said Wendy.

Lisa went to the kitchen. "Oh…okay." Things were definitely not going as planned.

But dinner proceeded fairly well. Charlie was clearly enjoying her father's company. Wendy was cordial and mostly non-intrusive. Lisa was not happy, but managed to control her displeasure. Charlie told Mark that she had come in second in her class spelling bee and had been awarded a set of colored pencils as a prize.

"That's fantastic!" said Mark. "Great job, Squirt!" Charlie beamed from ear to ear.

"In fact," said Lisa, "Mrs. Adamcyk sent home a note the other day reporting that Charlie was speaking up and participating much more in class lately."

"That's great news," said Mark.

"Well, that makes our little surprise even better," said Wendy.

"Surprise?" said Lisa. "What surprise?"

"Oh, well, we're going skiing this weekend in the Poconos, and we're bringing Charlie with us. It'll be a blast."

Charlie jumped out of her chair. "Wow!" She ran to hug Wendy. "Thank you! Thank You! Thank you! I can't wait!" Then she parodied skiing around the dining room. Wendy and Mark laughed heartily at Charlie's antics but Lisa did not.

"Well, that's very kind of you to invite her," said Lisa, "but she isn't available this weekend."

"What!" simultaneously exclaimed Charlie, Wendy and Mark.

"Why not?" said Charlie. "Why can't I go skiing?"

"Because you have rehearsals at the Playhouse this weekend. It's tech week Buddy, you know that."

"Shit!" said Charlie as she ran out of the room.

"Language!" Lisa called after her.

"Oh, c'mon…she can miss a couple of practices," said Mark. "It's not the end of the world."

"That's not the point. She made a commitment to the play. She has to learn the responsibility involved in that."

Mark stood up. "She's eight years old for fuck's sake. She's got plenty of time to learn about responsibility. Let her have a little fun."

"I really wish you had discussed this with me before hoisting it on her."

"*Hoisting it*!" said Wendy. "Like it's some kind of punishment? It'll be a great time for her."

Lisa stepped to Wendy and got in her face. "This does not concern you....at all. I don't even know what you're doing here. This was supposed to be a chance for us to reestablish our family ties."

Mark stepped between the two women. "Hey, I won't have you being rude to Wendy. She's with me now...just as that "Nick" guy is with you."

Lisa walked away. "I'll have you know, I broke it off with Nick....again in the interest of helping our daughter get through this rough patch."

"I insist that Charlie come on this ski trip with us," said Mark.

"You can insist and pontificate all you want. The judge placed Charlie in *my* custody...as you well know. She'll be fulfilling her responsibilities at the Playhouse this weekend."

"What a bitch!" said Wendy.

"You bet your sweet ass I am, Honey! When it comes to my daughter, I can be ruthless." Then Lisa executed a phony smile. "Thank you both so much for coming to dinner. I'll pass-on your goodbyes to Charlie." Lisa walked to the apartment door and opened it. "Please, do have a safe trip home." Wendy and Mark awkwardly exited and Lisa slammed the door behind them.

Lisa was shaking. She sat on the living room sofa and breathed deeply. The evening had been a disaster. She needed a few minutes to regroup before approaching her daughter. She knew that when she explained things to Charlie, the "wise-beyond-her-years" child would understand…at least she hoped so. Lisa really needed someone to talk to. She knew who she wanted to call. But, sadly, he was no longer an option.

***

Edward Morrison was mesmerized by the passing scenes displayed through the window of the Roadways bus on which he was a passenger. On a determined mission to settle accounts with his recently discovered father, he was making a preliminary day-trip to an unlikely destination…a remote playhouse in western New Jersey. Edward was a lifelong New York City resident and was unaccustomed to any non-urban locales. His assumption, as he set out on his pilgrimage, was that New Jersey would display very similar geography to his home base. And to be sure, as the bus exited the Lincoln Tunnel and traversed the communities of Weehawken, Secaucus, Newark and The Oranges, there seemed little to differentiate the *Garden State* from the grit of the "greatest city in the world."

But as the journey wound westward on Interstate Route 80, the passing terrain evolved. It became brighter and far less congested. Edward couldn't take his eyes off the beautiful homes and peaceful ambience of suburbia. He had heard of such residential sprawl, but to witness it somewhat overwhelmed him. Further west, it became even more picturesque; acres of farmland, kids playing in backyards, and cows in the pastures. These visions were all new to Edward Morrison…and he liked what he saw.

The end of the line for the westbound bus was the Hackettstown transit station. This municipality appeared somewhat developed, but still a far cry from the city. As Edward exited the bus, his map app indicated him to be approximately fifteen miles from the town of Lakeside…the home of the Town Square Playhouse … and Michael Morrison's upcoming performance. Edward's plan was to utilize a peer-to-peer ride sharing service like *TakeMe* to travel the final leg of his journey. What Edward didn't count on was the lack of *TakeMe* drivers in rural New Jersey. To his surprise, it seemed that everyone here drove his or her own vehicle. "Astounding!" he thought.

After waiting in the train station for over an hour, *TakeMe* finally arrived. The driver was a woman who appeared to be in her mid-forties. Her name was Kristi Andrianni and she was friendly…also quite chatty.

"Hey, how ya' doin'?" said the woman, "Sorry it took me a while to get to you. I had to pick up my kids from school before I could take any fares. I've got a seventeen year old son and a fifteen year old daughter…Kenny and Maggie. They're the best, but sometimes they drive me bonkers… You got any kids?"

"Uh…no," Edward replied. He was taken aback by Kristi's outgoing personality. His experience with drivers in the city had been that they rarely said anything…usually adrift in their headphones.

"So, we're headed to Lakeside, right?" asked Kristi.

"Uh, yes…that's right."

"Sweet little town, Lakeside." Kristi nosed her SUV out of Hackettstown. "Not a whole lot goin' on out there. But sweet…and quiet… *real* quiet. Mind if I ask your name?"

"Edward."

"Oh, Hi Edward….I'm Kristi. I guess I told you that already." Kristi let out with a loud, sustained laugh.

Edward smiled. He liked this lady. She was a big boned woman…voluptuous really, with auburn permed hair and bright brown eyes. She freely demonstrated lots of natural energy. It may have been the attraction of opposites, but Edward felt comfortable with her.

"Have you ever been to the Playhouse in Lakeside?" asked Edward.

"Oh, sure," Kristi answered, "lots of times. When my kids were little we went there to see *The Little Mermaid* and *Cinderella*...lots of shows."

"Any good?" asked Edward.

"Yes...we enjoyed them. Of course, I'm not exactly a theatre expert or anything. But I thought they were great. I've wanted to get back and see other things...but my husband, Joe, is kind of a stick-in-the-mud. If there's not a ball or a puck involved, he's not interested...ya' know?" Edward couldn't believe how nice and friendly this lady was. It eventually dawned on him that Kristi very much reminded him of his mother.

As they drove through Lakeside, Edward was impressed with the small town flavor. Tree lined streets, old fashioned courthouse with adjacent park, a diner, a gas station and finally...the Playhouse.

"Well, here we are," Kristi pulled to the curb in front of the Town Square Playhouse and smiled at Edward. "Pretty small scale, huh? Is it what you expected?"

"Honestly, I didn't know what to expect." said Edward. "I just wanted to get the lay of the land. I'm planning on coming out here to see a show soon. Can you wait? I'll just be a minute."

"Sure, I've got no place to be." Kristi turned off the ignition and pulled a paperback out of her purse. "Take your time."

Edward got out of the SUV, and approached the Playhouse. The marquee displayed the upcoming show information: "A Doll's House" - March 15 through 24 - SEASON TIX AVAIL. - townsquare.org. Edward stepped to one of the entrance doors. He tried to open it, but it was locked. As he peered through the glass framework he could see the interior lobby, festively decked out for the start of the new theatre season. Edward became cognizant of an inner sensibility…a destined reality appeared at hand.

16
See Saw
May 24, 2010

As Lisa Lesinski-Stratton held her newborn baby girl, she marveled at the creation she held in her arms. At 3:42 a.m. she had become a mom. She could barely believe it to be true. When her parents entered her hospital room, they were in tearful awe of what they saw. Lisa's mother, Ainsley, insisted on immediately holding the 6 pound, 9 ounce, Charlene. She cooed in baby talk of how she believed the baby's pink features resembled her own. Soon Lisa's father, Charles, reached out for his turn— indicating his strong belief that "Charlie" more strongly resembled him… "I am her namesake after all"

Lisa reflected on the happenstance of the moment. In spite of her joy, she couldn't help but contemplate the irony of the moment. Instead of completing her sophomore year at Atlantic University, she was a full-fledged wife and mother. Her ambitions of becoming a professional dancer and educator were now an afterthought…perhaps indefinitely. Though Lisa had no regrets at the time, she found the reality of her life quite astounding.

In the midst of her reverie, Mark came barreling into the room. He had been physically petrified in a permanent state of panic since the wee small hours of the morning. He carried a large gym bag containing a variety of Lisa's things...nightgowns, toiletries, makeup. "Charlie" arrived a little earlier than had been anticipated and the young parents were caught completely by surprise. Following the delivery, the new father had returned to the couple's apartment to get organized. Upon Mark's return, Charles passed his new granddaughter to her beaming dad, who delicately and proudly held her as he smiled with delight. Lisa cherished that vision. Times had not been easy for her and her husband. But now, she thought, maybe things would be better.

As Mark lovingly swayed Charlie in his cradled arms, Lisa flashed back to that awful morning, just about a year ago…a time that would change her life forever.

***

It was a little past 1:00 a.m. Lisa was in a sound sleep in her dorm room at Atlantic. She had been engaged in a particularly tough dance rehearsal for her upcoming summer tour and was totally bushed. She was suddenly awakened by the loud ring of her cell phone. She sat up in her bed immediately. "A call at this time of night can't be good," she thought.

"Who's calling at this hour?" mumbled Lisa's sleepy roommate, Lauren Benke.

"I have no clue," said Lisa. She gazed at the phone's ID and didn't recognize the number. "Great…it's probably a telemarketer."

Lisa considered not answering the call, but at the last minute changed her mind. "Hello…who is this?" It was Mark…but she barely recognized his voice. He was subdued to the point that Lisa wondered if he had been sedated. "What is it Mark? Mark are you all right?"

Mark's speech pattern was erratic to the extent Lisa had difficulty following the gist of what he was saying. "She's lying…it's not true…they're making the whole thing up."

"What's not true?" said Lisa. She was trying desperately to figure out what Mark was saying. "Start from the beginning. What happened?" After several minutes of questioning her fiancé, Lisa came to understand that he was in the county jail…charged with assaulting Wendy Phillips.

"She's lying," Mark continuously repeated.

“I don’t understand,” said Lisa.

“I’ll explain the whole thing when you get here,” said Mark.

“When I get there? You want me to come *now*?”

“Please…please!” said Mark. “Nobody will bail me out. I don’t want…I *can’t* stay here all night.”

Lisa was trembling. She was confused and had no real inkling of what was going on. “All right, I’ll get there as soon as I can.”

“Thank you…I’ve gotta go,” Mark’s phone abruptly went dead.

***

It was nearly 5:00 a.m. when Lisa arrived at the Warren County Jail. She was informed that Mark’s bail had been set at twenty thousand dollars. His release would require a certified check for $2,000 or cash to cover the bond. Lisa barely had enough money in her checking account to accommodate such a withdrawal. She knew she wouldn’t be permitted to withdraw that much cash from an ATM, and she would have to wait until the bank opened in order to certify a check. Lisa informed the corrections officer that she would return later in the morning to arrange Mark’s bail.

At this point, she really didn’t want to get her parents involved, but on the other hand, she didn’t want to sit in her car for several hours. So she went home. Although it wasn’t even 6 a.m. both of Lisa’s parents were up. As she entered the house she found them seated at their kitchen table sipping coffee and scanning the morning paper. To say the least, they were surprised to see her.
“What the heck are you doing home?” said Ainsley.

Lisa did her best to explain what had happened. She shared her plan to retrieve the necessary funds to post Mark’s bail as soon as the bank branch opened. Her parents were extremely concerned. They wondered what had caused Mark to assault Wendy. They were also confused as to why Mark's parents hadn't posted the bail.

"That's all I know right now," said Lisa. "If it's all right, I'm going to bring Mark here after I get him out." Lisa's parents agreed. But Lisa requested that they not question Mark about what had happened. "Let me talk to him about it in private, okay?" said Lisa.

"Of course, however you want to handle it, dear," said Ainsley, "but we're here to help however we can."

***

Mark Stratton paced the floor of his cell in the county jail. He had been doing so for the majority of the night and morning, occasionally sitting on the metal bed frame's hard mattress. He couldn't believe the situation in which he found himself. Just a year ago he had been the hometown football hero. He wondered how he could have fallen so hard, so quickly.

He knew he had made a huge mistake when, several months ago, he succumbed to the sexual advances of Wendy Phillips. Following his academic suspension from college, his inability to hold a job and his growing addiction to alcohol, Wendy's sexual healing seemed a welcome redress. He had been brimming with self-pity and Wendy offered him a safe haven.

But throughout the time of his affair, he never truly considered the risk he was taking with regards to Lisa. He rationalized that Wendy would meet his physical needs until after Lisa's European tour, at which point things would simply return to normal. But Wendy didn't see it that way. She wanted to go public regarding Mark's relationship with her. In her mind, she was now his girlfriend. She had even created the self-delusion that he had formally broken his engagement with Lisa, which of course, he had not.

On this night, in Wendy's bedroom, the couple had had a bitter argument. She was tired of being taken for granted. She insisted on a commitment from Mark.

“I love you and you love me!” said Wendy. “It’s time we made it official.”

“Wendy…what are you talking about?” said Mark. “I’ve never said I loved you! *Never!*”

Wendy slapped his face…hard. “You don’t love me…you just love having sex with me, right?”

Mark recoiled in anger. He tried to compose himself. “Look…you’re a great girl. We’ve had some good times. But that’s all it’s been. Fun. It’s been a fun time.”

“You bastard!” said Wendy. “You need to change your tune, and quickly.”

“Or what?” said Mark.

“Or I’m gonna tell your virgin fiancé, that you’ve been fucking me for the past three months.”

Mark lost control and grabbed Wendy by her arms. “You can’t do that! Please, Wendy...don’t!”

“Get your God damned hands off of me.”

Mark squeezed Wendy’s arms and gave them a shake. “Wendy, please!”

“Let go of me!”

Mark released Wendy, pushing her away from him and propelling her into the wall. Wendy grabbed her phone from the nightstand, dialed 911 and charged she had been assaulted by her boyfriend. When the police arrived, Mark’s explanation of what had happened fell on deaf ears. He was arrested and remanded to the county jail. Mark’s frantic phone calls to his mother and father went unanswered.

As he waited impatiently in his cell for Lisa's rescue, Mark wondered how he would explain this calamity to the love of his life.

***

Following her posting of Mark's bail, Lisa had to wait nearly two hours before her fiancé was released. When he finally entered the waiting room, Mark ran to Lisa and gratefully embraced her.

"Are you all right?" asked Lisa.

"I am now."

It was a silent ride from the jail to Lisa's home. As they entered the house, Ainsley Lesinski hugged her future son-in-law. "You poor thing," she said. Lisa's father, Charles, extended his hand to Mark and urged him to sit in the kitchen and have something to eat. Ainsley served coffee and Danish, which Mark seemed to appreciate. He hadn't eaten in nearly 24 hours. Then Lisa's parents retired to the living room, providing the privacy which Lisa had requested.

Lisa and Mark sat silently for a long time. Lisa was patient. She knew it would do little good for her to prompt an explanation. Whatever was to happen next would have to come from Mark. Finally he spoke. "Thanks again for bailing me out…I'll pay you back as soon as I can."

"There's no hurry. The important thing is that you're okay."

"Jail is a scary place," said Mark.

"I can only imagine."

There was another long silent gap. Then Mark blurted it out. " I was with Wendy last night."

"Oh?"

"She's had a crush on me for years."

Lisa's voice cracked as her eyes slightly welled up. "I didn't realize that."

"Oh, yeah, I never said anything because, I mean, what would have been the point…ya' know?"

Lisa didn't respond.

"Anyway, she got this idea in her head that she and I were together…which we absolutely were *not*. She said she was gonna tell you about it."

Mark waited for a response from Lisa…which again was not forthcoming.

"Well…obviously, I didn't want that to happen," Mark said.

"Obviously," Lisa repeated, with a hint of tone.

"Right…of course," said Mark, "so I approached her and gently took her by both arms. I pleaded with her not to say anything to you."

"And how did she respond?" asked Lisa.

"She called 911 and said I attacked her. But I *didn't*. I barely touched her."

Lisa got up from the kitchen table and walked to the sink. She looked out the window. "Anything else you want to tell me?"
Mark stood and went to her. "I love you. I want to tell you that."

"I love you too," said Lisa. "At least I think I do. But if things are going to work for us, I need you to be square with me. What the heck is going on?"

Now Mark became emotional…melodramatic…overly so. He stepped away from Lisa and then turned to face her. He garishly explained that since his exit from Wington he had had a rough time. He was down on himself…disappointed in himself. He was depressed. His mother was pressuring him for rent money. His father hadn't spoken to him. He found booze to be a convenient answer to his blues. He was unable to hold a job. He inhabited various bar rooms every day, where he would often encounter Wendy Phillips. "Wendy," he said, "was a good listener." Talking to her seemed to help him cope with his problems.

Lisa wanted desperately to believe her fiancé, but she was having trouble accepting his sincerity. She decided to probe a little deeper. "Now, I'm going to ask you a question and I want you to answer me honestly…no matter how much you think it may hurt me."

Mark cleared his throat. His voice was hoarse. "All right"

Lisa stared him squarely in the eyes. "Have you been intimate with Wendy?" Mark was unable to hold eye contact and looked away. He remained silent. "Have you?" said Lisa. "It will be better for both of us, if you tell me."

Mark finally returned Lisa's gaze. "Yes."

Lisa started to exit the kitchen. Mark caught up to her and grabbed her shoulders and turned her toward him. "But it meant nothing. *She* means nothing to me. I was so lonely…I missed you so much. I made a terrible mistake. It only happened once," he lied, "and I'm so sorry."

Lisa pulled away from him and left the kitchen. She ran to her room in tears. Mark waited a moment in hopes she might return. When she didn't, he left the house and started walking home.

***

Later that day, Lisa returned to the Atlantic campus. She had a lot to sort out. She ignored Mark's continuous attempts to call her. She didn't sleep well that night. The next day she found her classes to be a good diversion from the pain she was feeling. Later, she set off to rehearsal at the dance studio. To her surprise, Mark was waiting at the entranceway. Lisa attempted to walk past him, but he moved to block her path.

"Please…I have to talk to you!" said Mark.

"I don't think I can right now," Lisa replied.

"Please! Just give me five minutes."

Lisa looked down to the floor and then up to Mark. "All right. Go out to the bench in front of the building. I'll be right out."

"Thank you," said Mark as he headed out.

Lisa approached her choreographer and explained that she would be a few minutes late to rehearsal. She then found Mark sitting on the front bench. She sat beside him, but faced front. It was a warm, sunny April day…a stark contrast to Lisa's gloomy sentiment. "I feel numb," she said. "That's why I'm not sure having this conversation is a good idea. You've hurt me."

"I know. I'm sorry. I know I don't deserve your forgiveness. But I'm begging for it anyway." Lisa turned to Mark. She saw a sincerity in his face that had been missing in his earlier explanation. "I love you with all my heart," said Mark. "You are the only good thing that has ever happened to me. I know that's corny, but it's true. I would do anything for you."

"Blah, blah, blah…but, Wendy…" said Lisa.

"I made a mistake…a *bad* mistake. But yesterday, when you walked away, I could feel my insides collapsing. It reminded me of when that crazy teacher set out to hurt you. I couldn't let that happen, mainly because I needed you in my life."

Lisa recalled Mark's heroics. "I'll never forget what you did for me that day."

"Because I love you!" said Mark.

"I know you *say* you love me…and I *say* I love you. But being together has to be more than just the words we say."

"I know. You're absolutely right," said Mark. That's why, we can't wait."

"What? What do you mean?" asked Lisa.

"I mean…you have to come home and marry me…right away…today…tomorrow…as soon as possible!"

Lisa was flabbergasted. Her eyes widened in amazement. "I think you're *serious*!"

"I am absolutely serious! When you're not with me, I get myself into trouble. But if we're together anything is possible.

"But…what about *my* life…here?" said Lisa.

"It'll always be here to come back to. But right now, I desperately need you to devote yourself to getting *me* back on track."

The couple sat in silence for what seemed like a long time.

Lisa shook her head in bewilderment. "I can't believe I'm saying this…but if I were to agree to this crazy idea, you would have to promise to deal with the drinking."

Mark's face energized. "Absolutely! In fact, my lawyer told me that *Alcoholics Anonymous* is part of my plea agreement. I'll get past this and make you happy. I promise."

Lisa took Mark's hand. "It's not going to be easy."

"I know. But if you're with me, I know I can do it."

Lisa didn't make it back to rehearsal. She and Mark talked on the bench for the next three hours. The following day, Lisa withdrew from Atlantic University.

***

One week later, April 23, 2009, Mark and Lisa were married in a short civil ceremony at the Glennville Municipal Building. Both families were there to witness the event. Lisa wore her white chiffon prom dress. Mark dressed in his high school graduation suit. It was anything but a storybook wedding, but it didn't seem to matter. Lisa and Mark were the picture of youthful happiness.

Following the ceremony, all gathered at the home of Lisa's parents for a lovely catered wedding dinner. Before the meal was served, Mark's father toasted the bride and groom. "Here's to my son and his new bride. May you both live a long life together, full of happiness and good fortune. Congratulations!" All lifted their champagne, except Mark who sipped from his water glass. As he had promised Lisa, his journey to recovery had begun.

***

The first year of their marriage went remarkably well. Mark was an attentive husband who tried his best to provide for Lisa in every way. He had secured a job as a custodian at his old high school. Although the salary wasn't fantastic, it paid the bills. He also enjoyed being at the scene of his previous glory. There were still plenty of folks at Meadow Hills High School who remembered his athletic heroics. Lisa was happy too. Her initial uncertainty was quickly quashed. To her, Mark was living up to the faith she had placed in him. She was proud of his efforts and believed their past difficulties were fading away. Meanwhile, Lisa became employed at the Little Sprout Daycare Center, in Glennville, as a teacher's assistant. This position didn't pay very well either, but it was a good job for Lisa in that it held opportunities for advancement.

***

And then, just a year later, Lisa and Mark became a family of three. Their daughter, Charlene, better known as "Charlie," became the apple of their collective eyes. They truly adored her and showered her with love. But the new family dynamic brought with it new strains. Lisa had to take a leave from her job to care for her new daughter and the added family expenses were difficult to cover with only Mark's salary. Lisa's mother, Ainsley, helped out with child-care so, eventually, Lisa was able to return to the daycare center on a part-time basis.

In spite of its challenges, the young family happily edged along over the next few years. Lisa took on-line classes toward a teaching degree and had twice been promoted at Little Sprout. In addition to her duties as a teacher's assistant, she was now in charge of school enrollment. This was a big responsibility and Lisa handled it well. The owners of the daycare center liked Lisa very much and envisioned a bright future for her. But managing motherhood and her job became quite a balancing act. So far…so good.

Mark, meanwhile, was growing discontent with the tedium of being a school custodian. He applied for some other jobs, but found himself unqualified for most 21st century career paths. Lisa encouraged him to take some courses…perhaps in computer technology, to provide him more marketability. She even researched community college programs he could take in that regard. But Mark didn't follow through on these. So, as the years passed, he became increasingly resentful of his daily monotony.

Of course, both Lisa and Mark knew the best moments of their lives were those they spent together with their daughter. They didn't do anything fancy…no big vacations or extravagant outings. But a day at the beach, a picnic in the park or even a fun lunch at Harrison's Drive-in were joyous times.

But these occasions, it seemed, were becoming more scattered. Maneuvering work schedules and child care seemed to leave less and less family time. When Lisa worked the night shift, Mark was required to care for Charlie. As much as he loved his daughter, he wasn't thrilled with the prospect of being tied down with parental responsibility, following a long day at work. Also, unknown to Lisa, Mark had stopped attending *AA* meetings. He, in fact, had come to believe he was not really an alcoholic at all, but had simply stumbled in youthful stupidity. He maintained he had overtaken his demons. He was now cured he thought…which, of course, was not possible.

***

In September of 2015, Charlie began kindergarten at the Harris Street Elementary School. Everyone was excited, as well as, a little nervous. Lisa, along with her mother, had shopped for the cutest outfits, resulting in Charlie looking absolutely adorable. As Lisa and Mark tearfully watched their daughter enter the schoolhouse for the first time, neither could believe how quickly time had passed. Charlie took to school immediately and had no problem making adjustments. Of course, she had attended Little Sprout with her mom for the previous two years and had become well adapted to social interaction with other children.

The school was close-by the Stratton's apartment. There was no bus transportation available so it would be necessary for Charlie to walk to school each day. Obviously, as a kindergartner, she would require accompaniment. This caused a bit of havoc in the family schedule. School began at 7:30 a.m. - early. If Lisa was working the nightshift, she would easily be able to escort Charlie both to and from school…no problem. However, when Lisa was on the dayshift, she was required to be at work at 7:00 a.m. - so walking her daughter on those days wouldn't work. But… Mark's custodial shift at the high school didn't start until 8:00 a.m. Therefore…it would be left to Mark to accompany Charlie in those situations. Mark was reticent. He had enough trouble getting to work on time without any distractions. But there was little choice in the matter, so he reluctantly acquiesced. As it turned out, Mark walked Charlie to school every-other week…as would be necessitated by Lisa's schedule. He got used to this regimen and actually came to enjoy this special time spent with his daughter.

Everything seemed to be lining up pretty well. Charlie was totally enjoying her school experience and all the crazy logistics had fallen nicely into place. But then, one day, after seeing Charlie to the Harris Street School front gate, Mark turned and nearly bumped into Wendy Phillips. The encounter was quite a shock. "Woah! Excuse me," said Mark, in reaction to the near miss.

Wendy's face broke into an immediate smile. "Hi! How are you?"

Mark had not laid eyes on Wendy in years. In fact, there had been no interaction between the two since the fateful night of his assault arrest. "I'm doing okay," said Mark.

Wendy tentatively put her arms around Mark's neck. "It's so good to see you."

Mark responded by passively returning the hug. "Yeah, I guess it's been awhile."

Wendy's appearance had changed somewhat. She wore heavier make-up and wrinkly crow's feet could be detected around her eyes. Her arms were adorned with several flowery tattoos and her nose and tongue featured jeweled piercings. Mark was surprised by the changes, but reflected on the reality that his own appearance most certainly had altered as well. "What brings you here to the school?" asked Mark.

"Oh, my sister and her husband are on vacation this week," said Wendy. "I'm watching their house and caring for their son."

Mark hadn't noticed the boy standing beside Wendy. "This is Harry," said Wendy.

"Hi Harry, I'm Mark." Mark and the little boy shook hands.

Wendy handed Harry his lunch box. "You'd better get inside. You don't want to be late." She kissed his cheek.

"Bye, Aunt Wendy," said Harry, as he ran to the door of the school.

"My daughter goes to school here too," said Mark.

"How old is she now?" asked Wendy.

"Charlie's five."

"That's crazy!" Wendy gazed intently into Mark's eyes. "So…how is Lisa?"

Mark was effected by Wendy's glance. He was slow to respond. "Uh…oh…she's good. She's great!"

Wendy and Mark started walking together away from the school, making small talk as if there had been no history between them. In spite of their past bad blood, the fact that Wendy ultimately dropped the assault charge, provided Mark a far less complicated legal outcome. He had pled guilty to a simple disorderly charge and was released with a year's probation, as well as, required enrollment in an alcohol abuse program.

"Well, this is me," said Wendy, "or I should say this is my sister." They stood in front of a small green ranch house, with black shutters.

"This is really nice," said Mark. "We're saving to buy a house too. But, it's tough, you know?"

"I can just imagine," said Wendy. "It was good to see you." She started up the walk, but then stopped and called back. "Would you like to see the inside?"

Mark looked at his watch. "I'd better not. I've gotta get to work."

"Just come in for a minute," said Wendy. "I've got coffee on." She continued toward the door.

Mark looked around to detect any onlookers. As he didn't see anyone watching, he slowly followed Wendy up the walk.

***

Mark didn't make it to work that day. Upon his return, he told his supervisor there had been an emergency situation with his daughter. The explanation was accepted with a warning that future absences would be expected to adhere to policy procedures regarding personal leave. Over the next several weeks Mark called-in sick eight times. In addition, he was late to work almost every day. He was written-up for his tardiness and placed on probation. In addition, Mark was making frequent visits to the Cabin Tavern, where he would often meet-up with Wendy. Lisa was totally unaware of these developments, but noticed changes in Mark's personality. He seemed moody, she thought…quiet and withdrawn. When she tried to approach the subject with Mark, he veered away. "I'm fine," he said. "Fine."

Finally, after several warnings, Mark was dismissed from the custodial staff at Meadow Hills High School. Reasons cited included tardiness, excessive absences and suspicion of being inebriated on the job. Mark pleaded his case citing the hardship his firing would place on his family. But his appeals were denied.

That night, he had a difficult time explaining the situation to Lisa, especially after having spent the afternoon at the bar. Lisa was livid. She couldn't understand how Mark could have so slipped, after years of success. Of course, she didn't realize that Wendy Phillips was again involved in Mark's life…and he certainly wasn't about to volunteer that information.

After a long tearful talk, Mark promised Lisa he would return to *AA*. Lisa suggested they might also initiate marriage counseling. She thought it would benefit both of them and their daughter as well. Mark rejected this idea, insisting they were in no need of such intervention.

Over the next two years, Mark secured and subsequently vacated four different jobs. He worked as a gas station attendant, a grocery clerk, a bus driver and a used car salesman. He began each situation enthusiastically, but quickly became bored. Either he resigned or was fired from each position within a few months. In actuality, Mark spent more time unemployed than on the job. Also, his *AA* commitment was very hit or miss.

Lisa became more distraught. The lack of family income had created a huge financial challenge. She knew her marriage was failing, but was exasperated as to what she could do about it. In her heart, she still loved Mark, but his lack of initiative was robbing her spirit. She had made a good friend in Cailla McCormack, a co-worker at the daycare center. Cailla's brother, Jeb, owned a landscaping business, and offered to give Mark a job.

Mark was hesitant about the opportunity. He didn't like the fact that the job had been secured through his wife's connections. He held an old-fashioned notion that his role as a breadwinner should be self-navigated. Also, he considered the work belittling. He had mowed lawns when he was in junior high school. He resented the idea of regressing to his pubescent occupation.

But Jeb McCormack assured Mark that he wouldn't be pushing a hand mower. He would be in charge of servicing several high profile residential accounts. He would have access to the latest equipment and would be overseeing several co-workers. That last part sparked Mark's interest. He liked the idea of being "the boss." He accepted the job. Lisa held out hope that maybe this time things would work out.

***

Six months later it became abundantly clear that things indeed would *not* be working out. Although Mark was initially quite successful in the landscaping business, old demons reappeared and eventually took their toll.

Jeb McCormack, owner of Sunshine Landscaping, was happy with Mark as an employee. He was a real "people person" Jeb thought. He found Mark to be well liked by both the clients and the lawn crew he supervised. For the first month or so, everything was going great. Several of the residential customers were so happy with Mark's service, they referred their friends to the company. Lisa was proud of her husband's success. Everyone seemed content.

The only downside? Landscaping in the hot summer months was conducive to "a beer with the boys" at the end of the day. Mark and his crew made an after-work visit to the Cabin Tavern a regular occurrence. At first, even this seemed innocent enough…a round or two and then home. But, as time went on, Mark had trouble limiting himself. As in his past, the booze changed Mark's way of thinking. If his good service was building up the business, he thought perhaps he should *own* the business. Each night at the bar, he freely and loudly spoke of breaking off from Jeb…taking his clients and crew…and starting on his own. It became a regular talking point that expanded as the amount of consumed alcohol increased. In reality, it was probably unlikely that Mark would have the initiative or the means of following through with such a plan. But his boastful intentions got back to Jeb…who was not happy about it.

When Jeb confronted Mark about his plan, Mark denied it. "What do you mean?" said Jeb, "I've heard it from at least ten people…including members of your own crew."

"They're all lying. They're just jealous of me…that's all there is to it."

"No, Mark! It's not everybody else…it's you," said Jeb. "You're lying…and I can't have someone work for me who I can't trust."

"Jeb, I'm sorry," said Mark.

"I'm sorry too." Jeb walked away.

***

Mark was distraught. He couldn't go home and face Lisa just then. He would need time to fabricate some type of reasonable explanation for his getting the sack…again. He decided to figure it out at the bar. His plan was to stay there until Lisa went to work the night shift at the daycare center. That would give him plenty of time to come up with something.

As he lifted his third lager, he heard a text message alert… from Lisa. "Oh, shit," he thought. "Did she somehow find out what happened?" But no…she was simply reminding him to pick up Charlie from her playdate that evening at 7. Mark breathed a sigh of relief and took another swig.

Later in the day, Wendy joined Mark at the bar. By the time she arrived, Mark was pretty much in the bag. Through his slurring speech he ranted on and on about his sad, unfortunate life. Wendy was manipulative in her sympathy. She knew Mark craved absolution, and was happy to provide it. Mark embraced Wendy's solace, literally and figuratively.

As the afternoon transitioned into evening, the couple continued to commiserate with each other. Through the affectation of alcohol, Mark had once again managed to escape the reality of his life… and felt no pain. He hailed the man behind the bar, Marty Russ, who was the owner of the Cabin Tavern. "Hey, Marty, old pal, hit me up again," said Mark.

Russ, who knew Mark well, surveyed his condition. "I think maybe you've had enough, ya' know? You've been here since before noon."

"Oh, c'mon. I'm fine. I have a very high tolerance."

"I don't think so," Russ replied. "Besides, you wanted me to remind you when it was getting close to seven o'clock."

"Oh, shit, right. Thanks." Mark turned to Wendy. "I've gotta go. I've gotta pick up Charlie."

"Whoa," said Russ, "you're not driving anywhere." He held out his hand to Mark. "In fact, I'll take your keys."

"No...*I'm* not gonna drive," said Mark. He put his arm around Wendy. "*She* is."

"Well, what kind of shape are *you* in?" Marty inquired of Wendy.

"I'm fine," said Wendy. "I just got here a little while ago."

"Let me see you give her your car keys," said Russ. "And be careful."

Mark complied and the couple exited the bar. When they got out in the parking lot, Mark took his keys back from Wendy's hand.

***

It was a little before 8:00 p.m. when the phone rang at the Little Sprout Daycare Center. Cailla McCormack answered. "Yes...yes she is. I'll get her right away."

Lisa was reading aloud to a story-circle of children. At this time of night, it was challenging to keep the kids engaged. After a long day they were anxious for their parents to pick them up. Still Lisa pressed on, providing animated voices as she read *Gooseberry Park.*

Cailla approached her. "I'm sorry to interrupt you Mrs. Stratton, but there's a phone call for you." Lisa could see that Cailla's face was serious.

"Who is it?" asked Lisa.

Cailla leaned in and spoke very softly, “Glennville Police.” Lisa gasped, handed Cailla the book, and went to the phone.

A few minutes later, Lisa returned to the story-circle. “I’m sorry, Miss McCormack, but I have to leave.”

Cailla went to Lisa. “What’s going on?”

“I’m not sure. I have to get Charlie. I’ll call you later.” Lisa rushed out the door.

***

The police dispatcher had instructed Lisa to go to the intersection of Broad Street and Belvidere Avenue to pick up her daughter. As she sped the five miles to the scene she was frantic. Even though the dispatcher had assured her that Charlie was safe, the lack of any further information was causing Lisa significant distress. When she arrived at the scene, she saw one police car parked in front of Mark’s pickup , and another behind it. Mark and Charlie were standing on the curb next to the rear squad car. Lisa quickly parked and hurried to her daughter. When Charlie saw Lisa she burst into tears and ran to her. Lisa fell to one knee and embraced her daughter, assuring her that everything was all right. When Charlie’s tears subsided, Lisa looked questioningly up at Mark. “What’s going on?”

Mark spoke in a low tone. “I was pulled over.”

Lisa stood, still holding Charlie’s hand. “You’re drunk? You drove drunk?”

Mark interrupted. “Wait a minute…let me explain.”

Just then Lisa spotted her mother standing a few feet up the street. Cailla McCormack had phoned Ainsley Lesinski to alert her of the situation. Lisa walked Charlie to her grandmother, then turned to advance on her husband. Her face took a tortured grimace. “You drove drunk with your daughter in the car? You *fucker!* " It was all she could do to refrain from punching him. But refrain she did. Instead, she took a breath and stepped to the police officer standing near the squad car.

"What happened?" asked Lisa.

Officer Nick Riley of the Glennville Police department looked up at Lisa. "You're the wife?"

"For better or for worse," said Lisa in as negative a tone as she could muster.

"Well, Mrs. Stratton," said Riley, "I've arrested your husband for driving under the influence. His measured blood alcohol level is at .27…"

"My God!" said Lisa.

"He'll be spending the night in County. You can bail him out in the morning." Riley stepped to Mark and led him to the police car.

As Lisa watched Mark being ushered into the back seat, she noticed that he was joining another backseat passenger…Wendy Phillips. Lisa's face changed from beat-red to pale-white.

***

The next morning Lisa did not bail Mark out of the county jail. Instead she sought and found an apartment for herself and her daughter in the nearby town of Lakeside. Over the next month, she gradually moved to her new place as Mark served his 30 day sentence for the DWI. Lisa and Charlie had no contact with Mark while he was in jail. When he was released he was shocked to find that Lisa had left him.

Eventually, Lisa agreed to meet her husband at the Hiller Diner. They discussed a schedule for Mark's visitations with Charlie and the scope of his involvement in his daughter's life. They also renewed the possibility of marriage counseling. But this time it was Lisa who was reluctant. To her, the re-emergence of Wendy Phillips had placed a nearly insurmountable burden on any reconciliation.

In spite of this, the couple attended several counseling sessions over the next six months. Neither Mark nor Lisa found these to be very helpful. Mark had trouble assuming responsibility for his situation. Lisa simply believed she would never be able to trust her husband again.

The following July, after nine years of marriage, Mark and Lisa were divorced.

17
The Desert of Your Heart
March 8-16, 2019

After a lengthy peer through the locked glass doorway of the Town Square Playhouse, Edward Morrison backed away. He walked up, down and around the walkways surrounding the theatre. Nothing that he saw disputed the findings of his internet search: here he believed his long lost father would be performing in *A Doll's House* in one week. Since his mother's death, Edward had been obsessed with learning the details of his parental history. His conclusion that his father's desertion had caused his mother's demise, gnawed at his being.

Edward, of course, had no way of knowing that his father was no longer a member of the Playhouse company. Although the online press release clearly credited Michael Morrison as the actor playing *Torvald Helmer* in the Ibsen classic, the role had been quietly recast, with the correction never having been posted.

After perusing the Playhouse and its surroundings for ten minutes or so, Edward re-entered the *TakeMe* ride share vehicle which had conveyed him. The driver of the SUV, Kristi Andrianni, returned her paperback to her purse and looked at her passenger.

"All set?" she asked.

"Yes," said Edward.

Kristi was perceptive. She recognized that Edward's demeanor had changed since he exited her car…and not in a good way. As she piloted her vehicle on the eastward ride to Hackettstown, she began talking about herself and her family. Her jovial, good-natured manner again reminded Edward of his mother. He was strangely drawn to her. She was so appealing to Edward that he climbed out of his gloom and started talking…far more than usual. By the time they arrived in Hackettstown he had opened-up with Kristi well beyond that which was his custom. He told her all about his background, his education and his job. He even revealed that he had recently lost his mother. This hit a mark with Kristi. It was clear her sympathy was sincere.

As Edward departed Kristi's SUV, she wrote her personal cell phone number on her business card and handed it to him. "If you're out this way again, you can call me directly at that number. I'll get out to you as fast as I can."

"Thank you," said Edward.

Kristi flashed a warm smile. "And listen, Edward. If you ever need to talk…about your mom…or anything at all, just ring me up, okay?"

Edward was moved by what seemed a genuine act of kindness from a woman he barely knew. "Thank you, Kristi," he said. "Thank you very much."

***

The next day, tech week began for *A Doll's House*. Lisa arrived at the Playhouse with Charlie slightly before 2:00 p.m. Charlie was not a happy camper. Instead of enjoying a fun ski weekend with her father, she had been "*doomed to torture* in a *stupid* play, with *boring old people*, in which she appeared for *less than five minutes*." Lisa and she had engaged in a knock-down drag-out argument the night before. Charlie had begged her mom to reconsider and allow her to ditch tech rehearsal for the sake of the ski trip.

"How can you do this to me?" Charlie wailed, with tears flowing in torrents.

"Buddy, you freely accepted a part in this play…you have a responsibility to see it through." said Lisa.

"Bull shit!" Charlie screamed.

"Hey…!" said Lisa.

"Bull shit! Bull shit! *Bull shit!*" Charlie was out of control.

"All right…that's it. Go to your room. If we can't have a civil discussion about this, you'll just have to think about it alone until we can."

Charlie stomped her foot and exited to her room. "I *hate* you!"

So, as they arrived at the theatre for tech rehearsal, Charlie sullenly plopped herself into a back row seat, instead of following her mom to the front as usual. Lisa paused to look back at her, but then determined it probably best to allow her daughter to stew until she could bring herself to act like a person.

Director Sal Moretti addressed the cast prior to beginning the run-through. He reminded them there would, no doubt, be lots of stops and starts to work out technical issues. Fortunately, in *A Doll's House*, there was only one setting, so there would be no need to organize scenery shifts. Instead, he said, they would be mainly concerned with sound and lighting cues. Lisa turned and looked up at the light deck. There she saw Nick Curtis in place with other members of the technical crew. The couple's recent detachment had been weighing on her mind. She missed their talks at the diner getaways… she missed having his gentle ear.

When rehearsal finally began, Lisa was relieved. She was weary from worry…Charlie….Mark and Wendy…Nick. She was convinced that her focus on the portrayal of *Nora*, would block out her personal issues.

Unfortunately, it was not to be. Lisa was all over the place. She was unable to find any comfort in her physicality. Her posture was poor and imbalanced. Her blocking was off too. It was totally unmotivated and made no sense. Also, she was dropping lines left and right. Worst of all, she was hanging her fellow cast members out to dry. She had never had such problems…not in college…not in high school. In fact, she had not struggled so, even in her early *Doll's House* rehearsals. Moretti knew that something was up, but chose not to address it. He reasoned that perhaps Lisa was just nervous. Besides, he had his hands full dealing with all the technical problems he was having.

Charlie, still seated in the back of the theatre, also took note of her mom's sudden ineptitude. Her concern for Lisa kicked-in and pulled her out of her doldrums…at least temporarily. She moved down to the front row. During a break in the run-through Lisa sat next to her daughter. As she pulled a water bottle out of her bag, she caught Charlie's gaze.

"What?!" said Lisa.

"Nothing."

Lisa took a long swig and then, "Why are you staring at me like that?"

"What's going on with you?" said Charlie. "You're moving around up there like you've got ice cubes growing out of your feet."

"Oh, thanks," said Lisa. "That just bowls me over with confidence."

"That's sarcasm, right?" asked Charlie.

"Very, very good, Buddy. Apparently your vocabulary is expanding exponentially."

"Huh?" said Charlie.

“Never mind.” Lisa took another long swig of water.

“But, really, what’s up with you? You’re acting like you’ve never seen the script before!”

Lisa looked at her daughter. “It’s that obvious, huh?”

“Yeah…you can do better, Mom! I know you can!” Charlie put her arm around Lisa and smiled at her. “I don’t really hate you.”

“Thanks, Buddy.” This was the first warm moment between the two in several days. Lisa became aware that she was starting to tear-up. She stood and quickly wiped her eyes. “Okay…I gotta concentrate.”

Lisa continued to stumble through the rest of the rehearsal. She wondered why she was putting herself through such misery. “What a terrible mistake this was,” she thought. Charlie remained down front and tried to encourage her mom by providing lots of cute smiles and other positive cues. Lisa appreciated it, but it didn’t seem to help. By the end of the day, the whole cast and crew had become painfully aware and exceedingly concerned about Lisa’s apparent meltdown.

***

That evening Lisa mostly stayed in her bedroom. Charlie had completed a composition she had written for school and wanted her mom to check it over. She approached Lisa’s room and knocked quietly on the closed door. “Mom? Are you awake?”

“Yeah, c’mon in, Buddy,” said Lisa.

Charlie opened the door and found her mother seated at her vanity. “What are you doing sitting here in the dark?”

“Just thinking,” said Lisa. “I’m trying to muster up the courage to drop out of the play.”

"What? No, Mom, you can't do that."

"I'm terrible," said Lisa. "I'm gonna bring down the whole show."

"So, you had a bad day, so what? Nobody was very good today."

"Because of *me*! I was throwing off everybody," said Lisa.

"I don't think that's true. Besides…you told me I had to accept *my* responsibility. What about *your* responsibility?" Charlie sat on Lisa's lap.

"I know you're right, Buddy. I'm just really scared."

"You're a good actor, Mom. I'll bet you'll be better tomorrow."

Lisa hugged Charlie tightly. "I love you, so much."

"I love you too."

***

Edward Morrison dialed Kristi Andrianni's personal cell phone number. It was his fourth call to the *TakeMe* driver in a week. Edward had totally opened his heart and soul to Kristi and cherished the opportunity to unload his feelings to someone…to anyone. For her part, Kristi was surprised at the number and duration of calls from Edward. She hadn't expected her offer of availability to be taken up on such an immediate and extensive basis.

Edward had shared with Kristi his anger toward his mother for having hidden the truth about his father. At the same time, he felt massive guilt for harboring such feelings toward the woman who bore and raised him…who clearly loved him immensely. In addition, Edward was totally transparent regarding his hatred for his father. He truly believed his mother would still be alive, had Michael Morrison not abandoned her.

Kristi was quickly coming to the realization that Edward needed more than just a compassionate listener. She believed his needs were beyond her capabilities. She determined she would acquire the names of some counselors and discuss them with Edward at her first opportunity. But Edward's call today, was brief and non-therapeutic. He would be traveling by bus to Hackettstown on Saturday and would need a ride to Lakeside…to the Playhouse. Kristi agreed that she would accommodate him.

***

As tech week for *A Doll's House* continued, Lisa's performance hadn't improved much. Yes, she had retrieved command of her lines and blocking, but there was little passion in her delivery. Other components of the production had progressed nicely but Lisa's *Nora* was wooden. Lisa realized it…pitifully so. But try as she might, she was at a loss in fixing it. She reported to the theatre early each night and engaged in extra rehearsals with the other actors, but to little avail. She was simply unable to own the character.

After rehearsal one night, Moretti asked Lisa to stay. All week long the director had avoided pointing out Lisa's flaws in his corrective notes. He had hoped she was merely experiencing the nervousness that comes from being away from the stage for so long. But now, just days away from opening, he knew his intervention was necessary. The two sat in the front row of the Playhouse, chatting about this and that, as they had so many years ago at Meadow Hills High School. In fact, Moretti had known Lisa longer than anyone else in the cast. He complimented Charlie, who was seated a few rows behind them. He mentioned how impressed he was with her poise and presence.

"I think this has been a good experience for her," said Lisa, "right, Buddy?"

"Uh-huh," Charlie replied.

Moretti then related to Charlie how her mother had saved his butt, when she was in high school. "I desperately needed her as both a performer and choreographer in our production. But she had been denied permission to participate." He recalled how Lisa had courageously stood up to an unreasonable and ultimately *cuckoo* cheer coach and literally saved the day. "You showed incredible fortitude back then," said Moretti to Lisa. "After years of loyal service to cheerleading, you determined to stand up for yourself. Remember?"

"Oh, yes, I remember," said Lisa. "I still have the scars."

"You had been blindly obedient for many years to someone who clearly didn't deserve your loyalty," said Moretti.

"Yes…"

"Kind of like *Nora*, right?" Moretti smiled. The director referred to Lisa's character in *A Doll's Hou*se, who, for all *her* life had lowered herself to the whims and wishes of her husband and before that, her father. Finally, in a moment of epiphany, *Nora* raises herself up to become her own capable person.

"You think I was like *Nora*…when I was in high school?" asked Lisa.

"Yes…absolutely I do," said Moretti. "You demonstrated a reflection of strength that was beyond reproach." Then Sal Moretti recalled a warm-up exercise he utilized in his high school theatre arts classes. "Do you remember the rag doll?" he asked.

Lisa's drawn face smiled for the first time all night. "I remember."

Moretti looked back at Charlie, who was listening intently. "Rag doll was an exercise I used at the beginning of my classes," he said. "On beat #1, I asked the students to extend their arms as high over their heads as possible…step on their tiptoes and then…flex tightly." He stood up and demonstrated. The director continued. "Then on my call…beat #2, I instructed my students to drop and bend at the waist, dangle arms…wiggle fingers… and become as clear-minded and relaxed as possible." Again, Moretti showed the technique.

"Yeah…" said Charlie. "You were doing that the first night we came here."

"I still think it has a lot of value." said Moretti. "It helps prepare for stage both physically and mentally." Moretti then turned his focus from Charlie to Lisa. "But it also reminds us of our ups and downs…in our lives…and in our mission as actors to truthfully portray our characters."

"Uh-huh" said Lisa.

Moretti placed his hand on Lisa's shoulder. "It's that second beat…the release…when you determine your path." Moretti lowered his voice somewhat. "I've got a sense that you've been through some tough things. You're a strong woman, Lisa…don't forget that. Use those second beats to figure things out."

"I'll try," said Lisa.

Moretti stood and started to leave. Then he stopped and turned back to Lisa…almost as an afterthought. "You know, I'm not very religious…at all. But one thought has always kinda' stuck with me from my boyhood catechism classes. St. Frances deSales… he said 'we should remember to retire to the desert of our heart'…something like that."

Lisa looked puzzled.

"You've been stretching yourself very tight for a long time, Lisa—Beat 2…release… replenish your strength…and *Nora* will be there waiting for you."

***

Kristi Andrianni was troubled by her most recent phone call from Edward Morrison. He had asked her if she had any idea as to where he might acquire an unregistered handgun. After dismissing any thought that she would be able to help him in this way, she implicitly admonished him for even considering such an idea.

Edward's voice was raspy…almost unrecognizable. "You don't understand. I hate him. He killed my mother."

"Your mother had pneumonia. That's what you told me. How could your father have caused that?" said Kristi.

Kristi kept Edward talking for over an hour. His energy ran the gamut from loud aggression to quiet depression. Eventually, Kristi believed she had convinced Edward to abandon any notion of violence. But she was still very concerned. Kristi renewed her strong suggestion that Edward talk to a counselor. Although he didn't dismiss the idea of eventually getting some help, his only pursuit now was to confront Michael Morrison face to face.

Kristi was stressed. She understood that she was clearly dealing with an unbalanced individual. She considered contacting the police. But in her heart, she didn't believe Edward was capable of hurting anyone. There was, in fact, something about Edward that she liked. She was drawn to him, as he was to her. She wanted to help him…and was convinced she could. Their long phone call ended with confirmation that she would drive him to the Playhouse on Saturday night.

***

Sal Moretti's post-rehearsal talk with Lisa had been effective. She suddenly became aware of a powerful identity with *Nora*. For years, Lisa had exhausted every avenue to placate others…Mark, her parents, even Charlie. Most often her efforts were repaid with disparagement and other forms of condescension. And she just *took it…* Why? Moretti was correct in recalling Lisa's extraordinary mettle as a high school student. But, she knew she had lost a step. Like *Nora*, she came to the realization it was time to take care of herself.

When she got home from rehearsal, Lisa called her friend Cailla McCormack. She asked Cailla to cover for her at the daycare center the next day.

"Sure," said Cailla. "Are you sick?"

"No, not really…not at all. I just have to take care of some things," Lisa said.

"Anything I can help you with?" asked Cailla.

"Thanks. No, I don't think so. I've just come to the realization that I have to fix myself, before I'll be able to accomplish anything in my life."

"Good…that's good," said Cailla. "I'm with you all the way on that."

"You're a good friend," said Lisa.

"Hey, so are you! I'll see you at the show on Saturday."

***

The next morning Lisa surprised Charlie. As the eight year old scuttled through her morning routine, preparing for school, Lisa called her into the kitchen. "I just had an idea. How about if you and I spend the whole day together doing lots of fun stuff."

Charlie's face glowed. "Wow! That might be the best idea you've ever had, Mom! But what about school?"

"Well, everybody deserves an occasional personal day. I think today might be yours." Lisa said. "Besides, I've already called the school and told them you wouldn't be in."

Charlie let out a happy yelp, took Lisa by both hands and started dancing wildly around the kitchen. Mom and daughter had pancakes at the Lakeside Diner, did some vanity shopping at the Wainsburg Mall and bowled three games at Turnpike Lanes. They were totally enjoying exceptional quality time that had become so rare in recent months.

By mid-afternoon, they were both craving hot dogs. So, they made their way to Harrison's Drive-in. When they arrived, Charlie eagerly hopped in the front seat of her mom's Civic. They had fun teasing their car-hop and blasted their car radio as they enjoyed their lunch. They topped off their holiday with two rich hot fudge sundaes. "Oh, this is so good!" said Lisa.

"Ummmm!" Charlie replied. "This is fun, Mom."

"Sure is," said Lisa. "and believe me, Buddy, it's just the beginning. You and I are gonna spend a lot more time together like this from now on."

Charlie smiled and turned to face her mom. "The only thing that would make this better would be if Daddy was here with us."

Lisa placed her sundae dish on the tray attached to her car window. Then she put her arm lovingly around her daughter. "Daddy will always be part of your life, Buddy…a very *important* part of your life."

"You've told me that before…" said Charlie.

"I know…and it's true," said Lisa, "but it's a little different now."

Charlie's smile faded. "How?"

Lisa went on. "I used to think that there was a chance that all three of us would be together again…as a family."

"Yeah, that's what I want!"

"I know you do...Buddy. But I know now...that it's not going to happen. Your dad and I will always love each other, but in a different way...as your parents. But Dad has a new life now, without me. I want a new life too."

Charlie nodded.

Lisa faced Charlie directly and placed her hands on both of her daughter's shoulders. "My greatest wish for you is that you grow up to be a strong and capable woman. It means everything!" said Lisa. "I'm ashamed to admit that I haven't been very strong *or* capable lately. But I know it's time for me to get my act together. I need your help, Buddy."

Charlie looked up into her mother's eyes and smiled. "You've got it Mom. You're the best!"

Lisa and Charlie hugged, suggesting a new understanding and a shining future.

***

At that evening's rehearsal, Lisa's performance soared. She was like a different actor as she masterfully traversed the peaks and valleys of *Nora Helmer*. Particularly effective was her subtle portrayal of transition from the submissive housewife to the emerging feminist, realizing for the first time the optimum value of her own self-worth. As Lisa excelled, so did the other members of the company. Her new energy was contagious.

At the end of the night, Moretti was pleased. "Well, folks...we've got a show!" The cast and crew burst into applause. No one had been particularly confident that such an affirmation would be pronounced for this production. But Moretti's assurance meant everything. He was known to withhold such a stamp of approval until a show was clearly out of the woods. "Now, we still have a few details to work out," said the director, "but tonight we attained solid credibility." Moretti then read his rehearsal notes and discussed corrective measures. At the conclusion of his remarks,

Moretti provided positive comments for each cast member…but saved his final and particular praise for Lisa.

"Our *Nora* is the culmination of an incredible performance… inciteful depth of a very complicated character. Great job, Lisa!"

The whole company cheered in agreement. But no one shouted louder than Charlie.

***

There was a clear sense of relief among the cast and crew as they exited the theatre that night. The long tech week was over. Opening night was at hand. The late nights, the lack of sleep and the continual stress had taken a toll on everyone. But now, it all seemed worthwhile. A sense of accomplishment had been pronounced. All were eager to present the high quality performance they had worked so hard to attain. The haggard faces that had been present all week became unclenched… there were even some faint smiles detected.

Many cast members made it a point to compliment Lisa on her performance. Lisa was gracious as she accepted the encouragement. But in her heart, she was still worried. Yes, she definitely felt better than she had early in the week…but the notion that an audience would be in place the next night made her squeamish. As she turned to exit up the aisle, Lisa saw Nick walking toward her. The two hadn't spoken since the split, but Lisa had been thinking about Nick a lot. Though she was exhausted, she revved herself up and smiled. "Hey there, stranger!"

"Hi!" said Nick. "I didn't want to leave tonight, without congratulating you. You were amazing!"

"Thanks," Lisa said. "That means a lot."

Nick nodded and turned to leave when Lisa continued. "So how are things with you?"

“Oh, okay,” Nick replied, “not a whole lot happening…pretty busy at work …and school, well…”

Lisa cut him off. “Right…so listen, I wanted to tell you I found a *Sopranos* podcast.”

“Really?”

Lisa started walking Nick up the aisle. “Yeah, it’s cool. These two guys recap all the episodes and throw in their commentary. It’s really pretty funny?”

Nick was surprised by Lisa’s enthusiasm and at a total loss of anything to say. “Wow!”

“I’ll text you the podcast link. I think you’ll enjoy it.”

Nick became weak in the knees and stopped walking. “Maybe… we could listen together sometime.”

“Sure! That might be fun. I’ll have to let you know, though. I’ve got a lot going on right now,” said Lisa.

“Okay, sure.” Nick walked away with new hope.

Lisa turned to find Charlie trailing five feet behind her. She stepped back to her daughter, threw her arm around her, and headed toward the exit.

“Can I stay home from school tomorrow too, Mom?” asked Charlie, only half kidding.

Lisa laughed. “That would be nice, but I’m afraid we’d both be in trouble if we pulled that stunt again. But the weekend is just a day away, Buddy. It’s all good.”

Lisa and Charlie skipped out of the Playhouse, arm in arm…laughing all the way.

***

The next night a buzz of nervous excitement consumed the Playhouse. As the actors and crew arrived, all greeted each other with anxious smiles and well wishes. Lisa and Charlie entered the Playhouse front door and paused in the lobby to reflect on the artsy window boxes as they had done at the audition all those weeks ago. They both felt a sense of satisfaction as their journey approached its culmination.

As they entered the auditorium and walked down the stage-left aisle, they were greeted warmly by many of the new friends they had met along the way. They climbed the stairs onto the stage and then moved to its upper right corner, where they descended to the cellar dressing room. This was indeed perhaps the most unglamorous space imaginable. If one could visualize the most elegant dressing rooms found in Bette Davis movies or in 1940's backstage musicals, this was the opposite of that. It was an unfinished basement that had housed the old boiler heating system…run-down and worn. First time actors would gasp at what they saw. The Playhouse operators had, for decades, hoped to provide a facelift for the area, but other needs always seemed to take priority. However to the current inhabitants, the sad aesthetics were part of the charm.

As Lisa approached the crude make-up table, she saw that a bouquet of lilacs, labeled with her name, had been placed on it. Next to her bouquet was a smaller bunch labeled, "Charlie." Both labels were signed, "Nick." Lisa was moved by the gesture, and happy that Charlie had been included. But she had no time to be distracted. She proceeded to mentally prepare for *Nora*.

When the stage manager called "Places!" to signal that the show was about to start, Lisa climbed the stairs of the dressing room to the backstage-right area. This is where she would be making her first entrance. Charlie followed her mother and stood beside her. As the cast stood anxiously in the dark awaiting the houselights to dim, Lisa suddenly stretched her arms up as high and as tightly as she could… and then dropped at her waist, freely dangling her arms and fingers. She then stood up straight, inhaled and exhaled a deep breath.

Charlie was surprised, “Are you nervous, Mom?” she whispered.

Lisa looked her daughter squarely in her eyes, “I’m ready!”

***

Opening night was a jubilant success. The cast and crew stepped up and delivered a fulfilling performance. The company curtain call received a very enthusiastic reception. All the focus and diligence had appeared to pay-off…in spades. Lisa was exuberant. She had forgotten the high sensation of performance. What a feeling of accomplishment…on so many levels. Charlie too was very excited. This was all new to her, but she knew she liked it. Moretti made the rounds congratulating each member of the company. He approached Lisa. “Well, you sure nailed *Nora* tonight…big time. Congratulations!”

Lisa smiled. “Thank you, Mr. Moretti.”

“Will you please call me Sal? I’m not your teacher anymore.”

“Oh, yes you are,” said Lisa. “And thank you for having confidence in me.”

“It was the easiest thing I ever did,” said Moretti.

Lisa and Charlie were hugging each other in celebration, when Nick approached them.

“Hey, congrats…to both of you,” said Nick.

Lisa hugged Nick. “Thank you. And thank you for the lilacs. They’re beautiful…right Buddy?”

Yeah,” said Charlie, “thanks, Nick.”

"Sure…everybody's heading over to the Lakeside. You guys coming?"

Lisa and Charlie nodded to each other. "Okay…sounds like fun," Lisa said.

And it *was* fun. Lisa, Charlie and the *Doll's House* company enjoyed a wonderful celebration. And it was just the beginning. There would be another show the next night.

***

It was about 7:40 p.m., as Kristi Andrianni pulled her SUV into a parking space across the street from the Town Square Playhouse. Her *Take-Me* rideshare passenger, Edward Morrison, watched with wide-eyed interest, as patrons filed through the glass front doorways of the theatre for the Saturday night performance of *A Doll's House*. Occasionally, people would approach the 4 by 4 foot box office that bumped out from the front wall to purchase or exchange their tickets. But most audience members carried their home-printed admission tickets in their hands as they entered the venue. Kristi, had in fact pre-printed tickets for Edward and herself. She explained to Edward that as long as he required her for the return trip to the bus station, she might as well stay and see the show. In reality, Kristi was extremely concerned about Edward's state of mind and thought it best to remain close to him. They sat in the car watching the entering crowd until about five minutes to eight. "Well, I guess we should head in," said Kristi.

"Uh…yeah." Edward seemed detached.

"You okay?" asked Kristi.

"Uh-huh…let's go." Edward opened the passenger door of the SUV and got out of the car.

Kristi and Edward crossed the street and made their way through the theatre doors. As they entered the lobby, Edward couldn't look around hard enough…searching for evidence of his father, Michael

Morrison. But there was none to be found…no cast photos or even an indication of a cast list.

Edward was anxious as the usher led him and Kristi to their seats. The usher was a young woman in her early 20's. She smiled with upbeat personality as she handed Kristi and Edward their programs. "Here we are. Row C, seats 106 and 107…right on the aisle. Enjoy the show!"

"Thank you," said Kristi, as she and Edward took their seats.

"We're really close to the stage," said Edward.

"I hope these seats are all right," said Kristi, "I thought you'd want a good view, so when I bought the tickets I tried to get as far front as possible. "

"Mmm," Edward uttered.

"And you said you wanted to sit on the aisle, right?"

"Uh-huh…yes." Unseen by Kristi, Edward palmed his right pocket. Then, after looking around to see if anyone was watching, he reached into the pocket with his sweaty hand to grasp its contents, a 38 caliber Smith and Wesson revolver.

As Edward continued to nervously look around in all directions, Kristi scanned her program.

"Uh-oh," said Kristi.

"What?" Edward said.

"Did you say your father was playing the part of *Torvald Helmer*?" asked Kristi.

"Yeah," said Edward, "I think so. That's the husband, right?"

"Yes, but according to the program, that role is being played by someone named David James."

"What!" Edward blurted, as he searched his program. "Where?"

Kristi pointed out the cast list to Edward. "Shit" he said.

Edward Morrison had been planning for weeks this ultimate confrontation with his previously unknown father. Now, it seemed, everything was falling apart.

"Maybe he's using a stage name," said Kristi. Edward turned to Kristi, not really understanding what she meant. "Sometimes actors use different professional names. It could be that this David James is, in fact, your father, Michael Morrison."

Edward was confused and full of anxiety. Just then the house lights went out, causing Edward even more stress. Momentarily, the stage lights came up to reveal Lisa Lesinski-Stratton, as *Nora Helmer*, carrying packages and supervising the placement of a Christmas tree in the household setting. A few seconds later, the character of *Torvald Helmer* boisterously entered the scene.

Edward eyed the actor playing *Torvald* with intense scrutiny. He reached nervously into his pocket. But as the scene continued, it was clear that "David James" was *not* his father. This actor was barely 30 years old and certainly bore no resemblance to Edward. Edward furiously got up from his seat and stormed out of the theatre, banging into a metal trash can as he left. His noisy exit was a disruption to nearby audience members and caught the attention of several ushers. Kristi was taken totally by surprise. It took her a few seconds, but as she realized what was happening, she bolted up the aisle after him.

The actors onstage were unaware of the hub-bub and proceeded to deliver their finest performance so far. At the end of the night, as Lisa took her curtain call, she was shocked as the entire house rose in a fervent standing ovation. She was euphoric. She looked for Charlie, who was lined up on stage-right with the other children.

As the company took its third and final bow, Lisa caught Charlie's eye. They silently shared a poignant connection, which neither would ever forget.

***

When Kristi Andrianni raced out of the Playhouse in pursuit of Edward Morrison, she had to pause and catch her breath. In a short time, she had gotten to know Edward quite well. She fancied herself a fixer and had hoped to broker an amiable reunion between him and his father. It was now clear to both she and Edward, that this was not going to happen...at least not on this night. In spite of her affection for him, Kristi was painfully aware of Edward's instability. She feared what he might do. As she looked up and down the street outside the Playhouse, Kristi saw no sign of her young companion. The town of Lakeside encompassed a two mile radius consisting of a half-dozen tree-lined streets, running east and west...very small. In the next two hours, Kristi drove her SUV up and down these streets, dozens of times, searching and searching... for Edward Morrison.

***

After the show, the cast and crew of *A Doll's House* mingled with the many audience members who had stayed in the house to meet and greet them. Lisa was exhilarated. Her mother and father had attended the show and were both extremely complimentary. "You were wonderful. I was so proud of you," said Ainsley Lesinski. "The people sitting next to us were crying! Of course, I told them I was your mother."

Lisa smiled. "Of course!"

"I can't believe this is such a big deal. I guess you knew what you were doing, after all!"

"Thanks Mom," said Lisa, "you have no idea how much I appreciate that."

But even more exciting to Lisa, were the numerous compliments she received from complete strangers. An older, distinguished looking gentleman approached her with a broad smile. "Congratulations, Dear. You were spot on. I've seen this play many, many times…but I've never seen a better *Nora*."

"Thank you so much," said Lisa.

"Ibsen is challenging for contemporary audiences," the man continued, "but you managed to bridge the generations here tonight. Well done."

Lisa felt proud. She had set out on a journey to make a positive change in her life, and it was *really* happening. To her, it was almost like a dream. She made her way to Charlie who was on the other side of the theatre talking to her teacher, Mrs. Adamcyk.

"Hello there," said Lisa. "I didn't know you were coming to the show."

"Well, we couldn't miss Charlie's debut," said the teacher. "Actually, my husband and I are season subscribers to the theatre. We come to all the plays."

"Well, thank you," said Lisa. "It means a lot to both Charlie and me."

"Of course…and you were wonderful as *Nora*. Congratulations! See you Monday, Charlie!" Mrs. Adamcyk started exiting up the aisle.

"Thank you," said Lisa.

"Goodnight," called Charlie.

***

As Kristi Andrianni repeatedly traversed the byways of Lakeside, New Jersey, she had become far more familiar with the lay of the land of the small town than she could ever have imagined. Her search for the emotionally volatile Edward Morrison had yielded no results. She was frustrated and anxious. "Where could he possibly be?" she thought. In this tiny bucolic hamlet, he had seemed to vanish into thin air. As she approached the edge of town for at least the seventh time, she pulled over to the side of the road. She turned off the ignition and attempted to collect herself. She knew Edward was moving on foot so he had to be somewhere in town. "Unless," she thought, "he had somehow hitched a ride back to Hackettstown." After contemplating the situation for a few minutes, Kristi came to the conclusion that Edward was certainly still in town. "No one picks up hitch-hikers anymore," she reasoned.

As she restarted the car and prepared to continue her search, she noticed a dark street sign labeling a dirt road in front of her. She made the right turn onto Parkview Lane. She had somehow missed seeing this primitive thoroughfare in her previous go-arounds. It was rough going, lots of bumps and puddles. About a mile in, through an uninhabited wooded area, the road terminated to a dead-end parking lot. On the far side of the empty lot was a sign… "Welcome To Lakeside Municipal Park" … and in smaller letters… "Park Closes At Dusk." To Kristi, the dark abandonment was creepy. Her instinct was to turn the car around and "get the hell out of there." But instead she pulled into one of the empty parking spaces and again turned off the ignition. Without her headlights, the darkness became even gloomier.

Kristi turned on the flashlight of her cell phone and entered the park. As she scanned the area with the light, she could see several picnic tables and a few brick firepits. Clearly, this park was the site of fun-filled summer get togethers. But, now in middle March, there was no recent evidence of human visitation. As she continued to traipse through this dark park, strange things entered Kristi's mind. "I could be attacked by a bear or coyote," she thought. "No one would even find my body for months. What the fuck am I doing?!"

She raised the light on her phone and saw a lake in the distance… the lake for which Lakeside had obviously been named. As she proceeded toward the body of water, she spotted a large picnic table at water's edge. As she turned the cellphone flashlight toward the table, she gasped and recoiled. The shadow of a human form sat facing the lake. At this point, the vision of Kristi's children flashed before her. Nevertheless, she proceeded toward the mysterious silhouette.

She called, "Edward?"

There was no movement or response from the shadow, as Kristi inched closer. "Edward? Is that you?"

There was still no movement, but quietly came a voice, "How did you find me?"

Kristi quickly moved forward to the picnic table. When she reached it, she flashed her light on its occupant. She became quickly distressed at what she saw. Indeed, it was Edward Morrison…slumped and drawn. His face was flushed, his eyes were wet. There was not a glimpse of energy in his being. But the most troubling discovery…the Smith and Wesson revolver he was holding in his right hand.

"What's going on?" said Kristi. "What the heck is going on?"

"Would you turn the light out, please?" said Edward.

Kristi clicked off the phone flashlight leaving only dim illumination from the moon.

"I'm finished…done," said Edward.

"What?…C'mon!"

" I don't know who I am. And I have no one to *tell* me who I am."

"Stop! Stop it!" said Kristi. "You're a person...you're a capable person. Your mother saw to it that you grew to be a capable, strong, kind, human person."

Edward wiped his eyes. "Do I look strong and capable to you?"

Kristi moved closer to him on the picnic bench and put her arm around him. "Hey...you've taken a hard shot. Your mother was your salvation. Grief is unforgiving. You may feel a sense of isolation now and... you may need some help to get through it. But that doesn't mean the foundation your mother built around you isn't still intact. It is. I promise you, it is."

Edward stood up from the picnic table, and walked closer to the edge of the lake. Kristi followed him. "Do you think confronting your father would have helped you to know who you are?"

Edward gazed out over the dimly lit water. "Maybe...at least I might have found out why he abandoned me...us."

"What does any of that matter?" said Kristi. "He didn't know you. He clearly didn't *want* to know you. The reasons are inconsequential."

"That's easy for you to say," said Edward.

"I suppose so. But listen! I've known you for a week...and I feel I know you pretty well....far better than Michael Morrison *has* ever or *will* ever know you. And...I like you. I think you are a good soul.... You are someone I would be happy to introduce to my family."

Edward's gaze turned to Kristi. "Thanks."

"Until she died, your mother chose to have you believe your father was dead. She must have had a good reason for that. He *was* a non-entity to you. Guess what? He's *still* a non-entity, probably more so now than ever."

"I don't know..." Edward looked away.

"Sometimes we have to throw off the burdens that hold us down. It's never an easy thing to do. I've been there...many times. I know you can do this."

Edward again turned to Kristi, his face softening. "Will you help me?'

"Yes...of course I will."

Edward closed his eyes and threw his arms around Kristi in a long, emotional embrace. As they hugged, Kristi could feel the pressure of the gun in Edward's hand against her back. It frightened her. "You need to get rid of that," she said.

Edward moved another step toward the lake and tossed the revolver as far as he could.

In the pale night, Kristi and Edward watched the shadow of the weapon plop into the calm water.

***

At the Playhouse, Lisa had made the rounds to greet most of the audience well-wishers who had remained after the performance. She had received universal accolades and her morale was as high as she ever remembered. As the house had pretty much thinned out, she started toward the dressing room to change out of her *Nora* costume and into street clothes. But as she mounted the stage stairs, she spotted a smiling Cailla McCormack seated in the front row. Lisa quickly ran down the stairs and sat beside her friend.

"Hey, you," said Lisa, "I was looking all over for you."

"Well, I've been right here," said Cailla, "but I didn't want to interrupt your triumph." Cailla laughed and hugged Lisa. "You were absolutely fantastic!"

Lisa beamed with pride. “Really?”

“Of course, I was totally blown away…just like everyone else in this place.”

“Thank you. I’m so glad you were here,” said Lisa.

“I wouldn’t have missed it,” said Cailla. “Now listen, I’ve got something to tell you…about work. But I don’t want to distract you from your big night, so I can wait and tell you another time.”

“Good or bad?” asked Lisa.

“Pretty dog-gone good, if you ask me,” Cailla replied.

Lisa squeezed her eyes shut tight. “Lay it on me!”

“The Cartwrights were in today.”

“Uh-oh,” said Lisa, as she opened her eyes.

Richard and Michelle Cartwright were the owners of the Little Sprout Daycare Center. They had opened the Glennville facility ten years ago, and had since opened four additional centers in various parts of New Jersey. Although they kept close tabs on the operation, they rarely showed up in-person unless it was to fire somebody.

“No…it’s really good!” said Cailla. “They’re going to open a new place in Hackettstown and they want you and me to run it!”

“Really!” said Lisa.

“Yup…with a big raise….and, get this…they’re gonna pay for both of us to finish our degrees.”

“What? Holy Crap! That’s fantastic,” said Lisa.

“They’re coming back on Monday, to work out the details with us,” said Cailla. “You’re interested, right?”

“Are you kidding? Absolutely! My friend, you just made a good day even better.” The two women stood up in happy jubilation.

Cailla started out. “Great show! See you Monday.” Lisa waved as Cailla exited up the aisle.

As Lisa turned again toward the dressing room, she saw Charlie coming from that direction. Her daughter had already changed. “Grandma and Grandpa want to take me out for ice cream. Is that okay?”

“It’s pretty late,” said Lisa, “aren’t you tired?”

“Are you crazy?” said Charlie. “I’m flying! I mean, everybody loved the play. Grandpa slipped me a twenty…and some old lady asked me for my autograph! ”

“Wow!” said Lisa. “Nobody asked me for mine!” Mother and daughter laughed lovingly. “Okay, but tell grandma, ‘not too late,’ all right?”

“Okay. Are you going to the Lakeside?” asked Charlie.

Lisa saw Nick standing toward the rear of the house, waving at her. Lisa smiled and waved back. “No…I don’t think so…not tonight. I’ll be home waiting for you.”

“Okay, Mom, I love you.” Charlie hugged Lisa.

“I love you too, Buddy!” Lisa watched her daughter run up the aisle toward her waiting grandparents.

***

By the time Lisa had changed into her street clothes, there was hardly anyone left in the theatre. As she walked up the aisle toward the exit, she smiled and waved at Moretti who was up on the light deck. He flashed her a big thumbs up which she happily returned as she entered the lobby. Lisa paused at the display box for *A Doll's House*. As she contemplated the image of a woman locked in a birdcage, she recalled Charlie's initial reaction, "This is a weird play." But after living with *Nora* for all this time, Lisa didn't regard the play as all that weird. Not at all. For her, it had been an awakening; for *Nora*, and for herself.

As Lisa stepped away from the lobby display box and exited the Playhouse door, she was surprised to see Mark waiting for her. He had in his hands a bouquet of roses.

"These are for you," he said. "I thought you were terrific."

"Thank you, so much." Lisa smiled and accepted the flowers. They exchanged a somewhat awkward hug. They both recalled that their last encounter hadn't gone so well.

"I didn't even know you were coming tonight?" said Lisa. She looked around. "Is Wendy with you?"

"No…uh…no she couldn't make it," said Mark. "Listen, I didn't want to bother you inside. Everyone was so happy for you…and you deserved it all. But…I was hoping I could talk to you."

Lisa stepped away. "I'm pretty tired." She wasn't in the mood for another confrontation.

"It'll only take a minute," said Mark. " I promise."

"All right, I'm parked down by the bridge. Walk with me." She referred to the Pequest Bridge, covering the river that ran through the center of town. Because the only patron parking for the Playhouse was on the street, cast and crew members tried to park a good distance away, for the convenience of their customers. The bridge, and Lisa's Civic, were three blocks from the theatre.

There was an uneasiness as Lisa and Mark walked together. Finally, Lisa asked, "So what did you want to talk about?"

"Umm…I just wanted to say I was sorry about how things escalated the other week." Mark referred to the battle over Charlie's participation in the proposed ski trip."

"Well, I guess I'm sorry too. Charlie and I had a rough couple of days after that," said Lisa.

"I'll bet. I'm really sorry I put you in that position."

"Well, we got through it. In fact, Charlie and I ended up in a really good place…so it's fine."

"Good…listen….I want you to know that I'm going to break it off with Wendy."

As they reached the bridge, Lisa stopped walking. "I'm very sorry to hear that. I know how painful breakups can be."

"Yeah," said Mark, "I'm not sure how she's gonna' take it."

"It will be difficult for her, I'm sure. I can tell she cares for you a great deal." Lisa didn't want to cry. But she felt the urge. She turned away from Mark and looked out from the bridge over the river.

"Yeah…but the thing is, I don't love her. I never have. I love you."

Lisa's gaze remained away. She was slow to respond. " I love you too…I'm sure I always will."

Mark took Lisa by the shoulders and pulled her to him. But as he went to kiss her, she pulled away. "No. Not like that. You were my first love…you're Charlie's father…we've been through so much. I'll always love you for that." Lisa paused and again turned to look out from the bridge. "But I know now, that our life together is over. I feel really good about myself…for the first time maybe ever. There's so much I want to do in my life. I feel totally capable of accomplishing anything and everything. And I only have to answer to myself. "

Now Mark turned to look out over the bridge to the river. "Okay…I get it. It's my own fault."

"Sometimes things are just not meant to be," said Lisa. "There's no need to place blame. It is what it is."

"All right," Mark turned to face Lisa. "but, if you ever change your mind…"

"I won't!" Lisa cut him off.

"Bye." Mark turned away and started back toward the theatre and his car.

"Hey," Lisa stopped him. She walked to him and kissed his cheek. " I wish you the best."

"You too," Mark said. He turned and slowly walked away.

As Lisa approached her car, she stopped once more to look out over the Pequest Bridge. She felt an inner peace, as she reflected on her lot in life. She thought about the strength she had garnered from Moretti's spiritual allusion; "…remember to retire into the desert of your own heart…"

As she peered up at the moon, Lisa was oblivious of the SUV quietly passing behind her and its subdued passenger, casually eying her through his window. Never having met, but still, kindred souls passing in the night.

Made in the USA
Columbia, SC
20 September 2019